THE VANISHING

DAVID MICHAEL SLATER

Published by:
Library Tales Publishing
www.LibraryTalesPublishing.com
www.Facebook.com/LibraryTalesPublishing

For general information on our other products and services, please contact our Customer Care Department at 1-800-754-5016, or fax 917-463-0892. For technical support, please visit www.LibraryTalesPublishing. com

Library Tales Publishing also publishes its books in a variety of electronic formats. Every content that appears in print is available in electronic books.

978-1956769111
978-1956769241

PRINTED IN THE UNITED STATES OF AMERICA

The Vanishing

DAVID MICHAEL SLATER

WARNING: THIS BOOK MAY NOT BE
APPROPRIATE FOR YOUNGER OR HIGHLY
SENSITIVE READERS

"David Michael Slater in his novel *The Vanishing* has dared to imagine the unimaginable. His story involves a tragic end of innocence and the courage, leavened by a dash of the miraculous, that allows a young girl to navigate history's greatest nightmare, and to awaken from it with her sense (and ours) of human possibility still intact. A remarkable book."

> Steve Stern
> Author of *The Frozen Rabbi* and winner of the National Jewish Book Award

"I've long wondered whether any writer would have the courage to truly portray the sodden, mindless, pointless brutality of the Holocaust as it was. In *The Vanishing*, David Michael Slater has done just that, and I haven't been so moved by a book in a long time."

> Eric A. Kimmel
> 5-time winner of the National Jewish Book Award, Recipient of the Sydney Taylor Award for Lifetime Achievement.

"*The Vanishing* is a tragic, yet beautiful story that deserves a place on the shelves among some of the greatest literature penned on the Holocaust."

> Mark A. Cooper
> Author of the *Edelweiss Pirates* series

"*The Vanishing* is a vivid journey through every emotion in the human experience. It is heart-wrenching and hopeful by turns. Sophie Siegel is an incredible heroine, one readers will never forget. May your memories of this book be a blessing."

> Michael P. Spradlin
> New York Times Best Selling author of *The Enemy Above* and *Into the Killing Seas*

"Sophie Siegel wakes up one morning to find her mother sewing a yellow star onto her clothing. And so begins the descent of her family into the Nazi nightmare that will soon trap nearly all of Europe's Jews. David Michael Slater tells Sophie's story in this moving, compelling, and highly dramatic novel."

> Richard Zimler
> Author of *The Last Kabbalist of Lisbon* and *The Gospel According to Lazarus*

"This remarkable book seems to touch on every aspect of the Holocaust. Through the magic of Mr. Slater's cinematic writing, we accompany our invisible heroine to the ghetto, to the camps, to the forests, to the end of the war and beyond. *The Vanishing* is fierce and loving, devastating and compelling, a breathtaking blend of history, fiction, and magical realism."

　　　　Helen Maryles Shankman
　　　　Author of *They Were Like Family to Me*

"*The Vanishing* must be the most vivid work of historical fiction about the Holocaust that I have ever read. There were times I broke into a sweat at the intensity of it. David Michael Slater has done an incredible job in conveying the tragedy of the Holocaust and the triumph of the human spirit."

　　　　Doug Cervi
　　　　Executive Director of the New Jersey Commission on Holocaust Education

"*The Vanishing* took my breath away and held it until the very last page. Not many books on the Holocaust leave a reader crying and smiling, but this one absolutely did."

　　　　Felice Cohen
　　　　Author of *What Papa Told Me*

"Like all great fantasy, *The Vanishing* centers on human truths, just as a golem springs from the ground of human need. Through Sophie Siegel's eyes, we see both the brutal truth of the Holocaust and the essential and timely truth of how much human survival depends on persistent acts of resistance borne out of love."

　　　　Sarah Blake
　　　　Author of the NYT bestsellers, *The Postmistress* and *The Guest Book*

"David Michael Slater intwines the gruesome horrors of the Nazi Judenrein "cleansing of Jews" during World War II with a captivating tale of an invisible Jewish girl struggling to keep her best friend alive. Slater's artful use of fantasy, history, and folklore places *The Vanishing* in the literary tradition of Ursula K. Le Guin."

　　　　Ruth Tenzer Feldman
　　　　Author of the *Blue Thread* trilogy

"There is magic here... of a curious kind. David Michael Slater's brave, audacious decision to sprinkle a dollop of magical realism onto the horrors of the Holocaust offers a haunting reminder that there is hope in hopelessness, light in darkness, survival in struggle."

> Daniel Paisner
> Co-author of *The Girl in the Green Sweater: A Life in Holocaust's Shadow*

"There are books one reads and there are books one experiences. David Michael Slater's remarkable *The Vanishing* falls into the latter category. From the moment of Sophie Siegel's 'vanishing' to her stunning role in one final shocking death, this book takes hold of the reader and does not let go—not until the last page is turned and, indeed, not even then."

> David A. Poulsen
> Author of *Numbers,* winner of the Sakura Medal

"*The Vanishing* made me gasp and cry. Though not for the faint of heart, its blending of brutal realism with magic and folklore conjures a daringly hopeful story of friendship, devotion, and caring during the Holocaust. "

> Meg Wiviott
> Author of *Paper Hearts* and *Benno and the Night of Broken Glass*

"I read *The Vanishing* in one sitting because I was that invested in how Sophie Siegel's story lays bare the nightmarish realities of the German Holocaust. It's that powerful."

> Debra McArthur
> Author of *Raoul Wallenberg: Rescuing Thousands from the Nazis' Grasp*

"*The Vanishing* is a serious, powerful, and insightful exploration of the Holocaust that, using elements of fantasy, takes readers places that no memoir ever could."

> Michael Berenbaum
> Professor of Jewish Studies and Director of Sigi Ziering Institute at American Jewish University

"The beauty of *The Vanishing* is that, through elements of fantasy, it conveys the reality of the Holocaust in a deeply moving way. "
Belle Ami
Author of *The Blue Coat Saga*

"*The Vanishing* is the ultimate revenge story and one of the most memorable novels about the Holocaust I've ever read."
Nurit Wildenberg Stites, M.Ed.
Holocaust Educator

"*The Vanishing* is a powerful and important book that reaches straight down to touch the essence of our humanity."
Ian Lewis
Author of *The Ballad of Billy Bean*

"*The Vanishing* leaps into our imagination, allowing us to experience what young teens and children did during the Holocaust in a way that is both memorable and entices further conversation."
L.L. Abbott
Author of *Our Forgotten Year*

"There are many compelling novels about young people in the Holocaust, but none have taken a more original approach than David Michael Slater's gripping saga, *The Vanishing*."
Allan Zullo
Author of *Survivors: True Stories of Children in the Holocaust*

"Unflinching, honest, and riveting, *The Vanishing* is one of the most compelling novels of the Holocaust that I have read in a long time. It's a must-read."
Kathy Kacer
Author of thirty books about the Holocaust for young readers

"*The Vanishing* is a deeply moving, captivating account of the Holocaust as seen through the eyes of a child, Sophie Siegel, a truly brave and memorable character."
Sheryl Needle Cohn, Ed.D.
Holocaust Educator and author of *The Boy in the Suitcase: Holocaust Family Stories of Survival*

"*The Vanishing* is an unflinching evocation of the horrors of the Holocaust. Prepare to squirm, grimace, cry... and to believe in guardian angels."

> Jenny MacKay
> Author of *Children of the Holocaust*

"*The Vanishing* is a powerful and compelling blend of historical fiction and magical realism. This vital book is an antidote to ignorance."

> Jack Mayer
> Author of *Life in a Jar: The Irena Sendler Project*

"*The Vanishing* is a brilliant portrayal of an unimaginable time in history. With skillfully defined characters and rich, captivating descriptions, this is a must-read for everyone. I loved it."

> Shari J. Ryan
> USA Today bestselling author of *Last Words*

"*The Vanishing* is a gut-wrenching historical fantasy that doesn't skirt the horrors of the Holocaust. David Michael Slater's dark revenge novel will take readers on a haunting journey of an invisible girl as she struggles to save her beloved friend."

> Jennifer Voigt Kaplan
> Author of the Christopher Award-winning novel, *Crushing the Red Flowers*

"*The Vanishing* is a story of loyalty, revenge, and the possibility that human beings have as much capacity to love as to destroy one another. It offers a way to ask how we can transcend our worst contexts to shape a more humane and just future for us all."

> Rachel DeWoskin
> Author of *Someday We Will Fly*

"Sophie Siegel's brave heart and sheer grit compel readers to urgently follow her through the horrors of Nazi Germany on errands of mercy and revenge. Holocaust stories like *The Vanishing*, told in new and unexpected ways, are vital to the world—lest we forget. I fell in love with Sophie and really loved this book."

> Jennifer Elvgren
> Author of award-winning, *The Whispering Town*

"Unique, absorbing, and fast-paced, *The Vanishing* is an important book that will stay with readers well beyond its conclusion."
Gemma Liviero
Author of *Pastel Orphans* and *Broken Angels*

"*The Vanishing* kept me in the fictional dream from the first page to the last. With hints of *The World That We Knew* (Alice Hoffman) and *The Devil's Arithmetic* (Jane Yolen), it is a fantastical tale of the enduring power of friendship during our darkest history. David Michael Slater's charismatic protagonist, Sophie Siegel, will continue to own a piece of my heart."
Elaine Wolf
Award-winning author of *Camp* and *Danny's Mom*

"*The Vanishing* is a gripping, thought-provoking page-turner based on brutal historical events, told through the eyes of an extraordinary teen heroine."
Susan Goldman Rubin
Author of *Fireflies in the Dark: The Story of Friedl Dicker-Brandeis and the Children of Terezin* and *The Anne Frank Case: Simon Wiesenthal's Search for the Truth.*

"In *The Vanishing*, author David Michael Slater expertly tells the story of the Holocaust by weaving readers through a series of haunting locales that bring with them formidable characters, incomprehensible tragedy, and heart-thumping twists and turns. A page-turner, *The Vanishing* is reminiscent of Markus Zusak's *The Book Thief.*"
Julia Moberg
Author of *Presidential Pets, Animal Heroes,* and *Historical Animals*; former editor of the Children's Book-of-the-Month Club

"Sophie's journey in *The Vanishing*, from innocent schoolgirl and traumatized witness to avenging angel, is heartbreaking and harrowing, offering a glimpse at many of the most dreadful moments of the Holocaust."
Shannon Delaney
Author of *The 13 to Life* and *Weather Witch* series

"All things appear and disappear because of the concurrence of causes and conditions. Nothing ever exists entirely alone; everything is in relation to everything else."
— **Siddhartha Gautama**

"We refuse to disappear, no matter how strong and brutal and ruthless the forces against us might be."
— **Golda Meir**

PART ONE
THE TOWN

Sophie Siegel — December, 1941

orgetting she had slippers within easy reach, Sophie flung her covers off and climbed barefoot out of bed. She was wide awake and ready for her banner day. Having aced yesterday's mathematics exam, as of today, she was officially Top Student in her class—or at least she would be when Frau Volker chalked her name on the board, right on the top line inside the Triangle of Superior Students.

Sophie sat down at the vanity her Papa had built for her in his shop behind the house. He was a woodworker whose talents were much in demand, but he always had time to make her anything she needed, large or small. Everyone called him Big Benno because he was enormous. Sophie reckoned he might be the strongest man in the world.

Taming her unruly curls with the brush Papa had also made her, Sophie imagined what Frau Volker would say to her about being Top Student. It was hard to believe this was really happening. Sophie had never thought of herself as smart because she'd always done poorly in school, not that she'd ever put much effort into it. She'd been a social creature, far more interested in friends than academics. But gradually, that began to change when the Siegels moved from the City, where Sophie was born, to the nearby town of Weiler in August of 1938, only a few months before the pogroms erupted all over Germany — the violent riots that destroyed synagogues, Jewish businesses, homes, and schools. Some people were even killed. But there had been no pogrom in Weiler, which only proved how smart her Papa was for knowing it was hospitable to Jews.

Sophie was, of course, tremendously relieved to be safe in Weiler, but also terribly sad to have moved away from her friends. Even worse, it would be harder to see her two sets of grandparents, both of whom said they were too old to uproot themselves. Sophie was further distressed to learn that she was not good at making friends with kids she didn't know, especially since she was no longer attending a Jewish school. And so, with nothing else to do in class but pay attention — miracle of miracles — her lessons suddenly began to make sense.

However, Papa, who always had his ear to the ground when it came to politics, didn't like what he was hearing around their new home about the "Jewish Problem." So in August of 1939, he moved the family to Gemeinde, an even smaller town with about half as many Jews. There, Sophie became even more shy and more studious, and lo and behold, her lessons not only made sense, they struck her as interesting. She began to earn good enough marks to make her think she might be pretty smart after all.

But just when Sophie was getting comfortable, the Siegels moved *again,* in August of 1940, after a Jewish man was murdered in the street and no one bothered to find his killer. Papa took them to Ortschaft, a town of merely ten thousand, because he'd learned that it was known for leaving its Jews — all two hundred of them — to themselves.

Even so, when they arrived on Judenstrasse — the single long and dank alley of a street where all of Ortschaft's Jews lived — Sophie's parents informed her that while she could play with her Jewish neighbors all she wanted, at school she was to keep to herself. These were not instructions she'd been given in either Weiler or Gemeinde. But it was fine with Sophie, who had, by then, given up on the idea of making friends at school.

Sophie's parents also told her that she was not to be off-putting or standoffish, and that she was expected to be mannerly and well-scrubbed. Her Mama and Papa stressed that she wasn't to give anyone a single, solitary reason to think she wasn't an upstanding individual who could be counted on to do the right thing. This suited Sophie fine; she took pride in being an upstanding individual. From her first day of school in Ortschaft, all the way up to yesterday, her lessons were not only a cinch to understand and interesting, they were easy to remember. And now, at the wise old age of eleven, Sophie had transformed herself from an unremarkable student into a remarkable one. A Top one!

Sophie set down her brush and went over to her Papa-made wardrobe to swap out her yellow nightgown for her favorite yellow dress. But all the hangers inside were empty. Perplexed, she padded over to her bedroom door to peer into the main room, a combination kitchen and living room. She was expecting to see her mother, Bianca — or Bitty Bee, as everyone called her because she was so petite — standing at the counter, smearing jam on a slice of bread for her to scarf down on her way to school. Instead, her mother was sitting at Papa's blue table, bent over an enormous heap of clothes. This wasn't totally unusual, given that Bianca was a seamstress, but she never worked this early in the morning. And all of Sophie's dresses were in the pile.

Bianca was so focused on her needle and thimble that she didn't notice her daughter walk right up and stand next to her. She was finishing sewing a yellow star onto the breast of Sophie's wool jacket.

Sophie watched, enchanted by the welter of bright points in the tangle of mostly dark materials: cotton and wool dresses, skirts, button-down shirts, and sweaters. Upon looking closer, she saw that all the stars had the word 'Jude' on them —*Jew*. "Mama?" she said, now feeling the cold of the floor chill the soles of her feet. It shot up her legs and through her torso, into her arms, and right to the tips of her fingers. Sophie always got cold when she was nervous or afraid.

"Sophie!" Bianca yelped. She flashed her famous wide smile. But it wasn't so wide this time, and her normally soft lips appeared chapped. Her typically shiny black hair was tied up on her head in a dry, brittle mound.

"What is all this, Mama?" Sophie asked. "Have you been sewing all night?"

Bianca sighed and set Sophie's jacket on her lap. "It's the law now, Angel," she said, trying to sound cheerful, or at least not upset. "We heard last night. All Jews must wear a star on their outer garments when outside their homes." She fished one of Sophie's dresses from the mess on the table and held it out, the yellow one she'd lovingly embroidered with tiny flowers — she always seemed to know Sophie's mind. "Here," she said. "You'll have to get your own breakfast. I need to take the rest of these clothes back to the neighbors — before they have to go around naked all day." It was a joke, sort of, but Bianca didn't produce even a semblance of her infectious laugh.

"But — *why must we wear them?*" Sophie cried, refusing to take the dress and starting to shiver. "Will there be a pogrom here now too?" she asked. "Is this so they know who to hurt?"

Bianca's face fell. She took her daughter into her arms and began rubbing her back and shoulders to warm her up. "The Night of Broken Glass is over," she promised. "And this too shall pass."

"I won't wear one, Mama," Sophie said, trying to stop the tears in her eyes from spilling over. "They can't make me."

"Angel," said Bianca, softly, "they won't let you inside the school without it."

"But Mama!" Sophie cried, pulling out of her mother's arms. "I'm Top Student today!"

"You're... what?" Bianca asked. She blinked, trying to process this news.

"I wanted to tell you and Papa after school, when it was official. I'm the Top Student in Frau Volker's class! I've been working so hard since we moved here, Mama. Every day... You mean you haven't noticed?"

"*I — I —*"

"Mama! What do you think I've been doing every day after school in my room?!"

"Sophie," said Bianca, "I'm so sorry. Your Papa and I — we've been distracted. I should have been looking in on you more. You're just... you're never any trouble. But this... this is wonderful news." She smiled again, but once again, it wasn't a real one.

"Then why don't you look happy, Mama?"

Bianca, already weary, now looked pained. Sophie could see it in her mother's usually bright, saucer eyes. Her Mama seemed like she was about to say one thing but then decided to say another. "I'm very happy," she said. "Top Student is a tremendous achievement, something to be very proud of. Rabbi Hasendahl will want to know. We'll have a celebration when you get home this afternoon. I know your Papa will be very impressed... But Sophie, you must wear the star on your jacket and dress."

Sophie frowned while she tried to understand what was happening and what she thought about it. *Why should I be afraid to show the world I'm Jewish?* she wondered. She loved being Jewish: Shabbat, the holidays, the special foods — all of it. And yet, at the same time, she was sure that a star on her chest would feel like a dunce cap on her head. She didn't know what to do or how to feel, although she knew one thing for certain: nothing in the world was going to make her miss the day her name — Sophie Siegel — got chalked.

"Does Frau Volker know I'm Jewish?" Sophie asked, although she wasn't exactly sure why. She didn't know whether her peers knew because she rarely interacted with them.

Bianca nodded.

Sophie snatched the dress from her mother's hand and said, "Good. Then the class should know her Top Student is a Jew."

"I'm proud of you, Angel," Bianca told her. "Like Rabbi Hasendahl always says: *Live in such a way that brings honor to our people.*"

Sophie poked her head out of the front door. The wind bit into her cheeks as she watched some of the neighborhood kids heading down the street with their stars on their coats. She hurried out onto the cobblestones, shouting, "Arno!" to the back of one of the bundled figures. But Arno, a boy a grade ahead of her, did not stop.

Sophie turned to see a tall, pink bundle coming her way. Even without the eye-catching coat, she knew it was Lea Malka Mankewitz, a gorgeous high school girl with an almost regal bearing about her. She was the most beautiful person Sophie had ever seen. Her face was strikingly pale and her hair strikingly black. All the Judenstrase kids resented Lea Malka for the attention she got at school from everyone: teachers and students, Jews and gentiles alike. But at the same time they craved her attention. Sophie, herself, was afraid even to talk to her.

Despite her anxiety, Sophie plucked up her courage and chirped, as brightly as she could, "Lea Malka!"

Lea Malka stopped short in front of Sophie, apparently startled out of her thoughts. She looked surprised to find herself where she was.

"But —" Sophie said, shocked to see that on Lea Malka's long pink jacket, there was no star. "But — they won't let you into school!"

Lea Malka gave Sophie a hard, almost imperious look, said

nothing, and walked away.

Flummoxed, Sophie turned around and saw another girl who was a few years younger and who had a mole on her cheek. "Gisela!" she called. But Gisela was walking with her head down and refused to look up as she passed. Unlike Lea Malka, she did have a star on her coat. Disconcerted, Sophie stared at Gisela's back as the younger girl hurried along and then at the other kids further down the street. Normally, kids walked to school in wisecracking clusters, but today every single one of them was walking alone, silent. The crunching of snow under their boots echoed eerily on the street.

Sophie, starting to sweat despite the cold, was relieved to see Giddy Goldfarb coming out of the house attached to hers. Giddy was just eight years old, but he was Sophie's only real friend in Ortschaft. Every time his mother had to leave him alone to deliver washing to a customer, she sent him to Sophie's house. He was immature, but in an amusing way, and if she put a book into his hands, he wouldn't disturb her for hours at a time. Besides, he was adorably tiny and had an adorably round doll's face with ears that stuck out like the handles on a pitcher.

Giddy was walking with his head down, and he had his arms wrapped around himself even though his coat was a heavy one. "Giddy!" Sophie cried before he barreled right into her. "Watch out!"

Giddy stopped just short of colliding with Sophie. He looked up with his big, long-lashed eyes just under the edge of his wool cap. Sophie expected to see his crooked, goofy grin, but his mouth was a pinched-up line. Without so much as a nod of recognition, Giddy veered around Sophie and walked on, still hugging himself.

This was too much. Sophie chased after him, grabbed his shoulder, and turned him around. "Giddy!" she said. "Why won't you say hello?"

"Leave me alone," he grumbled, mostly to the ground.

Sophie saw now that Giddy wasn't exactly hugging himself, and in any case, it certainly wasn't to keep warm. One of his hands was scrunching up part of his coat, the part with a yellow star on it.

Giddy saw Sophie seeing this — and ran. He looked like a fool, slipping and sliding over the cobblestones without his arms for balance. And sure enough, after maybe ten comically awkward strides, his boots went out from under him and up into the air. He landed hard on his back.

Sophie hustled over to help Giddy up, but it was difficult because he still wouldn't unwrap his arms. It was like trying to tilt up a miniature, rosy-cheeked mummy. But once he was on his feet, Sophie took his wrists and lowered his arms. Giddy wasn't hurt, but he was crying.

"It's okay," Sophie said, putting her hand over the star on his chest. "This too shall pass. And in the meantime, maybe these will actually help. In Germany, I mean. Think about it, everyone should know that Jews are good students and good people who never cause any trouble."

Giddy wiped snot from his nose with the back of his reddened hand and said, "Do you really think so?"

"I really do," Sophie promised. "So let's walk to school and behave in such a way that brings honor to our people."

Giddy wiped his nose again and nodded, obviously comforted by Sophie's words. Seeing this, Sophie felt something new in her life, something she thought that parents must feel: a responsibility to say whatever was necessary to reassure their children. And somehow, she felt certain that saying such things made them more likely to be true.

Giddy held his snotty hand out to Sophie, who took it, after only a moment's hesitation. Hand-in-hand, they trudged off down the street.

On normal days, there was an unspoken agreement between all the Jewish kids: they'd walk together down Judenstrasse, but only until they neared Schulstrasse, the main road that led to the schoolhouse. Several side streets branched off of Judenstrasse before that intersection, and the kids, without comment, would stagger their entry into them so as not to emerge among all the gentiles in a pack.

But today, Sophie and Giddy ignored that practice and walked together all the way to the corner at Schulstrasse. They turned at the intersection to find the street, as usual, hosting a parade of satchel-carrying kids. Except today the parade was, rather than a raucous flow, a frozen line. The gentile kids, two or three hundred of them, were lining the sidewalk, watching as the few dozen Jewish kids went past them. Fat flakes of snow wafted softly down upon them all.

Sophie wanted to run straight home, but Giddy was looking up at her, wordlessly imploring her to make this alright. He had his free hand clasped over his star again. "Let's go," she said, squeezing his other hand. "We don't want to be late."

So they walked.

Sophie's heart was beating wildly when they neared the closest bunch of gentile kids standing in front of the first in a long line of shops — five kids dressed just like she and Giddy were, but at the same time nothing like they were because they weren't wearing stars like targets on their chests. Sophie's ears burned under her hat. She'd never felt so conspicuous.

When she and Giddy got closer to the crowd, Sophie was relieved to recognize one of the students, a chatty, strawberry-blond girl from her class who was friendly to everyone.

"Good morning, Ilsa," Sophie said when they reached her.

But Ilsa didn't say good morning back, and she wouldn't meet Sophie's gaze. Her bright blue eyes were on the star, as if it were an open wound. Sophie swallowed into a dry throat that wouldn't let her repeat her greeting. Over Ilsa's shoulder she saw Herr Schmitt, the butcher, standing like a statue at the window of his shop in his permanently greasy apron. She raised a hand to him, but he did not move.

Now Sophie felt like a statue, but Giddy squeezed her hand and pulled, and then they were walking again.

Along the half mile walk to school Sophie said hello to every statue on the street and raised a hand to every statue in every shop window: Herr Schafer, the baker; Herr Hoffman, the grocer; Herr Becker, the liquor store man; Herr Krause, the newsagent; Herr Berger, the tobacconist...

Not one acknowledged her.

At the steps of the schoolhouse, there was a disturbance of some sort. When Sophie and Giddy got closer, they saw a ring of boys and girls in a circle; there was a fight happening in the middle. Sophie tried to pull Giddy around the crowd and up the edge of the steps.

Just then, the Recktorin, Frau Schneider, a fearsome, heavy-set woman in her sixties who wore her hair in two long, incongruously youthful braids, barged into the ring of cheering spectators. "What is going on here?" she demanded.

Now Sophie could see that a big boy had a smaller one in a headlock, choking him. The smaller boy already had a black eye and was bleeding from his nose.

"Let him go at once!" Frau Schneider ordered the bigger boy, who obeyed.

"Frau Schneider," said the boy, out of breath from his exertions, "he's a Jew. He came to school with no star."

Frau Schneider turned her withering attention to the smaller boy, whom Sophie now recognized as Simon Horn, a spindly teenager, three years her senior.

"I'll never wear it!" Simon swore.

"Simon Horn!" commanded Frau Schneider. "You will go home this very instant, and you will not return until you are ready to obey the law. Do I make myself clear?"

Simon, who'd been ready to fight the law and a school bully, was not ready to fight Frau Schneider. He girded himself up the best he could, then walked down the steps through the parted crowd and back into the street.

"You," said Frau Schneider, pointing a plump finger at the bully. "Get moving!" Then to everyone, "All of you, get moving! Do not be late!"

Sophie dashed inside with Giddy and got him to his class. She was almost late to her own, for on her way, while passing a high school room, she saw a flash of pink and stopped to peek inside. There was Lea Malka, sitting erect at her desk in the very front row, still wearing her starless jacket.

Frau Volker was a short, stout woman in her fifties with unstyled hair and a penchant for wearing brown, shapeless dresses. She had a stern demeanor, and was generally strict with her students, but she wasn't altogether humorless. And while she was quick to correct and criticize if she thought it necessary, she wasn't stingy about doling out a compliment when it was warranted.

Today, for Sophie, it was warranted.

The incident outside was forgotten. The stars were forgotten. Even Giddy was forgotten. To Sophie, sitting in her hard seat, the only thing that existed in the world right now was the chalkboard waiting for her name.

Frau Volker swiped her hands down her ruddy cheeks the way she always did. It was an odd but harmless habit her pupils enjoyed. "Good morning, class," she said.

"Good morning!" the entire class said back, swiping their hands down their own cheeks, a gentle tease they never missed a chance to administer — the entire class, minus Sophie, who was staring at the Triangle of Superior Students.

"Please stand to practice saluting our Führer," said Frau Volker.

The chairs slid back, Sophie's a second or two later. But she stood up with everyone else, and with everyone else, shot out her right arm, straight from her neck, with her hand flat and fingers extended, then called out, "Heil Hitler!" Only, she didn't say it. Her lips had formed the words, but her voice would not pronounce them the way they had every single morning since she'd come to Ortschaft.

"Again," said Frau Volker, who was a stickler. "With more oomph, please."

"Heil Hitler!" the kids yelled, trying to outdo one another.

Sophie tried again, but again, made no sound. Panicking, she looked to see if Frau Volker saw. Her teacher's daunting blue eyes were aimed right at her, but her normally severe face was a blank slate.

"Again," said Frau Volker. "With pride!"

"HEIL HITLER!"

Sophie tried so hard this time that she felt her face turn hot red. Her eyes watered, but no sound emerged. She tried to sneak a look to her right to see if Bruna Muller, the flaxen-haired girl she shared her long wooden desk with, had noticed her difficulty. Bruna was looking straight ahead, at the Nazi banner above the board at the front of the class.

"Please take your seats," said Frau Volker, sitting down at her desk.

The thirty students all sat down in their wooden chairs and slid them forward. The scraping, like the crunching of the snow on Judenstrasse, sounded too loud in Sophie's ears.

Sophie took a deep breath. It was time for the Top Students to be updated. Frau Volker would do it before saying another word. Even if there was no change to the names or their arrangement, she would go to the pyramid, erase them anyway, and put them back up. Everyone had to earn their recognition every day.

But Frau Volker didn't get up. She swiped her hands down her cheeks. Stifling their snickers, the class did the same. When Frau Volker swiped her hands down her cheeks again, the class, outright giggling now, did the same.

Frau Volker normally reacted to the mimicry with a good-natured shrug, but she didn't even seem aware of it now. She seemed distracted. Sophie's heart began to pound when she reached out and picked up a piece of chalk from the little wooden box on her desk. She tapped it on the desktop.

Sophie could hardly breathe.

Just then, someone knocked on the classroom door, which opened without invitation. Fraulein Werner, the school secretary, came into the room pushing a projector on a rolling cart. Excitement spread through the class. It was very rare that they got to see any sort of film.

"Children!" said Frau Volker, brightening up, "I almost forgot. We have a treat this morning." She got to her feet, then pulled down a screen that was attached to the wall behind her desk.

"What is it, Frau Volker?" a girl asked. It was Ilsa. "What will we see?"

"Children," said Frau Volker, making her way to the back of the classroom, "this morning we are blessed to see and hear from the greatest man in the world, our Führer, Adolf Hitler."

When Fraulein Werner left the room, Frau Volker explained to the delighted class that they'd be watching the Führer's most famous speech, and that it would inspire within them everlasting devotion to him and to the Fatherland. Sophie scarcely heard any of this. She was too upset that the chalking had been interrupted before it had even started. What if they skipped it today and her grades fell before tomorrow?

Frau Volker turned the classroom lights off and switched the projector on.

A black and white image of Adolf Hitler appeared. He was approaching a podium standing between two others. Three larger ones were on a higher level behind him, all with uniformed men standing at them. There were even more men standing to both sides of the platforms.

For a moment, the film showed an auditorium packed with men in uniform, then it returned to the podiums. On the wall behind them hung a hulking eagle clutching a swastika in a circle that seemed to be emanating beams of light in all directions. Adolf Hitler, wearing a tie under a long, side-buttoned coat, began to speak.

Sophie turned her attention back to the Triangle on the chalkboard, which she could still see unchanged in the projector's flickering light.

Abruptly, her attention was recaptured when she heard the word *Jew*, spat out like something foul. She saw Hitler actually spitting as he ranted and raved, "The peoples of the earth will soon realize that Germany under National Socialism does not desire the enmity of other peoples. I want once again to be a prophet. If the international finance Jewry inside and outside of Europe should succeed in plunging the peoples of the earth once again into a world war, the result will not be a Bolshevization of the earth and thus a Jewish victory —" Sophie didn't much understand any of this, but then Hitler, pointing repeatedly at his podium, proclaimed, "but the annihilation of the Jewish race in Europe!"

With that, the projector was switched off, and the lights switched on. Sophie looked around at her classmates, all of whom were in awe as they clapped and clapped and clapped. Someone began cheering, and then everyone joined in.

But Sophie's eyes were fixed on Frau Volker making her way back to her desk.

The students began to settle down. It was finally time for the chalking.

Frau Volker stopped at her desk and turned to face the class. She ran her hands down her cheeks. The class did the same. She sighed. Then she turned and approached the portion of the board where the Pyramid of Top Students was chalked, at the far-right side of the room. She stood, her broad back to the class, and sighed again. Sophie, once more, could hardly breathe.

Frau Volker took up an eraser from the board ledge and carefully wiped away the names in the pyramid. First, she erased the third Top Student: Gunter Schulte. Sophie, feeling a tingling running up and down her spine, assumed his name would not go back up. Next, Frau Volker erased the second Top Student: Bruna Muller, Sophie's deskmate. And then the former Top Student's name turned to dust: Otto Huber.

The class was hushed now, waiting to see if there were any changes today. Frau Volker wrote Otto Huber on the third line.

Wow, Sophie thought, *he must have really slipped up.*

On the second line, Frau Volker wrote, Gunter Schulte. Sophie peeked at Bruna, who didn't seem to realize she had fallen off the board and was trying to suppress a triumphant smile.

Sophie held her breath as Frau Volker held the chalk up to list the Top Student. When she traced out an S, Bruna gasped and looked at Sophie with narrowed and now icy blue eyes.

But at that very moment, there was another knock on the classroom door.

Frau Volker turned around as the door opened to reveal Frau Schneider and a Nazi wearing a swastika armband. The sight of the Nazi caused the class to titter with excitement again. He was tall, broad-shouldered, fair-haired, and had eyes like azure diamonds. He was as handsome as a man could be. Behind Frau Schneider and the Nazi stood a group of Jewish students. Giddy was one of them. He looked right at Sophie with wide eyes.

This should have worried Sophie, but her only concern was the chalkboard.

"Please excuse the interruption to your class, Frau Volker," said Frau Schneider. "I hope your students enjoyed the film. But I need to speak with Sophie Siegel, if I may."

All as one, the entire class looked to Sophie, whose face went white.

"Sophie," said Frau Schneider, "please step into the hall."

But Sophie remained in her seat, eyes locked on the board, blood thrumming in her ears.

"Sophie...," said Frau Schneider.

Sophie could not take her eyes off the S on the top line in the Pyramid of Top Students. She heard herself say, "Frau Volker, you didn't finish Top Student."

"Sophie," Frau Volker said, running her hands down her cheeks. "Did you not hear? Frau Schneider is asking to see you."

"You must chalk Top Student, Frau Volker," Sophie said.

"She only pretended to Heil Hitler!" Bruna mewled into Sophie's ear. "And she didn't clap for his speech!"

"Silence!" Frau Schneider demanded.

"Top Student, please, Frau Volker," said Sophie. "Please finish writing my name."

Frau Volker looked at Sophie, then at Frau Schneider and her guest.

"And she has been cheating from my papers!" Bruna cried.

Frau Volker now looked pointedly at Sophie and asked, "Is this true?"

"What is this about?" asked the Nazi.

"She thinks she is Top Student!" Bruna told him. "But she is a cheater, and she is a Jew!"

"That is preposterous," the Nazi scoffed, making his way through the class. "You, girl, stand up," he said as his shadow fell across Sophie's desk.

Sophie leapt to her feet. "Frau Volker!" she shouted. "You must chalk the Top Student's name! My name! You must do it now!"

"This is positively ridiculous," said the Nazi. "Come with me."

A hand grasped Sophie's wrist and pulled her to the front of the class. Frau Volker, looking pale, stepped to the side.

"Now, Frau Volker!" Sophie insisted. "Now! Now! Now —!"

The Nazi slapped Sophie across the face, stunning her into silence. "Children," he said to the class, "look here." He grasped Sophie's hair and pulled it up above her head like she was a bunch of carrots. "Look at the tall forehead," he said. "We know from science that this indicates laziness." He let the hair fall. The class nodded in full agreement.

The Nazi pinched Sophie's ear and pulled it out, painfully. "See this wide ear that has a point along the top?" he asked. "This indicates selfishness." He let the ear go and added, "The hooked nose reveals deceitfulness." More nods. But Sophie's nose was not hooked. It looked like most everyone else's in the room.

"This bulge below the lower lip," the Nazi continued, poking Sophie in the chin, "shows a jealous disposition." Then he looked back at the class — he had their rapt attention — and said, "Taken together, these traits indicate irremediable stupidity. Children," he concluded, "it should be obvious why the mere idea that a Jew could be Top Student is nothing less than laughable."

While the class laughed at the mere idea, the Nazi turned to Frau Volker and asked, "Who is Top Student?"

Frau Volker, perspiring heavily, stepped to the board. She promptly turned the S she had written into a B and finished chalking the name Bruna Muller.

Bruna stood and curtsied.

"No!" Sophie wailed, finding her voice again. "That's not right, Frau Volker! That's not right!" The Nazi grabbed her again, but this time she struggled against him. She went on wailing, "Chalk my name, Frau Volker! Chalk my name!" until he dragged her out of the classroom.

That night, Sophie lay in the dark, reliving her mortification. The pain she somehow managed to shunt aside while it was happening, and then again while walking back home with Giddy and the rest of the Jews, was now lacerating her. A clammy mass under her blanket, she touched her forehead, her ears, her nose, her entire face. And she felt ashamed for doing so. She knew that nothing that awful man said was true, but it didn't really matter. The class believed every word. She hated that man. She hated her class. She hated Frau Volker and Frau Schneider. She hated that school.

But what she hated most of all was that she was not allowed to go back.

Sophie heard a scratching through the wall next to her. Then several light taps. Then more scratching. "We don't need a secret code, Giddy," she sighed. His bed was on the other side of the paper-thin wall.

"Your forehead isn't tall," Giddy said.

"Thanks, Giddy," Sophie said, sitting up.

"And your ears aren't pointy."

"Thanks, Giddy."

"And your nose isn't bent."

"Thanks, Giddy."

"But even if all those things were true, you would still be beautiful."

A lump in her throat prevented Sophie from saying thank you again. She burrowed back under her blanket and mashed her face into her pillow to muffle her crying. She was crying because Giddy wanted to comfort her, but also because she hadn't realized the Jewish kids in the hall had witnessed her humiliation too.

Giddy didn't say anything more and soon, she heard him snoring.

Sophie was still crying when her door creaked open. She knew it was her Papa from the smell of wood shavings that was a permanent part of his person. She loved that smell.

Even so, she wasn't coming out from under her covers.

Benno sat down on her bed, causing it to sink dramatically. Despite herself, she felt soothed. She knew he was going to tell her a story.

"In the Sixteenth Century," her Papa started, in his low, resonant voice, "in Prague, there was a great and powerful rabbi called Judah Loew ben Bezalel, who, from the mud of the river Vltava, created a giant, which he brought to life through spells and incantations."

Sophie lay still, listening.

"This giant — this golem," her Papa said, "was eight feet tall and had the strength of a hundred men."

"That's even bigger and stronger than you," Sophie couldn't help but respond. "What did it do, Papa?"

"The Jews of Prague became his people, so he protected them. No one ever bothered them again."

Sophie came out from under her covers and sat up. "Is that the end of the story?" she asked. She couldn't see her Papa, but his presence in the dark was huge.

"That is the end," he told her. "They lived happily ever after."

"Why did you tell me such a short one, Papa?" Sophie was trying to decide whether or not to be annoyed. She liked the story.

"You are my angel," Benno said, putting his heavy hands on her shoulders and squeezing them gently, "I will be your golem." He leaned over, kissed her on the top of her head, then went out of the room.

Sophie lay back down and fell asleep.

Sophie Siegel — April, 1942

The Jews in Ortschaft, all of whom were laborers of one sort or another, lived in shabby but meticulously clean, three-room attached wooden row houses on Judenstrasse — the only exception being Rabbi Hasendahl and his wife Sarah, who had two residences with a door in the wall that normally divided them. The extra space housed a small synagogue, a library, and a meeting room.

Sophie and Giddy were in the musty, humid library on a warm, late April afternoon, combing through the eight rows of crowded and totally disorganized bookshelves for something new to read. Giddy had become attached to Sophie's hip since they'd been expelled from school. He was at her door in the morning to hinder her sock-mending; he was there after lunch to make her trips to the market for fruits and vegetables take longer; and he was there in the afternoon at the library, so she could read to him. Sophie didn't mind spending all her time with Giddy since she'd lost interest in the other kids on Judenstrasse. She read to him for hours every day and somehow never tired of it. In fact, the more she read, the less tired she felt.

The problem was they'd read everything they could find that was appropriate for children — the stories of Y.L. Peretz and Sholom Aleichem, the folktales in the *Mayse-Bukh,* several compendiums of Hasidic tales for children, and every story about the Bal Shem Tov they could find. It was looking like they'd have to start reading them all over again, which Sophie thought wouldn't be the worst thing in the world.

"Just those left," Giddy said, popping up next to Sophie in the aisle where she was rummaging through the stacks of books. He was pointing to the top shelf of books, which neither of them could reach.

"Those are just prayer books," Sophie said.

"Maybe not *all* of them?"

"But how are we supposed to —?"

"Put me on your shoulders."

Sophie didn't see why not. Giddy was still every bit as pint-sized as he'd been when she moved to Ortschaft. She got on her knees and let him throw his legs around her neck, then she stood up. There was nothing to it. There was nothing to him! This must be how her Papa felt when he did this for her.

Unfortunately, all the books up there were, in fact, prayer books. She walked Giddy to all the other top shelves, but alas, more prayer books.

Giddy didn't care. He was having fun on Sophie's shoulders. "I'm a giant!" he declared.

"You're a golem," Sophie said, turning down an aisle they'd already walked through.

"I'm a what?"

"In the Sixteenth Century, in Prague," Sophie told Giddy, "there was a great and powerful rabbi called Judah Loew ben Bezalel, who, from the mud of the river Vltava, created a giant, which he brought to life through spells and incantations. This giant — this golem — was eight feet tall and had the strength of a hundred men. The Jews of Prague became his people, so he protected them. No one ever bothered them again. They lived happily ever after."

"I'm a golem!" Giddy cried. "Legs! Start stomping Nazis!"

So that's what they did. Sophie stomped up and down the aisles of books while Giddy waved his arms around, bellowing in his childish voice, "Stomp! Stomp! Stomp!" each time Sophie took a step. He was so dramatic about it that Sophie wound up doubled over laughing, which sent Giddy rolling onto the floor. That was funny enough to send her rolling as well. Sophie laughed until she realized she couldn't remember the last time she laughed. She sat up, sobered by the thought.

"They're all dead," Giddy said from his back, not laughing at all.

Just then, footsteps, many footsteps, thundered in through the Hasendahls' front door. The Judenstrasse men were there for what had recently gone from a weekly meeting to a near daily one.

"Ugh!" Sophie sighed, collapsing onto her back. It was too late to hide. She typically heard the men debating well before they came inside, which gave her time to get herself and Giddy situated behind one of the rows of shelves in the back of the room. Hiding was necessary because Mrs. Hasendahl shooed away any remaining kids when the meetings began.

Not being in the house made it rather difficult to eavesdrop.

And here was Mrs. Hasendahl now, right on schedule. Sophie closed her eyes and waited for the kindly eviction. The door to the library opened, but strangely, no such order came. Sophie opened her eyes to see Giddy sitting cross-legged, looking up at the hefty Mrs. Hasendahl standing in the door, gazing absently into the library, evidently lost in less-than-cheerful thoughts. Her normally jovial face was squinched up tight. She was a smiler, even when she had to say something difficult. Surely, she was about to look down and see the two children on the floor less than ten feet in front of her, or so Sophie thought. But instead, Mrs. Hasendahl brushed some crumbs from her apron, then shut the door.

Pleasantly surprised, Sophie got up. What a stroke of luck!

"Ugh," said Giddy. He got up too and grabbed the largest story collection he could find and sat down with it on the long, uncomfortable wooden bench bolted to the library's rear wall. He knew Sophie would ignore him for the next hour.

Sophie went to the wall shared between the library and the meeting room and flattened her ear against it. These meetings filled her with anxiety, but she listened in on them anyway because she'd have more anxiety if she didn't. Her Mama and Papa would tell her nothing about anything that was going on. She knew they meant well, but it galled her to no end that all they ever said to her was, "Let us worry about it." Lately they'd been telling her to try to enjoy this extra free time because she may never have it again, which made her feel even worse. There was nothing Sophie could say or do to make them understand that, for her, worrying about the worst was worse than knowing about the worst. The only thing keeping her together since losing school was her faith in Papa always knowing when to relocate them. If he didn't think it was time to move again, things must not be so bad.

Every community meeting went the same way: the men complained about the Nazi's latest affront to their dignity as human beings, and Rabbi Hasendahl would counsel them that this dark phase in history couldn't last; that Hitler was a buffoon who'd be out of power before long; that things couldn't get much worse before they got any better; that they must be patient, have faith, and trust God.

Sophie had heard him say these things after the town crier banged his drum on the street, announcing that Jews could no longer socialize in public places; she heard him repeat them when they were barred from entering public buildings. She was quite sure he would say those things regardless of what was going on.

"Let us begin," said Rabbi Hasendahl. He was a soft-spoken man in his sixties, with tufts of white hair on either side of his otherwise bald head that shaped themselves into a copious white beard. He knew everything about everything, and so his congregants had taken to calling him "The Beard of Wisdom." Everyone had to strain to hear him when he spoke, but this only made them listen harder. Most of the time, the thin walls on Judenstrasse were a source of irritation to Sophie, but now she found she appreciated them. "I understand," the rabbi said, "that Benno would like to address the group."

Sophie tensed. Her Papa attended every meeting, but he'd never spoken up before. He was like that, quiet — but only because that's how he gathered information. He never spoke unless he was sure he knew what should be said. He often told her that if you aren't constantly running your mouth, when you do decide to speak, people will listen.

"The time has come to leave Ortschaft," he said. "For all of us."

"No!" Sophie gasped, but there was no chance anyone could hear her over the tumult that met her Papa's declaration.

She heard Israel Bokser shout, "Nonsense!"

Then Levi Bernstein cried, "What a wholly irresponsible and alarmist thing to say!"

Hirsh Finkel: "Go where?!"

Joseph Dressler: "Take your bravado somewhere else!"

Finally, Ruben Linker shouted, "Ortschaft has been my home for generations, and I have as much right to live here as any gentile!" and then, "Benno would understand what that meant if he didn't run away from every place he's ever lived at the first sign of trouble!"

Someone called for quiet. It was Mr. Goldfarb, Giddy's father. This didn't surprise Sophie. Whenever there was an argument and he was around, it got resolved. And the Jews in Ortschaft were always arguing. Truthfully, everywhere Sophie had lived, the Jews were always arguing. Even though Mr. Goldfarb was a fisherman, he was almost never without some scholarly book or another; he was very clever. His knowledge certainly paled in comparison to that of the Beard of Wisdom, but Sophie saw that people often approached him with their problems first. She thought maybe they were afraid to bother the rabbi unless they had no other choice.

"Benno must be given a chance to explain himself," Mr. Goldfarb said once the men calmed down. "Do we not want to hear his reasoning before attacking him? Isn't it possible he knows something that we do not?"

A reluctant grumble passed through the room.

"Benno," said Rabbi Hasendahl, "please, say what you have to say."

"As you all know," Benno said, but then paused. Sophie knew he was taking in a deep breath to make sure his words came out exactly so. "I do commissioned work for customers all over town," he continued when he was ready. His powerful voice sounded like he was on Sophie's side of the wall, standing right next to her. "Including," he added, "some of our wealthier and better-connected neighbors."

"You heard something?" Rabbi Hasendahl asked.

"Herr Weber," Benno explained. "He took me aside after I finished a trunk for his wife. He said to me, 'Benno, Frau Weber loves your work. Says she's never seen better. We will need to make some... confidential arrangements going forward.' When I asked him why, he told me that on Monday, three days from now, Jews will be excluded from all aspects of economic life. He said he did not approve of these new prejudicial laws."

If Benno's initial remarks caused an uproar, this information set off a near riot. The crowd called Benno a liar, and that such a law would be a death sentence. Benno said that's precisely what he assumed it was. He was called a fearmonger who moved from town to town spreading false rumors. He was accused of being a self-hating Jew.

Sophie barely resisted the urge to pound on the wall. What was wrong with everyone? Her Papa was trying to save them! She was so furious that she forgot how much his words had scared her.

At last, when not even Mr. Goldfarb could get things back under control, Rabbi Hasendahl spoke and, despite his soft voice, his clamoring congregants settled down to hear what he had to say. "Benno," he said when he could be heard, "you are a good man. What exactly are you proposing?"

"That we — all of us," Benno said, "gather our belongings, before they are taken from us, and go into the woods. We are practical men: we will provide for ourselves and our families until this is over." He sounded so calm, so confident — the way that made

Sophie feel safe in such a scary world. But his words didn't affect the men the way they did her.

"What about the gangs of Hitler's thugs they say are roving the countryside and wandering through the woods?" shouted Joseph Dressler. "Maybe you, the Jewish Bear, can fight the Nazis all by yourself. But you are not going to get us all killed!"

"Here is what you will all do," said Rabbi Hasendahl with gentle yet unchallengeable authority. "Two things. First, you will all go home and celebrate the day of rest with your families. The Nazis will not take Shabbos from us. Second, Sunday morning, you will collect all your debts and perhaps sell anything you don't need to accumulate some extra money. You will buy as much food as you can, and you will tend to your gardens. Such a law may be meant only to make a point, a point I cannot begin to imagine, but I believe it will be temporary. And here is what I will do: Benno mentioned that Herr Weber does not support such laws. If that is the case, it is very possible that he is not the only one. I will go to the Burgermeister and plead our case. That is my decision, and it is final."

Not one voice rose in defiance of this decree, not even Benno's. There was only the scuffling of boots as the men left the meeting room, and then the house. Sophie, livid about the treatment her Papa had been subjected to, peeled her hot ear from the wall and turned around to find Giddy standing right behind her. Tears were streaming down his face. He'd heard everything.

Instead of crying with him, which she sorely wanted to do, Sophie put her hands on Giddy's shoulders and gripped them firmly. She fixed her eyes steady on his. "You are my angel," she said, "I will be your golem."

The Judenstrasse men traipsed down the cobblestones in an agitated mob, waving their hands and arguing vociferously. Sophie's Papa was right in the middle, the calm eye of the storm. None of them noticed the golem stomping past them on the far side of the street.

Sophie stomped quickly, not in order to get home before her Papa — he'd soon be making rounds up and down the street to do small repairs for the same neighbors who were probably still insulting him — but because she needed to be home to help her Mama prepare for Shabbos.

After taking Giddy back to his house, that's exactly what Sophie did. Bianca prepared dinner — chicken soup — and Sophie swept the floors, dusted the furniture, and set the table, all while biting her tongue. It took all her willpower to keep from sharing what she'd learned from the meeting.

While she and her Mama sliced vegetables for the soup, Bianca said, "Sophie, you're so quiet. Is something wrong?"

"Mama," Sophie said, "I don't feel well. Would it be okay — I'm not hungry — if I missed Shabbos tonight? I'd just like to go to bed." It wasn't really a lie. Sophie wasn't hungry much lately, and now that she was out of the library and away from Giddy, her exhaustion had caught up to her.

Bianca, her lovely face creased with concern, fussed over Sophie, putting the back of her hand on her daughter's forehead.

"It's not serious," Sophie said. "I'm just tired."

"Of course, I understand," Bianca said, taking her hand away. "Go lie down, Angel. Perhaps you will feel well enough to join us later."

After forcing her own fake smile, Sophie went to her room, closed the door, and fell onto her bed. There was no way she could get through an entire Shabbos meal without exploding, knowing what she knew while Papa didn't say a word about it.

Sophie finally heard her Papa come home and, despite her dark mood, she found herself mouthing the words he always said to her Mama: "Bitty Bee, you are my light and my life, the reason I go out in the morning and come home at night." She heard him lift Mama up so they could share a kiss, then he set her back on her feet, whispering, "We need to talk."

"Oh, dear," said Bianca. "Let's light the candles first. Sophie is in bed. She's not feeling well."

"Nothing worrisome?" Benno asked.

"Nothing worrisome," Bianca confirmed.

Sophie heard her parents sit down at the table. She listened to them chant the Shabbos blessings that welcome the day of rest. Her favorite part was when her Papa recited the praise of a woman and told her Mama she was more valuable than rubies — and when her Mama recited the praise of a man and told him he was gracious, merciful, and just. Then she listened to her Mama bless and light the candles and her Papa say the blessings for wine and bread. She felt a pang of regret for denying herself some of her mother's delicious challah while the traditional bread was still fresh out of the oven.

Bianca served the soup. Sophie could hear her parents' quiet slurping.

"Delectable, my darling," said Benno.

"Thank you," Bianca replied. "Now tell me what you have to say."

Benno told her what he told the men at the meeting. "And they reacted," he said when he was done, "exactly as the men reacted in Weiler and Gemeinde. Exactly. Right down to calling me a self-hating Jew. I ask you, my love, how can a man be expected to fight the Nazis *and* the Jews? It is too much of a burden." But then, just as Sophie felt her fingertips begin to freeze, he added, "Even so, I will bear it."

"We will bear it together, my love," Bianca said. "But this new law?" she asked. "This is, like the others, for all of Germany, no? So where are we to go? Is there a town ready to defy the Führer?"

"Beautiful Bitty Bee," said Benno, which is what he called her when he was trying to be persuasive, "we can survive on our own. In the woods. I will build us a shelter, many shelters. We can move around as we must. And I can fish and I can hunt. We will wait the bastards out."

"I —" Bianca said, "I just don't know if I could... live in the woods?"

"But Bee," Benno said, so calm, so reassuring, "you do want to live?"

Sophie could no longer restrain herself. She flew off her bed, threw open her bedroom door, and stormed over to the Shabbos table. "Is anyone going to ask me what I think?" she demanded.

"Oh, Sophie," Bianca sighed, "this conversation was not meant for you to hear."

"Well, I heard it!" Sophie cried. "And I heard the meeting too! I've heard all the meetings!"

One of Benno's thick, dark eyebrows went up. She could see him try to soften his features for her because even his face was strong. He had pronounced cheekbones, a proud nose, and a firmly set chin. He sighed deeply and said, "Sophie, Angel, you will not be part of this discussion. And that is final."

"Why?!" Sophie pleaded. "Doesn't my opinion count? I'm not a child anymore, Papa! I'm a very serious person!" She would have shouted her opinion at the top of her lungs right then and there — had she known what it was.

"Sophie," Bianca said, "it is for that very reason you may not play a part in making the very difficult decision that lies before us."

"I don't understand!" Sophie whined, feeling the temperature in her body drop.

Benno took Sophie into his massive arms. She wanted to resist, but she couldn't if she tried, and she needed his warmth and love. "Sophie," he said, "if you tell us you want to go, and it turns out badly for us — you will blame yourself. If you tell us you want to stay, and it turns out badly for us — you will blame yourself. It is our responsibility to make such decisions for you."

The tears Sophie didn't shed in the library came at last. She felt belittled. And also more cherished than she ever had in her life. Nonetheless, she released herself from her father's embrace and huffed back to her bedroom. She slammed the door behind her and hurled herself back onto her bed.

And then, she tiptoed back to listen at the door.

Sophie heard her parents talking again, but in hushed voices that were hard to make out. She was ready to charge out of her room again when she heard her father's voice speak to her through the door.

"Sophie, our little spy," he said, making her face flush, "we have decided to stay. Your wise mother has convinced me that if Herr Weber — and perhaps others — mean to continue to commission my work privately, I can ask for my payment in the form of food or medicines, or anything else we may need and, anything our neighbors may need. That way I can both keep us safe and live in such a way that brings honor to our people."

Then she heard her Mama's voice just as close, "Go to sleep, Angel. We love you, always and forever."

Sophie walked back to her bed and climbed under the covers. She did fall asleep, but it took a long time.

Sophie Siegel — November, 1942

Sophie lay in bed, entombed in her covers against the cold with her pillow over her face. There was no chance she was getting out of bed today, even though she was ravenous. She was skipping the day. But just as she was about to drift back into a hungry sleep, a series of scratching sounds came from behind the prayer book-sized door in the wall about five feet above her bed. It was followed by a series of taps, then a few more scratches.

"No," Sophie said.

The scratches came again.

"I said no."

Scratch. Tap. Scratch.

Sophie freed an angry eye from her blankets and cast a per-turbed look up at the little door. "You can knock like a normal human being," she said. "Or just talk."

When the Jews in Ortschaft were banned from earning their livings — on the very day Benno had predicted they would be — the already close community leapt into unprecedented collective action. A representative from each family met at Rabbi Hasendahl's every morning and shared what their household needed. The information was then taken to every home and anyone who had those items to spare returned them to the rabbi, after which they were redistributed by Mrs. Hasendahl. Money was pooled and talents were bartered. And so, while living conditions deteriorated quickly, they did not become dire.

That is, until the Jews were forbidden to leave their homes.

When word got out, every family on Judenstrasse cut a hole in their adjoining walls — one on either side of their attached homes. And so, the exchange of essentials continued, although at a rapidly diminishing pace, for every day there was less to share. They'd all have been long dead by now if not for the buckets of murky water and baskets of unsellable fruits and vegetables dropped off at their doors every other day by the Town Council — along with a puny pile of kindling so their homes could be heated for an hour or two each day.

It also helped a bit that Herr Weber did, in fact, continue to commission work from Benno covertly, although his payments were nothing but a few extra fruits and vegetables that found their way into the Siegel's bucket — which were then shared around.

More scratching, tapping, scratching. Slightly more insistent now.

Exasperated, Sophie stood up, blanket over her shoulders like a cape, and opened the little door her father installed over the hole he cut out.

A skinny hand slid through the open door on the other side, holding some folded-up papers. Sophie looked round the hand and saw Giddy's pale face and jug ears. He was kneeling on his dresser so he could see through the hole.

"Happy birthday, Sophie," he said.

"Giddy!," Sophie cried. She'd forgotten her own birthday. Evidently her parents had as well, and the realization sent a stab of resentment through her. She'd told Giddy when her birthday was shortly after they'd met, and it never came up again. But he remembered it last year, and now he'd remembered it again.

Sophie took the papers and unfolded them. They were pages torn from a book he must have found in his house, pages that told the legend of the golem of Prague. She could hardly speak.

"I had to sneak them out before my dad burned the book," Giddy explained. All the books in every house, Sophie knew, save the prayer books, were used as fuel not long after winter hit, as was all superfluous furniture. "Maybe you can read it to me some time," Giddy said.

"Every night," Sophie promised, closing the door on Giddy's goofy grin.

Sophie refolded the pages and tucked them into the pocket of her nightgown. She got her slippers on, then, keeping the blanket wrapped around herself, went hesitantly out of her room.

"Happy birthday, Angel!"

Sophie's parents were sitting in the living room on the brocade upholstered couch Papa made. Cloaked in their own blankets, they'd been waiting for her to emerge from her bedroom. Sophie forced a smile, but she wanted to cry. Her Papa was still big, but now he was also skinny and sallow. Her Mama was still pretty, but now in a haunted, hollow-cheeked sort of way. And since thread had become scarce, her soiled nightgown was coming apart at the seams. Sophie's was too.

What wasn't?

"Come," Bianca said, waving Sophie to Papa's matching armchair. Sophie saw something small on the coffee table, hidden under a dish towel. Seeing it made her realize she could smell it as well. She quickly sat down, trying to determine whether she was imagining the scent of honey and lemon... or was it orange?

"Sit, sit!" Benno said, gesturing impatiently. So Sophie sat. Bianca twirled the towel away to reveal a small piece of honey cake on a plate.

Sophie put a hand on her heart. Every family on Judenstrasse must have contributed to this tiny delicacy.

"We love you, Angel," her Mama and Papa said at the same time.

Sophie wanted to eat that cake more than she'd ever wanted to eat anything in her entire life. Her stomach was dying for it. Her mouth filled with saliva, but she pushed the cake on its napkin across the table so her parents could have the first bites.

Bianca and Benno shook their heads. "It's *your* birthday," they said, again together. Because they knew she'd do exactly that.

"I'm the birthday girl," Sophie retorted. Because she knew they'd say exactly that. "And I insist."

Bianca reached for the cake and broke it into three equal-sized pieces. She had to use her fingers because she'd sold the family's utensils, a wedding gift from her parents.

"You first," Bianca said to Sophie.

"You first," Sophie said back.

"Hold on," said Benno. "I think we should tell her first. It will make the cake taste even better."

"Tell me what?" Sophie asked.

"Tonight, just after dark," Bianca told her, "we will go. We will live in the woods until Germany regains its sanity."

"We're leaving?" Sophie asked, not because she didn't understand what her parents were telling her, but because she needed to absorb it. "But what about my Oma and Opa and Bubbe and Zayde?" Sophie asked. "We haven't gotten a single letter from them in forever! How will they know where we are?"

"It has been painful not being able to communicate with your grandparents," Benno admitted. "We have to trust that they are okay, and that when this is over, we will be able to see them again."

"But — but —" Sophie stuttered as the full implications of this decision hit her. "I — I can't leave Giddy! He needs me! Can the Goldfarbs come with us?"

Benno and Bianca looked at one another, then back at Sophie.

"We can ask," Bianca said.

This calmed Sophie down considerably. "Okay," she said, putting on a brave face. Giddy would come. He would not take no for an answer from his parents, she was sure of it. "Okay," she said again, trying to make it so. "Can we eat the cake now?"

"First," said Benno, "your other present."

"Another present?"

Benno took something out of his pocket, something on a lanyard, like a necklace. But when he handed it to her, Sophie saw it was not a necklace, but rather a wooden whistle with exquisitely carved angels' wings on its sides. When she looked closer at what at first appeared to be feathers on the wings, she saw it was actually the letters of her Hebrew name, Tzofia.

"Oh, Papa!" Sophie cried, throwing her arms around him. "It's lovely!"

"But also practical," said Benno. "Try it."

Sophie let go of her Papa, put the little treasure between her lips and blew. What came out was a rich tone that felt like honey in her ears.

"I love it, Papa."

"Now, Angel," Benno said, "when we leave tonight, or any time after — if you ever get separated from us — you are to blow the whistle and we will find you. Do you understand?"

"Yes, Papa," Sophie said. "As long as Giddy comes with us. May I ask you something now?"

"Yes, Angel."

"Can we have the cake?"

Benno and Bianca laughed. "Of course!" they both said.

But before any of them could pick up their piece, someone pounded on the front door so violently that Sophie dropped her whistle.

At once, all three Siegels were on their feet, their blankets fallen, their faces ashen.

"Open up!" a man shouted at the front door, banging harder. "At once!"

They had a plan for this: the back door. Out into the street. Scatter. Meet at the well beyond the market. But when the Siegels turned toward their back door — their escape! — someone banged on that too. "Open up!" a second man demanded. "By order of the

Führer!"

Sophie began to shake uncontrollably.

"*Big Bennnno!*" the banger at the front door called. "*Bitty Bee!*" sang the man at the back.

These men knew her parents' nicknames, but they were not from town. They were Nazis.

Benno and Bianca exchanged grim yet determined looks. Without a word, Benno lifted Sophie's shivering body and carried her across the room and into the coat closet.

The pounding got louder, more vicious.

"OPEN THE GODDAMN DOOR!"

Benno set Sophie down, draped her coat over her shoulders, then gripped them tightly. He looked directly into her eyes, and then, in a voice so grave that it made Sophie feel unsteady on her feet, said, "Do not come out of this closet, no matter what happens. Do you understand me, Angel? *No matter what happens.*"

Sophie, her mouth dry as bone, her limbs locked up, could only nod.

The moment Benno shut the closet — or rather, tried to, it never closed completely — Sophie heard both doors to her home kicked open. She could see a sliver of the main room, and standing there a few seconds later, were four Nazis garbed in gray. They wore jackets with belts and red and white armbands with swastikas. They wore peaked caps and had long guns across their backs. Pistols were holstered on their hips.

A fifth Nazi stepped into view, a tall, paunchy, pale-faced soldier with diamond shapes on his lapel. The leader. He shot out his arm and shouted, "Heil Hitler!" Then he finished his salute with a smirking sort of sneer — a grotesque, open-mouthed expression of some kind that revealed many broken teeth.

Bianca and Benno hesitated, transfixed by the man's grisly mouth. But then both shot out their arms and, with much less enthusiasm, they muttered, "Heil Hitler."

This seemed to amuse the men.

"Oh," the leader said, "I think we can do much better than that. Again, please."

Bianca and Benno did it again, this time shouting, "Heil Hitler!"

"Again."

"Heil Hitler!"

"Again! Like your lives depend on it!"

"Heil Hitler!"

"Wonderful," said the leader. "It warms the heart when dogs show due respect to their Master."

"Welcome to our home," Bianca said, her voice splintering like one of Benno's logs when he hit it with an ax. She was smoothing her nightgown, trying to turn on her famous smile. "We don't have much," she added, "but we would be pleased to share what —"

"So, this is Big Benno," the leader said, ignoring the offer. "I've seen much bigger." His men sniggered. None of them were anywhere near Benno's size. They all kept their hands near their guns.

"Sir," Benno said, "is there anything we can —?"

"But Bitty Bee!" the leader interrupted, turning to her. "Now, here is a Jew who lives up to her billing. Tales of your beauty do you no justice. A pearl among swine!"

"Please," Benno said, his voice now urgent and fearful. "Do anything you like with me, but please..."

Sophie had never heard her father sound scared before; she clenched her teeth to keep them from chattering.

The leader turned back to Benno and said, "Get down on your knees and beg, dog."

"Please," Bianca said, "we would like to cooperate. You need only tell us what you —"

"Use my name," the leader told her. "Dieter Wolf. I want to hear it on your lovely lips."

"Dieter Wolf," Bianca said. "Please. Dieter Wolf. We would like to cooperate."

Dieter Wolf grinned, exposing his jagged teeth again. "Sounds nice, doesn't it, men?" he asked. "She would like to cooperate."

Like a pack of hyenas, the men snorted and nodded.

Benno dropped to his knees on the worn living room rug. "I beg of you," he pleaded. "Please don't hurt my wife."

Bianca began to cry. Sophie tasted bile in her mouth — she was going to throw up.

"So this is the famous Jewish Bear," said Dieter Wolf. "A sheep in wolf's clothing, as I expected. A dog in sheep's clothing, in wolf's clothing!" he added, guffawing at his own joke. The men guffawed with him. "I guess he won't put up a fight," Dieter Wolf sneered. Then, to Benno, he said, "Come here and lick my boots, sheep dog."

Sophie put her hands out to brace herself in the closet; her legs were starting to fail her.

"Please, no!" Bianca cried. She took a step toward her husband, but one of the Nazis grabbed her by the hair and bent an arm behind her.

Benno looked at Dieter Wolf. Then he looked at his wife, who was crying. He turned away from her, set his jaw, then crawled to Dieter Wolf's feet and licked one of his boots.

"Oh, that's not nearly good enough," said Dieter Wolf. "My boots are dirty from walking through this shithole town. I'd like them clean, please." When Benno hesitated, he said, "Or perhaps Bitty Bee is better with her tongue."

Benno leaned back down and began licking the boot. He licked it all over. For too many minutes, he licked it while his wife wept. Sophie could see her Papa's hands balled into fists beside Dieter Wolf's boot, his knuckles white. When Dieter Wolf was satisfied, he had Benno lick his other boot clean. The Nazis laughed.

Benno sat back on his knees.

"You make me sick," Dieter Wolf said, and spat something foul in Benno's face.

Benno winced, but instead of wiping it off, he began to recite the most important prayer of their religion, the Shema. "*Shema Yisroel...*" Sophie knew this meant her Papa expected the very worst. She wanted to cry out, to tell him he was her golem, but she didn't dare open her mouth, even if she could.

Dieter Wolf's lip curled over his broken teeth. With blue eyes blazing, he sprang forward while tearing his pistol out of its holster. Without pause or hesitation, he shoved the barrel into Benno's mouth and pulled the trigger.

A hole in the back of Benno's head burst open with a spray of blood and brain. His body slumped over with a sickening thump on the rug.

Sophie felt her mind trying to wrest itself out of her body. Her legs had given way, yet she managed to stay on her feet. Her outstretched arms had remained locked in place, her hands pressed against the walls of the closet.

Bianca had watched her husband's murder in disbelief, her mouth agape and distorted, a rictus of horror and incomprehension. She was trying to scream, but could only produce a wet, choking sound. The Nazi who'd seized her was holding her up by her hair.

"The punishment for circumventing the Führer's laws is death," Dieter Wolf said. "As Herr Weber has already discovered. He will no longer be illegally soliciting your husband's work. Which is convenient since your husband is no longer available."

Now it was Bianca who spat, but a feeble spume of spittle was all she could muster, and it fell well short of Dieter Wolf's feet.

Dieter Wolf nodded.

The Nazi holding Bianca threw her to the floor. Then he and his three partners, in an organized but animal frenzy, tore off her nightgown and undergarments. They held her down while Dieter Wolf had his way with her.

Over their hooting and urging, Bianca screamed long and hard enough to shred her vocal cords.

Sophie wanted to close her eyes, but she had long since lost control over any part of her body. Instead, urine streamed down her leg as her mind tore itself free.

When Dieter Wolf finished with Bianca, she turned her head from the floorboards and looked at Sophie's unblinking eye through the cracked open closet door. Her bloodied lips formed a soundless word: *Angel.*

Dieter Wolf, back on his feet and buckling his belt, turned to his men and said, "Who's next?" But before any of them could volunteer he said, "Never mind. I don't like to share the good ones."

And then he shot Bianca in the face.

At this, the others got a turn. They shot her too: in the throat, the chest, the gut...

Finally, Sophie's body collapsed. Her arms went limp, and she fell to the floor in the closet. The sound was swallowed by the gunshots.

When it was quiet again, one of the men cried out, "Cake!" Then came the sounds of a mad dash.

"Stop!" Dieter Wolf shouted. "There are three pieces!"

Silence met this observation.

"Idiots! There is someone else here! Check the other rooms."

Sophie's hand, of its own accord, went into the pocket of her robe. It found something: the pages Giddy had given her. Sophie flattened them on the floor, and while the men ripped her home apart, she read them, waiting for her fate.

"Ah ha!" said Dieter Wolf.

Sophie stood up when the sliver of light coming into the closet went dark.

She had to say goodbye to Giddy, so she quietly scratched the closet door. Then she tapped on it. Then she scratched it again.

The door whipped open.

When Dieter Wolf did not immediately drag her out, Sophie looked into his eyes. He seemed to be staring right at her. But his expression was blank, then disappointed, then annoyed. He was wearing Papa's whistle.

"Smells like piss," Dieter Wolf snarled, lip curled in disgust. "These Jews live like pigs."

Then he shut the closet door.

"No one is here!" one of the other Nazis said. They were all back in the main room.

"We'll check the records," Dieter Wolf said. "Take care of it at loading tomorrow. Let's go. The day is just getting started. Bring the cake."

In high spirits, the Nazis left the Siegels' home.

When they were gone, Sophie sat down again. She heard something, faintly at first, a scratching and knocking coming from somewhere in the house. She listened as it steadily grew louder and louder, more insistent and plaintive. She knew, of course, that it was coming from her bedroom wall.

Early the next morning, Sophie was still sitting in the closet when she heard the crier out on Judenstrasse announcing that all Jews had two hours to pack their belongings, one piece of luggage per person, and to report to the street for relocation.

So for the next two hours, Sophie listened to her neighbors' lamentations as they rushed to and fro, echoing through her house from both sides. And when the two hours expired, she listened to Nazis in the street barking orders at people to line up with their papers ready.

Sophie heard her front door open. She looked out of the closet and saw Giddy standing at the threshold of her home, wrapped up in his jacket and hat, his eyes popping wide at the sight of her parents lying dead on the floor in pools of blood, her mother naked. She could see him gather every bit of courage he had to take a few steps into the house. He put his hands over his eyes but fanned his fingers just enough to avoid the bodies.

"So — Sophie?" he whispered, standing by Papa's blue table.

"I'm here," said Sophie, her voice, a husk.

"Sophie?" Giddy said again, as if he hadn't heard her. "Please don't be dead, Sophie. Please don't be dead. Please don't be dead."

"Giddy!" Sophie shouted. "I'm not dead. I'm in the closet."

"Please don't be dead. Please don't be dead."

Sophie hadn't thought for a moment about why Dieter Wolf pretended not to see her, but now... She got up, letting her coat fall from her shoulders, and stepped out of the closet. "Giddy," she said, "I'm okay."

But Giddy walked right past her into the kitchen and looked behind the curtain that hung in front of the cupboards beneath the sink, a place she knew he liked to hide in his own house. Then he headed for her bedroom with his hands splayed open over his eyes again. Sophie walked behind him saying, "Giddy! Giddy!" Just before he went into her room, she put her hand on his shoulder and turned him around the way she had on the street last winter, the day their lives began to unravel.

Giddy dropped his hands and gasped, looking astonished and afraid and as if he were looking right through her. But then someone else was calling, "Giddy! Giddy!" Someone desperate — Golda Goldfarb, his mother, who had come into the house through the open front door. She was a tall, angular, athletic-looking woman. When she collapsed at the sight of Sophie's parents, it seemed to play out in slow motion. When Giddy ran to her, she grabbed him and pulled his face to her neck to prevent him from seeing what he'd already seen.

"Where is Sophie?!" Golda cried, although Sophie was standing right in front of her, now at a complete loss. Why didn't they see her?

"She's not here, Mama," Giddy said into her hair. "She got away. She got away. She got away."

"From your lips to God's ears," said Golda, standing up with Giddy in her arms. "Baruch dyan ha-emmet," she whispered, the prayer one said upon learning of a death. Then, backing out of the house with her eyes averted, she said, "Big Benno and Bitty Bee, may your memories be for a blessing. And dear God, please protect that angel of a child."

Once Giddy and his mother were gone, Sophie went to her room, threw off her yellow nightgown, and, after cleaning herself up, put on her favorite yellow dress, the one her Mama embroidered with tiny flowers — after ripping the star off of it.

Back in the living room, she picked up the blankets her parents had dropped and carefully laid one over each of their bodies. "I love you, Mama," she said as she covered Bianca. "I love you, Papa," she said as she covered Benno. "Always and forever."

Then, after ripping its star off, she put her coat back on and went out into the street.

Three large horse-drawn wagons sat on the cobblestones of Judenstrasse. Sophie's neighbors were crowded on the wagon beds, clinging to their bags, suitcases, and satchels. And those that weren't, like the Goldfarbs, were getting screamed at. Everyone looked adrift and afraid.

The five Nazis were all there. Sophie also saw a gathered crowd. The town's gentiles had come halfway down Judenstrasse to watch what was happening. She could see Bruna Muller, holding her mother's hand, smiling.

"Leave me be!" someone cried, a girl.

Sophie turned to see one of the Nazis, who'd been manhandling people into the back of one of the carts, dragging a girl away by the arm. A girl in a long pink coat. Lea Malka. Sophie had not seen her since all the Jewish kids had to walk home in disgrace after being expelled from school. She remembered being slightly surprised that Lea Malka hadn't been allowed to stay, with or without a star.

"Leave me be!" Lea Malka cried again, but she was no match for the Nazi, who hauled her to Dieter Wolf.

"Look here," the Nazi said. "This girl has no star."

Dieter Wolf was incensed, but then he got a longer and better look at Lea Malka. "Stand where you are and do not move if you wish to live," he told her. "Where are your parents?"

"My — my father," Lea Malka said. But she couldn't say anything else. She pointed at the cart she'd been pulled away from, where her father was waving wildly for her to come back to him.

"Bring him here," Dieter said to his man, who went back to the cart and yanked Lea Malka's father from it. His name was Emanual, but everyone called him Manny. He was a small, bespectacled man with an unpretentious air about him. Everyone respected him for doing his best to raise Lea Malka by himself after her mother died when she was only six. When he was delivered to Dieter Wolf, he reached up to put his arm protectively around his daughter's shoulders. "Please sir," he said to Dieter Wolf. "It was an... accident. It fell off."

Before Dieter Wolf could reply, shouting came from another of his men.

"Get back here!"

Sophie turned to see a woman trundling away from another wagon toward the now empty houses.

"Stop!" Dieter Wolf ordered.

She stopped and turned back to him — it was Mrs. Hasendahl! Sophie saw her smile, but it was a smile of abject terror. "My husband has forgotten his Tanakh!" she cried. "It — it is a very special book! A priceless heirloom!"

"Sarah, leave it be!" someone called in a strangled voice. It was Rabbi Hasendahl. He was trying to get out of his wagon, but his people held him back.

"A gift from his grandfather!" Mrs. Hasendahl called to Dieter Wolf. "Please! I will be right back."

Dieter Wolf nodded, so Mrs. Hasendahl hurried back into her house. The rabbi stopped struggling, apparently satisfied, but Sophie knew better than to think Dieter Wolf capable of kindness. Meanwhile, Lea Malka and her father stood next to him, arms around each other now, waiting to learn their fates.

Mrs. Hasendahl came back outside clenching a leather-bound book to her chest. She tried to make haste for the wagon, but Dieter Wolf stepped in front of her and put out his hand.

"May I see this priceless heirloom?" he asked, feigning politeness.

Mrs. Hasendahl reluctantly handed him the book. There was complete silence on Judenstrasse, as the Jews in their wagons and the gentiles on the street waited to see what would happen.

Dieter Wolf opened the Tanakh, looked at the Hebrew words inside for maybe a second, then dropped the book like it might burn him.

Then he unzipped his trousers and urinated on it.

"No!" roared the rabbi, his weak voice well past its limit. Again, he had to be restrained in the cart.

Mrs. Hasendahl slapped Dieter Wolf in the face.

Sophie sprinted toward him, having no idea what she was going to do. But before she could reach him, Dieter Wolf shot Mrs. Hasendahl in the heart.

Everyone in all the carts cried out in horror as she fell down dead.

"Sarah!" the rabbi wailed. "My Sarah! My Sarah!"

"Okay! Go!" Dieter Wolf shouted to the wagon drivers. "Rid us of these vermin!"

Sophie wanted to grab his gun, to shoot him dead, but the wagons were leaving. She raced after the one the Goldfarbs were huddled in and climbed into the back before it got moving too quickly.

While the gentiles stepped to either side of the street to let the carts through, Sophie settled into a spot next to Giddy, who was whispering, "Don't be dead. Don't be dead. Don't be dead." Then, looking at the gawking faces as the cart passed them, Sophie seemed to lock eyes with a beaming Bruna Muller, still holding her mother's hand. But just then there came the sound of another gunshot.

Sophie looked back to see Manny Mankowitz lying in the street next to Mrs. Hasendahl.

The last thing Sophie saw of Judenstrasse was Lea Malka in her long pink coat, falling to her knees beside her father's body. For a long time, as they were carted away, the Jews of Ortschaft heard her wails echoing off the cobblestones.

PART TWO
THE GHETTO

Sophie Siegel — March, 1943

Sophie shouldered her way through the crowd on the street, heading out on her morning acquisition run. The ghetto was so overcrowded that there was no difference between the streets and sidewalks to its trapped residents: emaciated phantoms in rags, who spent their days shambling hither and yon in search of whatever it was they needed to make it to tomorrow. No one was allowed to work, so Sophie never really knew where anyone was going. Unless it was to a food line, she assumed it was to beg, borrow, barter, or, like her, steal.

The day the Jews of Ortschaft were unceremoniously deposited into the twelve blocks of the Stadtgebiet ghetto, Sophie discerned the basics of her situation. Her clothes, while on her person, were as invisible as her body. Putting objects into her pockets or concealing them in her fists rendered them invisible too, but simply holding or touching something did not. She used her newfound ability to filch food for herself, which gave her the energy to filch more for Giddy.

Her initial attempt to help him did not go well. Sophie stole a handful of carrot and potato peels from the soup kitchen and tucked them into Giddy's pocket. She cried to see his tears of joy when he found them there. But he showed the peels to his parents — it didn't occur to Sophie that he would do that, but of course he would — and they reacted with anger and suspicion. So that was the end of that. Eventually, she hit upon the idea to supply the Goldfarb's entire apartment with extra rations. They lived in one of the nearly twenty identical, unfinished concrete housing complexes that made up the ghetto. They'd been built, or mostly built, Sophie learned, before World War I, when the population of Stadtgebiet was growing rapidly. When the economy crashed, the construction simply ceased, and now the "apartments" were just empty concrete boxes with no plumbing, perfect for a ghetto. Sophie had heard many Nazis say it was far too good for Jews.

The Goldfarbs shared their tiny apartment, which was meant for two people, with a pair of elderly couples: the Brenners and the Rosensteins. This meant the food Sophie scavenged was shared seven ways, but there was nothing she could do about that other than to bring as much as she could. And so at some point every day, handfuls of potato peels and beets, and sometimes even hunks of bread and cabbage, would show up in a paper bag inside their door.

These daily gifts prompted both bewilderment and appreciation. Roz Rosenstein decided that the Jewish Council, the committee nominally in charge of the ghetto, was secretly looking out for her husband, Herman, because he had been a community leader in their hometown. Herman thought she was right. Sophie thought they were delusional. The Brenners, Aron and Selma, were always praying. They insisted that God was providing for *them* because their faith in Him was superior to everyone else's in the ghetto, and that they should thus be thanked for generously sharing with their faithless roommates. Sophie thought they were delusional too.

After she got what she needed for the Goldfarbs every morning, Sophie went to poach more food for her neighbors from Judenstrasse. So far she'd managed to locate Arno's and Gisela's apartments, as well as the Horns', the Dresslers', the Finkels', and the Boksers'.

Sophie also tried to give a little extra to Rabbi Hasendahl; he was a shattered man since losing his Sarah, and it broke her heart to see it. He almost never came out of his apartment and denied to anyone who asked that he was a rabbi. He was belligerent, so much so that the four others assigned to his apartment moved out, preferring to cram in with the already crammed rather than to suffer his company. He was left to lie on the floor alone, day after day, plucking out his beard hairs and talking to Sarah as if she were there. Sophie brought him food every day, which he accepted without wonder or gratitude.

But then, one day, Sophie saw him working in the soup kitchen, chatting amiably with those he was serving. It was like his sorrow had burned itself out and he was himself again, although he would still not answer to the word, "rabbi."

It was usually possible to pull off three food heists a day, and with her third haul, Sophie would try to feed anyone she came upon who appeared close to death. She'd spent most of her days — sunup to sundown — for the last four months, walking the ghetto streets and haunting the halls of the housing complexes, slipping vegetable peels into the hands and mouths of people too hungry and weak to fathom such miracles. Despite her unrelenting efforts, people were dying all the time, but because of those unrelenting efforts, Giddy and his parents weren't among them.

Sophie wedged her way out of a crowd and turned down a less busy street. They'd never been named, but she no longer had any problem knowing where she was. Here there were also many, many people, but they were standing in a long, orderly line on the sidewalk, waiting for their turn at the soup kitchen. The line reached all the way down the block and would do so until the kitchen closed at dusk.

Sophie stopped raiding the soup kitchen once she learned it was a charitable enterprise run by fellow Jews. Fortunately, she discovered that there were other lines for food that was distributed by Nazis from the back of trucks first thing in the morning and then again at noon. The few Jews with money could buy limited but desirable food items from these trucks. Everyone else could use their ration card, which entitled them to just enough nutrition to starve slowly to death. It was from those trucks Sophie now stole her rations. She was on her way to one now.

As Sophie was passing the soup kitchen, she saw Golda Goldfarb. This wasn't surprising; most people in the ghetto spent most of their days in one food line or another. But Golda was carefully carrying a dented metal bowl, which was likely filled with watery soup. This was surprising because Sophie, who'd been in the Goldfarbs' apartment many times, knew no one there had such a bowl. Perhaps it had just come into Golda's possession, but Sophie was doubtful as she watched her walk down the street; she was taking it somewhere. Not back to Giddy, Sophie noted. She was walking in the wrong direction.

Curious, Sophie followed Golda, who now walked like her back had gone bad. She really didn't look much heartier than anyone else on the street, even with the extra food she was receiving. Like many others, her skin had gone flaky and her hair, which had been black, was turning a weak shade of red. Sophie felt her own face. Her skin felt normal, so she assumed she was eating enough. She touched her now long spirals of hair, wondering if they were still black. Would she ever see them again? Refusing to speculate, Sophie followed Golda down the street, around a corner, then toward an apartment building.

There was a man standing in front of it as Golda approached. It was Mr. Goldfarb. Mendel was his first name. He had lost his glasses, and because of his faulty vision, he now walked around with a squint. Like his wife, Mr. Goldfarb appeared to be in poor health. He had the same flaky skin, and his formerly brown hair was turning dirty blond. Until now, Sophie really hadn't had an opportunity to look them over in the daylight. Mr. Goldfarb was carrying a brown paper bag; he'd already been to a food truck this morning.

Mendel and Golda, without a word of greeting, turned and walked into the housing complex. Sophie followed them inside, wondering what was going on.

Golda walked down the hall, balancing her bowl. Sophie walked behind, trying not to peek into the apartments she passed. None had doors because they'd never been installed. Some had sheets hung in their place.

Sophie saw the Goldfarbs enter an apartment, so she followed suit. It was empty but for one very old, very fragile-looking man lying on a blanket on the floor. The apartment was fit for maybe six people, but Sophie counted eleven other blankets.

"Good morning, Mr. Nusbaum," said Golda.

The old man made no reply.

Mendel sat down next to Mr. Nusbaum and helped get him into a sitting position, propped against the wall. Golda sat down as well and began feeding him from her bowl, holding her spoon to his lips so he could slurp its contents. Mendel took some food out of his bag, placing a single drooping carrot, a malformed potato, and a crust of bread next to Mr. Nusbaum. Then he rolled the top of the bag over again. It looked like there were still a few things in it.

Sophie backed out of the apartment, angry and frustrated. So Golda and Mendel were giving up rations they could get for themselves to make up for the rations she got for them. Only Giddy, it seemed, was getting something close enough to avoid looking like the walking dead.

As irked as Sophie felt, she also couldn't help but swell with pride as she rejoined the crowd on the street. Every day, she witnessed such breathtaking acts of sacrifice. Giddy's parents, like so many others, were living in a way that brought honor to their people.

Sophie stopped to watch two men from the Sanitation Committee carrying away an old woman on a stretcher. She must have died on the sidewalk. The crowd had parted to give them room, but otherwise no one took notice. Dead bodies were a regular sight everywhere in the ghetto: the streets, the stairwells of the housing complexes, the apartments, even the hastily constructed outdoor latrines. The horror of coming upon a corpse had devolved into mere annoyance by the depressing frequency of it. During the winter months, frozen bodies had to be removed from the sidewalks each morning.

The day Sophie arrived, she overheard a Nazi say there were six thousand Jewish cockroaches in this ghetto, but she figured at least a thousand had died since then. The actual cockroaches, though, were thriving.

Sophie walked up behind the men carrying the body and got close enough to see the woman's face. "Goodbye, Mrs. Garfunkel," she whispered. "May your memory be for a blessing." She had made a point to learn as many names of the residents of the ghetto as she could, especially of those with nowhere to sleep but the streets. Who was going to remember them? Sophie figured having their names spoken one final time, even in a voice that made no sound, was important. Maybe their departing souls, invisible as she was, could hear her.

Despite the Sanitation Committee's best efforts, the ghetto reeked of urine and feces. The streets and sidewalks were nearly always covered in garbage. Worse, they were permanently splattered with human waste because there weren't enough latrines. People stood in line for them as long as they were able, and then did what they had to do wherever they could — or they emptied the pots they used wherever they wanted. If people were lucky, maybe once a week, they were able to wash with warm water at the tea house, but the ubiquitous stench was an unignorable reminder that shame about bodily functions was now a forgotten concept. Sophie walked on, compulsively covering her nose with a hand. The smell was awful. It was disgusting. Revolting. Repulsive. There really were no words she could think of to describe it, and there was no getting used to it

Sophie finally reached the line at the food truck. This one snaked down the street and even around the corner. The truck had swastikas painted on its doors and a covered bed that was open in the back, where two Nazis were checking ration cards and handing out brown paper bags.

"I'd like a steak," said a man at the front of the line. "On the rare side, please." He had little round glasses with one fractured lens and wore a beret. Sophie looked closely at him to see if he was crazy — finding people who'd taken leave of their senses was not unusual. The man was looking up at the Nazis in the truck with, it seemed, complete sincerity.

The people in line behind him — who were typically ornery and impatient — traded covert smiles. The Nazi, a burly, mustachioed brute, was apparently not amused. He leaned out of the truck and hit the man in the side of the head with an open hand, knocking him to the ground.

The man managed to get up after the blow. "Perhaps just the usual then," he said, holding out his ration card.

"Fuck off," said the Nazi.

The man bowed, then turned and walked away to the shaking heads of others in line.

"Pepi Schenkel," someone said when he'd meandered away. "Lost his marbles, I guess. What a shame."

Sophie climbed into the truck, thinking she'd have to track Pepi down later and give him some extra food. She maneuvered past the two Nazis and stood among the various open crates of half-rotted fruits and vegetables. While they were busy dealing with the people in line, Sophie stuffed all her many pockets with them — the many pockets of a shirt she'd stolen out of a truck much like this one. She made sure to overstuff them.

Sophie was about to make her escape when she noticed a bunch of paper bags sitting on the floor toward the front of the truck. These bags were already full and had names written on them. She went over and looked at one that said, "Kohn." Intrigued, she peeked inside and her eyes popped: eggs. Actual eggs. Sophie couldn't remember the last time she'd seen one. They were not part of normal rations in the ghetto. In fact, they were forbidden. David Kohn was the head of the Jewish Council. Did that entitle him to special privileges? She supposed it did.

Sophie was still contemplating the eggs when the bag was picked up by one of the Nazis, a younger man with a pockmarked face. Her heart skipped a beat as she stepped back, nearly falling over some crates. She managed to steady herself just as he took the bag to the open back of the truck and gave it to someone in line: David Kohn. Then the brute with the mustache shouted, "We are taking a break!" and pulled a tarpaulin down over the back opening. Sophie, breathing heavily, sat down and tried to make herself small. She'd never gotten stuck like this before.

"Jesus," said the brute, "I couldn't take the smell anymore! They are worse than reptiles in a zoo!"

"We aren't going to get into any trouble, are we?" asked the Nazi with the pocked face.

"No," said the brute, with some annoyance. "I've told you how this works. Zinter is in on it. He gets half the bribe. You get a quarter of my part, for keeping your mouth shut. If you want to get something going with another shop in town, I'll take a quarter of yours."

"Maybe Braun at the apothecary would be game."

"Everyone's game."

Sophie Siegel — June, 1943

Three months later, Sophie was crouched in Herr Zinter's grocery, waiting for him to switch the light off behind the counter. Once he did so, Sophie knew she would have exactly thirty-three seconds to get away undetected. This was her ninth time robbing him, and he always closed up the same way. The food in the shop was incomparably better than the nearly rancid fare the Nazis brought into the ghettos. Soon after she'd begun delivering Zinter's pilfered produce to the Goldfarb's apartment, Sophie began to see improvement in everyone's health. Giddy seemed the most improved; he'd become much less wan and lethargic. Sophie only wished she'd gotten this idea earlier.

Luckily, Herr Zinter, an elderly gentleman, was both plodding and hard of hearing. The moment he turned off the light, Sophie carefully, delicately, opened the front door to avoid jangling the bells dangling from its handle, stepped through the threshold, and closed it just as softly behind her. Then she ran. The street was dark at this late hour and no one was about — Herr Zinter was always the last to call it a night. But even with his poor eyesight, Sophie didn't want to give him any opportunity to see a rucksack too big to hide under her clothing — especially one stuffed with his fruits, vegetables, bread, and dried meat — floating down the street.

Sophie turned the first corner she came to, then walked quietly in the shadows through the quaint cobblestone streets of Stadtgebiet. They were very much like the quaint cobblestone streets of Ortschaft, which were very much like the quaint cobblestone streets of Gemeinde and Weiler. She made her way past well-stocked shops, then through a tree-filled neighborhood full of charming townhouses topped by red tile roofs and fronted by well-tended gardens. Then she made her way down some less affluent avenues, where the homes were smaller and much closer together — and then, finally, onto the road that led to the ghetto.

When the gate came into sight, Sophie stopped to look at the silhouette of a Nazi with a rifle on his back. Did he care about what was happening on the other side of that gate? Did he really hate the Jews? Or was he just doing what he was told to do because that's what people did? The sign above him, ominously lit, read: "Jewish Residential Area: Entry Forbidden."

Not for me, Sophie thought.

Leaving the ghetto every night was never a problem. Sophie simply waited until the guard at this one and only entry/exit checkpoint had some reason to open the gate — Nazis were constantly going in and out — then she'd walk right through. But coming back with the rucksack was more complicated.

Sophie turned onto a side street that ran north and parallel to the ghetto and walked along the fence. The Nazis had erected fences — tall wooden posts connected by twenty lines of barbed wire — enclosing the twelve square blocks. But for some reason, they neglected to use the already existing wall that ran east to west at the north end of the ghetto as the barrier. The wall bordered a long dirt field that had been intended to be a cemetery. Instead, they ran their fence just in front of the wall — inside the ghetto — a foot or so. Sophie had no idea why they bothered, but she had learned that if the Nazis were nothing else, they were thorough. Although, they weren't thorough enough to realize that an invisible person, with a visible bag, could very well sneak along said space between that wall and their fence. Then, that person could use, say, a pair of wire cutters stolen from the hardware store to snip two barbed wires at the base of a post. Unless someone was standing in the dirt field, no one would see. Stupid Nazis.

Sophie wedged herself behind the fence and sidled her way to the first post. Then she kicked the bottom two wires out of it with one of the reinforced toes of the work boots she had also stolen from the hardware store. She dropped down, rolled through the exposed space, got up, then kicked the wires back into place. Then she walked swiftly across the dirt field — which was now actually being used for its intended purpose, a cemetery, albeit one where Jews could dig only unmarked graves.

At last, Sophie was safely back inside the ghetto.

The streets were silent this late at night. Sophie stopped to put a crust of bread into the hands of an old woman sleeping on the sidewalk, Mrs. Plesser. Then she walked the rest of the way to Giddy's complex and up five flights of foul-smelling stairs.

In every apartment Sophie passed, dark figures could be seen sleeping on the floor, practically shoulder to shoulder. Someone let out a long, disconsolate moan that made her shudder. A baby cried; she shuddered again. There were very few babies left in the ghetto. *It must be a new arrival,* Sophie thought. *It won't last long.*

The few new mothers she'd seen were too malnourished to produce any milk — and there were more than a few infants in the field of unmarked graves.

When she reached the last apartment on the right, Sophie peeked in. There were seven people sleeping on the floor — the Brenners, the Rosensteins, and three Goldfarbs. Giddy was squeezed up tight between his parents.

On her knees, Sophie emptied the rucksack just inside the door. Then she stood up and walked back down the hall. But as she entered the stairwell, a commotion erupted behind her — people running.

And then came shouts.

And now, the sound of violence: grunting and screeching and skin smacking skin.

Sophie ran back down the hall. There was a clutch of shadows in the dark, all moving into the Goldfarbs' apartment. She fought her way inside, into a mass of flailing bodies.

"Thieves!" someone cried in the mayhem.

"Thieves!" Sophie heard Mr. Rosenstein shout back.

"I told you they were stealing in here!" a man cried. "Stealing and hoarding!"

Sophie wedged her way through the melee and got elbowed in the head and kneed in the thigh for her efforts. But she found Giddy, curled in a fetal position against a wall. She lay her body over his and waited for the brawl to end.

It stopped as quickly as it started. Feet pounded out of the apartment, then down the hall. All was quiet except for the groaning of the original occupants.

Sophie got off of Giddy, who sat up, sniffling.

"Is — is everyone okay?" asked Mrs. Goldfarb in a tremulous voice. "Giddy?"

"I'm okay, Mama," Giddy said. "I was safe the whole time."

"I'm okay, too," said Mr. Goldfarb.

"I'm okay," both the Rosensteins said.

"Me too," said the Brenners.

"Let's just go back to sleep," said Mr. Goldfarb. "The food is certainly gone."

Everyone laid back down in the dark. Sophie could hear them all trying to get their breathing back to normal. She was doing the same.

A few moments later, a young boy's voice came from the hall. "Giddy? Are — are you okay?"

"I'm okay, Leo," Giddy answered.

"Good," was the reply, which was followed by the sound of padding feet beating a hasty retreat. Sophie didn't know that Giddy had made a friend. For some awful reason, she felt a rush of jealousy, which filled her with remorse.

The heavy breathing in the room slowly gave way to anxious silence. But then, suddenly, Mr. Rosenstein said, "What does your God have to say for himself now, Brenner?"

"God," said Mr. Brenner, "had nothing to do with those — those pirates attacking us."

"So he's responsible for giving, but not taking. Do I understand that correctly?"

"I doubt you understand anything correctly, Rosenstein."

"Well, there's no doubt in my mind," said Mrs. Rosenstein. "That was an attempt to assassinate you, darling. The food was merely a pretext."

"Good lord, you're both insane," said Mrs. Brenner.

"We're insane?" both Rosensteins jeered.

"Enough already," said Mr. Goldfarb, but weakly. "Can we just be thankful that we're all alive? That, for at least one more day, we can argue about such things?"

"Yes," said the Brenners.

"Yes," said the Rosensteins.

"Well said, dear," said Golda, reaching out to touch her husband's shoulder in the dark.

And with that, everyone fell silent and, eventually, asleep.

Normally, because the apartment was so crowded and she couldn't sleep for fear of getting stepped on or tripped over, Sophie slept in the prop room of the theater in the center of the ghetto. Although she didn't sleep well there either because her dreams were so often haunted by her parents. They were usually running through the woods, screaming for her. Sophie would be nearby, blowing her whistle over and over and over again. Sometimes Mama and Papa wouldn't find her. Other times they came to where she was but could not see her, even though she stood right there in front of them. In those cases, Sophie found herself unable to move, and so they'd run on, crying out her name while she blew her whistle.

Tonight, Sophie wasn't going to leave Giddy alone. She slid into the space between him and the wall and draped an arm over his back, clutching him tightly. They slept that way all night.

An ear-piercing scream shocked Sophie out of sleep in the morning. She leapt to her feet with her heart in her throat. It was Golda Goldfarb, on her knees next to her husband. "They killed him!" she cried. "They killed my Mendel!"

Mr. Goldfarb lay on the floor, unmoving. Light from the apartment's single window illuminated a gash on his head and some blood pooled on the floor beneath him. He was dead — his face stony, his body stiff. Sophie stood looking down over him, aghast. Mr. Goldfarb had obviously been struck in the brawl — and hadn't wanted to bother anyone about it. And now he was dead.

And it's my fault, Sophie thought.

Mrs. Goldfarb wailed. Giddy, sitting on the floor with his hand on his father's chest, whispered, "Don't be dead, Daddy! Don't be dead. Don't be dead."

Loud footsteps sounded in the hall, and two members of the Jewish ghetto police appeared at the apartment door. Their clothes were as shabby as everyone else's, but they each sported armbands with a blue star and carried batons. "We have a report of a disturbance here last night," one of them said, a scarecrow of a man with a beard that seemed to have no intention of growing in. He then saw why Golda Goldfarb was screaming.

The policemen ordered everyone out of the apartment, including Golda, who would not stop wailing, "They killed my Mendel! They killed my Mendel!" Giddy, who was still groaning, "Don't be dead. Don't be dead," refused to move. Sophie, dizzy, helped him to his feet and guided him with the others into the hallway, where their neighbors had gathered to gawk.

The scarecrow policeman examined Mr. Goldfarb and quickly pronounced him dead. Golda went mute and slid down the wall onto the hallway floor. Giddy dropped down next to her, quiet now. Sophie sat between them and took one of each of their hands in hers, which neither seemed to notice. Sophie wanted to scream and cry, but all she felt was an icy bitterness taking hold of her heart.

The other policeman, a bald man with a disturbingly protruded chest, stepped into the hall and demanded to know what happened.

"They killed him," Golda said, but it came out in a voice that wasn't hers.

"They are thieves!" someone in the crowd of pests and murderers shouted. "They steal food! Always, they have extra!"

Sophie had not known they'd all known. How could they know? From what she'd seen, everyone in Giddy's apartment took every precaution to dole out and consume their mysterious bounty promptly and secretly.

All the same, she should have known. Everyone knew everything about everyone in the ghetto.

"Is this true?" the scarecrow policeman asked.

"It's true!" someone cried. And then it seemed like the entire hall was shouting, "It's true! They are thieves!"

"Look!" a man cried. "Look at that fancy bag. Who has such a fancy bag?"

Sophie cringed. The rucksack. She'd used it as a pillow.

"Quiet!" the scarecrow policeman demanded. He'd come out of the apartment with the bag, fascinated by the quality of it. "So, perhaps it should not come as a surprise," he said to one and all, "if an apartment full of crooks turned on each other? As we know, there is no honor among thieves. Maybe one thief stole from another and there was revenge?"

The bald policeman turned to the Rosensteins and Brenners. "Perhaps a trial is necessary?" he suggested. The four of them blanched. Then he looked to the crowd and said, "Perhaps one of you stole from the thieves and murdered one of them when they resisted?"

This was met with gasps.

"Sir," said Herman Rosenstein, stepping forward. "There was an unfortunate accident. Mr. Goldfarb fell, on account of his stunted vision. He lost his glasses. There were many witnesses. The cut, as you saw, was small, and he thought nothing of it. So naturally, neither did the rest of us. He must have suffered brain damage that killed him overnight."

The scarecrow policeman looked at the Brenners. "Is this true?" he asked.

"Yes," they both said, avoiding eye contact.

The policeman looked down at Golda, who was still on the floor with her hand in Sophie's. Without looking up, she said, flatly,

"Yes. True."

"Is this true?" the scarecrow policeman asked the crowd.

A resounding, "Yes!" was the reply.

"And this bag?" the scarecrow policeman asked.

"We have no idea," said Herman Rosenstein. "Please, take it away."

This seemed to satisfy the policemen, even to please them. The bald one said, "I guess it's settled then."

The scarecrow policeman put the rucksack on his shoulder, then he and his partner went back into the apartment and picked up Mr. Goldfarb's body. They carried him off like a drunkard in the street. As soon as they were in the stairwell, everyone but Golda, Giddy, and Sophie retreated to their apartments. No one had the temerity to offer an apology or condolences.

From inside, Sophie heard Mr. Rosenstein say, "You better thank me, Brenner, not God, for what I just pulled off. We were all about to be accused of murder."

"I am thanking God," Mr. Brenner replied, "for helping you pull that off."

"Oh, for crying out loud."

Sophie continued massaging Golda and Giddy's hands on the floor, wondering how things had gone so horribly wrong.

As if hearing Sophie's thoughts, Giddy, his voice a croak, said, "Yesterday, behind the latrines, I gave Leo half of a magic carrot."

As dictated by The Jewish Council, corpses, once discovered, must be buried within the hour. And so, hardly thirty minutes later, Sophie stood with the Brenners, the Rosensteins, Giddy, and Golda in the field of unmarked graves at the edge of the ghetto. They watched as the Burial Committee — two hunched men who didn't look long for the grave themselves — dug one for Mendel Goldfarb. Rain was falling steadily, but it came as a relief on such a hot day. It made the digging easier as well.

Nearly all of the Jewish rituals pertaining to burial had been suspended by the Council in the name of preventing the spread of disease. And because the materials to make them were simply not available, there were no shrouds or pine boxes. And in most cases, there wasn't even a service at the graveside. The rabbis in the ghetto were far too busy ministering to the barely living to conduct any ceremonies for the dead. There were only three of them, one of whom was Rabbi Hasendahl, and though he was vastly improved, he still refused to act in that capacity.

Sophie winced watching the poor Burial Committee struggle to get Giddy's father into his shallow grave without dropping him. She was glad to see that Golda was not paying attention. She was simply standing by the graveside, holding Giddy's hand, looking out over the ghetto fence and wall, into the nothingness. Giddy watched though. Sophie wanted to run to him and, like his mother had once done, cover his eyes.

Once Mr. Goldfarb was finally in the grave, Mr. Brenner offered a few hasty prayers from memory. Then, after everyone ceremonially tossed some dirt into the hole, and the burial men began filling it up again, he and Mr. Rosenstein told Golda that she and Giddy were no longer welcome in the apartment.

"We're sorry," said Mr. Rosenstein, "but word is already around that your son told another boy about our previous good fortunes. Either we will all be branded as thieves, or just you. There will be less suffering this way."

It took all she had for Sophie to resist kicking him. She swore at him instead, but Golda, who hadn't uttered a single word since they'd left the housing complex, simply nodded.

"But where will we go, Mama?" Giddy asked.

"God will provide," said Mr. Brenner.

"Damn right He will!" Sophie seethed. But just then she noticed four boys at the far end of the field digging into the mud with their bare hands, and there was suddenly something she had to do.

When the Brenners and Rosensteins walked off in the rain, Golda finally spoke. "I will go find us a new apartment," she said with no emotion and without looking at Giddy.

"What should I do, Mama?" Giddy asked, looking up at her with rain running down his face.

"You have school," she said. "And you are already late."

"I don't want to go."

"School is a blessing. Go."

Giddy wouldn't go, so Sophie took his hand and tugged at him. For a moment, he was startled, but then he just gave in, as if he had no will left to resist whatever direction the world wished to drag him.

When Sophie first discovered that classes were being secretly taught in the ghetto, she couldn't believe it. Not because of the risk — teaching was illegal and punishable by death — but because nothing seemed more ridiculous than starving teachers wasting what little energy they had instructing starving kids who could hardly sit up straight. However, she changed her mind after seeing Giddy and his eight classmates study with Hani Ferber, a delightful woman in her fifties with kind eyes and an apparently indestructible optimism. When she taught children mathematics with nothing but her fingers, or when she taught them new words through pantomime, or sang prayers with them — it was as if she and the kids somehow forgot where they were, at least for a little while. At least on days when there wasn't someone coughing up phlegm or blood.

At first, Sophie couldn't conceive of what difference it could possibly make to the Nazis if schools operated in the ghetto. But after watching Giddy's class for a few days, she understood perfectly: learning restored some level of humanity, even happiness, to people whose souls they wanted to extinguish.

Sophie had to guide Giddy all the way from his father's grave to Hani's apartment. The closer they got, the less she had to pull him along, and when the kindly teacher saw his face, she opened her arms, and he ran into them.

Older kids attended classes as well, all over the ghetto, six days a week. Once Sophie discovered in which apartments they were held, she decided to shop around. She knew that getting smarter, getting wiser, would make her more able to make a difference. So she moved from class to class, always seeking more interesting subjects, eventually making her way up to those for the oldest and most advanced students. At last, she found the one she didn't know she was looking for — and she found it when she wasn't even looking. She'd been checking in on Rabbi Hasendahl one day, a few weeks ago, and discovered the reason for his improved attitude. He was teaching four boys in his apartment — the same four boys she'd just seen digging with their hands in the field of unmarked graves: Solomon, Jashel, Mattias, and Jakob.

When she neared the rabbi's building, Sophie saw the boys exiting, and since they were all heading off in different directions, she knew they were returning to their apartments to clean up as best they could. It had stopped now, but while it had rained, every bucket in the ghetto — every container that could possibly hold water — was left outside. They'd be looking to use some to get the mud off their hands and arms.

A few minutes later, the rabbi came outside for one of his daily constitutionals. The moment he was out of sight, Sophie hotfooted it into his complex, ran up to the third floor, and into his apartment, putting all thoughts of Mendel Goldfarb out of her mind. She was getting good at blocking out thoughts she didn't wish to entertain.

In Sophie's interactions with Rabbi Hasendahl in Ortschaft, he'd always been kind to her. He usually had a joke or an amusing story to share. But with his students here, he was always serious. She wasn't sure if that was because he'd lost his wife, or if that's just how he taught. She suspected a bit of both. He spoke as softly as ever, but, as always, with absolute authority. It was obvious why he'd been called the Beard of Wisdom, although the nickname no longer applied. He no longer had a beard: judging by his perpetually red and bumpy cheeks, he was still plucking out his whiskers by hand.

The rabbi devoted entire classes to lectures on one of the many great Jewish thinkers. So far, he'd discussed Philo Judaeus, Saadia ben Joseph, Maimonides, and Spinoza, among others. The boys always asked the same question after each lesson: how would so-and-so explain why God is letting this happen to us? Sometimes the rabbi — who would only respond to the boys if they called him Abe — had a guess. Though sometimes he did not. No one was ever satisfied in either case. Often, Rabbi Hasendahl reminded the boys that a Jew's obligation was to ask questions, not to demand answers. "Although answers are nice," he always admitted.

To encourage complete honesty and to establish open lines of communication, the rabbi had the boys leave anonymous questions for him, although this was a challenge without anything to write with or on. He devised a solution: every time it rained, the boys were required to go to the field of unmarked graves and carry as much mud as they could back to his apartment to smear on the walls. Rabbi Hasendahl would then leave his home and invite the boys to etch their questions into the dried mud with a stick while he was out — a 'question stick.'

The little closet of an apartment became a cave of questions, mostly more intimate versions of the boys' public concerns: Am I going to die? Does God hate me? What did we do to deserve this? There were also less fraught questions about their changing bodies and unclean thoughts about girls. Sophie was glad no one could see how they made her blush.

Today, after watching Giddy watch his own father buried, Sophie decided it was time to ask her first question. She picked one of the sticks up off the floor of the now empty apartment, and on a blank, dry wall, scratched it out in oversized letters. Then she hurried out to complete another errand so she could be back before class started at noon.

The children who were not in classes were on the street, scavenging or begging. Sophie avoided a bedraggled bunch of them as she headed back through the packed ghetto streets toward the theater.

Another thing that astounded Sophie about the ghetto was that the residents put on some kind of event or show almost every night: poetry readings, dance reviews, musical performances, lectures, and even full-length plays. Since Sophie no longer had anything to read — and thus no other worlds to escape into — she turned eagerly to the theater.

On one of her first nights in the ghetto, Sophie followed a line of people headed to a performance, and so she'd seen her first play since moving out of the City: *A Midsummer Night's Dream*. It was performed by a cast who'd done the entire show from memory, and it was glorious.

Sophie was enchanted, even with costumes that were no more than strips of fabric worn in clever ways, and even with sets that were non-existent. She couldn't help but head backstage after the show to get a closer look at these skin-and-bone souls who somehow found the energy and passion to transform themselves into beguiling characters, if only for a few hours. That was how she discovered the prop room and its piles of fabric. They made for a good enough bed.

And that was also how she found the room the Jewish Council used for its daily meetings.

Sophie entered the theater and immediately heard loud voices. She feared her plan would be derailed by the presence of the Councilmen, but now she saw that the voices came from but one person, standing on the stage. It was Pepi Schenkel, wearing nothing but rags and talking to himself. Sophie had not been able to find him after his antics at the food truck got him hit in the head. She saw that he'd sustained a bruise on his temple that had yet to heal.

"Can I take your order, sir?" Pepi said. Then he replied to himself: "I'd like a steak. On the rare side, please."

He'd said that same exact thing at the food truck. Sophie looked on, fascinated, as Pepi conducted a conversation with himself, walking back and forth on the stage.

"Absolutely, sir. We are here to provide whatever you prefer."

"Very well, then."

"Right. A steak, very well done."

"No, I asked for it rare."

"Very well then."

"No!"

This was funny. Can you be crazy and funny? Sophie wondered. But she didn't have time to consider Pepi's mental health. While he continued to talk to himself, she walked carefully on the creaky wooden floors to avoid alerting anyone to her presence.

The room was empty, which was a relief. Sophie had spied on many meetings, so she knew that the Council was in charge of all the committees in the ghetto. Aside from receiving reports, they brainstormed ways to distribute food and supplies, or to promote hygiene, or to settle disputes more efficiently. They also held trials for Jews who committed crimes that did not interest the Nazis. They were as weak and exhausted as the people they were serving, probably more so.

Sophie took a slip of paper from her pocket and laid it in the dead center of the room's long wooden table and, with a pencil she'd stolen from Herr Zinter's office in the back of the grocery store, wrote another message that couldn't be missed. Then she hurried out.

Class was in session when Sophie got back to Rabbi Hasendahl's apartment, sort of. The rabbi and the boys alike were all standing in contemplative silence, pondering Sophie's big question.

Can you teach us how to make a golem?

Sophie stole in, curious to see what would happen.

Rabbi Hasendahl turned to look the boys over, as if trying to determine who'd asked the question. The boys looked each other over, clearly wondering the same thing.

The rabbi sighed.

"I don't want to spend much time on silliness," he said, "but I did promise to answer every query, no exceptions. And while I am tempted to do so in this case by simply saying no, I will respect the larger question, which is, I think, can we induce God to intervene in our situation? Also, because I love a good coincidence: golems are made from mud. Please sit down."

Sophie and the boys took their seats on the floor. And then Rabbi Hasendahl introduced the class to Kabbalah, a mysterious word Sophie had come across once or twice in the Ortschaft library but hadn't understood. The rabbi explained that it referred to ancient Jewish mysticism. Sophie was interested to hear that Kabbalists perceived God, not as an entity you could have a personal relationship with, but more as an ineffable concept with which you had to come to terms. But she was most intrigued to learn that there were so-called Practical Kabbalists who attempted "white magic" with incantations, amulets, and the summoning of angels. And the creation of mud monsters.

"The golem," Rabbi Hasendahl said, "is simply a personification of the Jewish will to resist oppression. According to legend, the golem, formed from clay or mud, was imbued with life when a mystical word was written on its forehead."

"What's the word, Rabbi Hasendahl?" asked Solomon, a perpetually smudge-faced bundle of tatters who rarely spoke.

"Please, it's Abe," the rabbi insisted. "But in any case," he added, "I am not going to share the word. It's just a word, of course, but I don't want to encourage you to ascribe any supernatural power to it. Many Jews have gotten carried away by such mishigas."

Jakob, a nervous boy with jumpy eyes, raised his hand.

"Yes?" the rabbi said.

"The golem," Jakob asked, "must it be made of mud or clay?"

"A golem is made of mud or clay," said Rabbi Hasendahl, "according to the stories. And if one was inclined to dig deeper, if you'll pardon the pun, into such symbolism, you could do worse than recognize that Adam, the first person, was created from *adamah,* or earth. But, if your larger question is, does a magical being who protects the Jews have to be made of mud — why should it? Why not a Behemoth? Why not a friendly dybbuk?"

Jashel, an intense boy with close-set eyes and an aquiline nose, asked, "What's a dybbuk?"

"Oy," said the rabbi. "It's said to be a malevolent spirit, the dislocated soul of a dead person. But why not something totally new? Something more befitting of the times? But enough of this," he sighed, waving his hand, as if to shoo the discussion away. Then he said Kabbalah and everything connected to it was rubbish and he'd not speak of it again. What they were doing in his apartment was illegal — they could lose this precious time at any moment, possibly forever, so it behooved them not to waste another second on such trifles.

"Yes," Sophie said. "Why not something totally new?"

"And so," said Rabbi Hasendahl, "let us begin properly. Jakob?"

Class usually began with the rabbi asking for a report of good deeds.

Jakob said, "I did my sister's chores for her last week because she was not feeling well."

After an approving nod, the rabbi said, "Solly?"

"I carried luggage to an apartment for a new arrival," said Solomon.

"Jashel?"

Jashel said, "I stood in line at the food truck for a man whose feet wouldn't let him do so," he said.

"And Matty?"

"I did not complain about being hungry," said Mattias, whisking his long hair away from his eyes and offering a shy smile.

"Wonderful," said Rabbi Hasendahl. "Tell me again, why do we do these mitzvahs?"

Sophie was always impressed with this ritual check in, but she'd never heard any discussion about why they did it. She assumed because they were commanded to live in such a way that brought honor to their people.

Jashel raised his hand, and when the rabbi looked at him, he said, "Because all the knowledge and wisdom in the world means nothing if you do not help others."

"Correct," said Rabbi Hasendahl. "Very much true. But let me suggest something else, something perhaps in some ways quite the opposite."

The boys leaned forward to hear what he was going to say.

"Helping others," said the Beard of Wisdom, "is the only true way to help yourself. Put another way: it's a blessing to be a blessing."

"Yes," said Sophie.

A small boy in only dirty shorts abruptly burst into the apartment, his face soaked with tears. "Sol!" he cried. "Sol! Bubbe and Zayde! They're dead!"

Solomon was on his feet. "What — what — what?" was all he could get out.

"They bought some — some meat — from a man," said the boy, who had to be his brother. "It was bad, Sol! The meat was bad! They're dead!"

The three other boys stayed where they were, heads down so as not to witness Sol fall apart. Which he did. Sol bleated an animal-like scream, and then passed out.

"Sol!" his brother cried.

Rabbi Hasendahl rushed to Sol, and with strength he didn't appear to have, picked him up into his arms, as if he were a toddler. As Sol came to, the rabbi gently walked with him to the door. He stopped at the threshold and turned back for a moment. "*Emmet*," he said to the boys, who all looked up at him, confused. "That is the word one must inscribe in the clay to give life to a golem. It means truth."

And with that, he carried Sol to his family.

The three boys looked at one another, uncertain what to do, but then Jashel got to his feet. He picked up a question stick and scratched the Hebrew word onto a wall. As soon as Matias and Jakob saw what he had done, they picked up sticks and scratched the word too.

And then they scratched it again. And again. And again.

Their faces were stern. No one spoke. They went on scratching in silence.

Sophie watched the boys work until the apartment walls were covered with the word. Then she went quietly out. Feeling the numbness that was becoming all too familiar, she walked through the crowded streets, heading back to the theater to see if her other efforts had produced better results.

Five members of the Jewish Council sat around the table in the meeting room backstage. The full committee was there, minus its head, David Kohn. Sophie, standing at the open door, saw him coming her way. Everyone seemed uncomfortable. The note was gone, which Sophie hoped meant they'd seen it.

David was surprisingly young to be the head of the Council. He had a large gap between his front teeth, which was ironic because he'd been a dentist. He left the door open after entering, per Sophie's written instructions. "It's one," he told the group as he took a seat at the end of the table. "Are we really going to do this?"

Sophie noted that the Council members, despite looking run-down and ragged, had relatively healthy-looking skin. She guessed maybe they were all bribing the Nazis for eggs.

"I've been trying to decide if playing along could hurt us in any way," whispered Karl Meyerhof, a broad-shouldered man who'd been a kosher butcher. "And I can't think of any reason not to see what comes of it. We're already sending smugglers out of the ghetto. What's one more? Especially if he's as talented as he claims to be."

"And, obviously, we are desperate," whispered Moshe Epstein, a rail-thin former watchmaker.

"So, we are agreed?" asked David Kohn.

The men nodded, though they all seemed skeptical.

"So be it," David sighed. Then he cleared his throat and said, as if making a sacred pledge, which was what Sophie hoped he thought he was doing, "We agree to find for Golda and Gideon Goldfarb a new apartment, which they may live in by themselves, and to make sure they are well cared for." He paused, then continued in something more like his normal voice: "What we need is... everything, of course — every type of provision — but at this time, we are in dire need of medicines, of any and every kind. Disease is running rampant through the ghetto, and if we don't get it under control, soon enough, we won't need anything at all."

The next morning, Sophie woke up in the prop room to the sound of banging. She got up from her nest of fabric and followed the noise to the courtyard outside the theater. There was a group of Nazis — ten of them — erecting some very tall posts on platforms. They had six up and were working on a seventh. Sophie's heart sank. They were fencing off the theater, and she was sure she knew why. Besides education, only one thing separated humans from animals: culture. And so now they were taking that away too. Sophie walked up to one of the Nazis and was about to kick him in the shin when she thought the better of it. Instead, she bit down on her bitterness and headed for the ghetto gate. She had more important matters to tend to right now.

The apothecary was located next to the grocery on Marktstrasse. It was owned and operated by a widower in his fifties, Herr Braun, a stooped man who walked with a cane. Sophie had been sitting in a corner of his shop all day, watching him serve a steady stream of customers, mostly women, who came in to purchase medications, toiletries, cosmetics, stockings, hot water bottles, hair pins, and toothpaste. They talked about infuriatingly mundane things: neighborhood gossip, the bother of increasing shortages caused by the war, and the offensive smell coming from the ghetto. Not one person all day said anything about what was happening to the people living inside it. Not one. Sophie had to resist the urge to kick about a hundred shins.

Instead, she ate her ire by gorging on fistfuls of candy when no one was looking. The rest of the time she spent eyeing the medicines sitting on their shelves behind the counter, waiting for her.

Finally, at closing time, Herr Braun locked the front door and set about his end-of-day rituals. Methodically, he straightened up his products in their displays, slowly swept the floor, then tallied up his sales in a ledger at the front counter.

At last, he took up his cane and left the shop, locking the door behind him. Sophie stayed behind, for tonight she needed more time to gather her spoils. She was not going to fail to impress the Council.

Sophie stood up and stretched her back, then walked carefully to the rack of leather bags. She was caught off guard when she chose a satchel that smelled very much like the one she used to carry to school every day. Before. When she had parents. Sophie didn't want to think about her parents. They belonged to another Sophie, the before-Sophie. She fended off their memories and made her way behind the counter, careful not to knock over any displays.

Using her steady hands in the darkness, Sophie found the shelves of glass vials full of medicines and carefully filled the bag. Each one clinked against the others as her stockpile grew. When she was done, she stuffed the bag with aprons she knew hung behind the counter on the wall, just in case she dropped it on the way back to the ghetto.

Now for the great escape.

There was a door behind the counter which led to the large

room where Mr. Braun kept his inventory and mixed his medicines. Sophie entered and waved her hand above her head until she felt a rope and pulled down the ladder to the attic. Once it was in place, she climbed up quickly with her supplies. She couldn't pull the ladder back up but figured it didn't matter — there was no chance this theft would go unnoticed.

Sophie was going to lower herself from the window at the back of the attic, down to the alley below. She'd formulated the plan when Mr. Braun's teenage son, Heinrich, had stopped by earlier in the day and was told to retrieve something from above. Sophie had followed him up there and discovered boxes of old sheets, perfect for tying into a rope she could use to shimmy down.

But as Sophie headed for one of the boxes, she heard shouting on the street below. She moved to the front window and her pulse spiked. Nazis with flashlights were rushing down Marktstrasse — pairs of them were entering every shop. Two were heading to the door right below her. Sophie backed away, panicking. She ran to the window at the back of the attic, thinking maybe she could just jump. But there were Nazis waving flashlights around the alley too.

Sophie made a move for the attic ladder but froze when she heard the shop's front door slam open and men rush inside. She felt her fingers and toes turn to ice.

"Hold on!" Mr. Braun hollered. "Let me get to the light!"

It dawned on Sophie that this was a stakeout of all the shops on Marktstrasse. The shopkeepers obviously knew they were being robbed on a regular basis. She leaned against a wall and slowly sat down, trying to stay calm.

Light filtered up into the attic from the lamps below.

"My medicines!" shouted Mr. Braun. Then, "The attic!"

Moments after that, men were climbing the ladder.

The attic light switched on, momentarily blinding Sophie. When her eyes adjusted, she saw two Nazis looking around. One was a young redhead, the other an older blond with a cleft chin.

The blond Nazi picked up the satchel and looked inside. "I found your medicines, Herr Braun!" he called, then took it down the ladder. Sophie cursed this bad timing and worse luck.

"Thank you!" Herr Braun cried. "But... the thief — he must have been hiding in the store when I closed — and you say no one left."

The blond Nazi rushed back up the ladder, shouting, "He's still here!" The redhead went into high alert, turning in a slow circle as he surveyed the attic. Sophie remained seated against the wall. She rubbed her arms and legs against the spreading cold.

But the men could see that no one was hiding in the attic. There was nothing there but tables and shelves full of boxes too small for anyone to hide in. Even so, the pair poked through some of them as they stalked silently around, as if they might sneak up on the burglar. For a long and terrifying few seconds, the redhead stood directly in front of Sophie, who was too cold and too scared to do anything but shake. If he had taken just one more step, he would have kicked her. But he hadn't. Instead, he turned and continued his fruitless investigation.

"There is no one up here, Herr Braun!" the blond Nazi finally shouted down into the shop.

"But that's simply not possible!" Herr Braun shouted back up.

The Nazis looked at each other, mystified. "Let's check the windows," the blond said. He went to the rear of the attic. His partner went to the front. Both attempted to open them, but evidently, they were painted shut.

The blond went and leaned over the ladder. "Herr Braun," he called down, "our thief is either hiding in the shop or has vanished into thin air."

"No one is in the shop!" Herr Braun cried.

"Maybe there's something to all this talk about Jewish black magic," the blond said to his partner.

"I used to know some Jewish families," the redhead said. "Seemed like decent enough folks who..." He stopped mid-sentence at the sight of his partner's narrowed eyes. "Which goes to show," the redhead said, changing his tone, "how they can manipulate your mind."

The blond nodded, then climbed down the ladder. Sophie heard the redhead let out a breath he must have been holding. Then he climbed down too.

When the ladder was again raised and the attic once more shut, Sophie felt some warmth come back into her limbs. All the same, she stayed where she was, hugging her knees to her chest.

When Mr. Braun and the two Nazis finally left the shop, Sophie got up and went to the front window. She wasn't surprised to see the blond station himself on the street below; nor was she surprised to see the redhead take up position in the back.

Sophie paced all night, constantly checking the street and alley, but neither man left his respective post. She was hungry. Worse, she was worried about Giddy and Golda. What if they'd gotten thrown out of their new apartment? And what if she would no longer be able to steal anything from town? The Committee said there were other smugglers. Were they all foiled now?

Sophie paced and paced and paced.

Not long after the sun came up, Sophie heard shouts from the street. She went to the front window and saw the blond Nazi walking off with his partner. Even so, she was still too afraid to attempt her escape.

By midday, Sophie was faint with hunger and just about ready to break the window and climb down to the alley when Herr Braun's son came once more to the shop. As luck would have it, he once again got sent up to the attic. As soon as he climbed off the ladder, Sophie climbed down to the main floor.

Herr Braun was in the back room, working at a table with his head down over the mess of vials she'd stolen temporarily. Sophie sneaked into the empty shop and took as many new vials from the shelves as she could fit into her pockets, then slipped out into the street.

Passing the grocery, she grabbed two apples and ate them greedily on her way back to the ghetto.

Sophie sensed something was wrong well before she neared the gate. During the day, the ghetto was cacophonous: you could hear shouts or cries or the engines of trucks — always something. But right now, there was nothing but an eerie silence in the air.

And the gate was wide open.

And the guard was gone.

With extreme trepidation, Sophie tiptoed through the gate. The streets were empty, as if it were the dead of night rather than midday. She made her way to the closest housing complex. Silence. She went through the halls, peeking into open rooms. The usual blankets and other paltry possessions — all gone.

Sophie returned to the street. She stood, turning in all directions, looking for something, anything. A painful headache was solidifying in the front of her skull. Had there been a mass escape? She dared to let herself hope. But no, she would have heard alarms last night if that were the case. All hell would have broken loose — the whole town would be overrun with Nazis by now. She headed to the theater.

The moment it came into view, Sophie froze. The muscles in her arms and legs went numb. She saw the poles the Nazis raised yesterday. They had not been building a fence. Each pole had a perpendicular platform on top, turning them into oversized Ts. There were 10 in total and, from seven of the structures, bodies hung by the neck.

Like a sleepwalker dragging herself through an intolerable dream, Sophie had to force her feet forward. When she finally got close enough to the theater, she saw the faces.

All six members of the Jewish Council.

Each had a sign around their neck that read, "Smuggler."

And then Sophie saw the seventh body.

It was Rabbi Hasendahl.

The sign around his neck said, "Sorcerer."

The ground shifted under Sophie's feet. Her vision blurred. She leaned forward, placing her hands on her knees, waiting and wanting to black out.

A long, loud horn sounded from somewhere beyond the fences.

A train?

Sophie straightened up. Flooded with adrenaline, she sprinted back across the ghetto, out through the unguarded gate, and back into the streets of Stadtgebiet. The train depot was many blocks beyond Marktstrasse. She sprinted in its direction, gutted, trying to outrun the image of the rabbi's lolling head. She wished the ground would open up and swallow her whole. But, no. Giddy needed her.

So Sophie ran.

"Rabbi Abraham Hasendahl!" she screamed as tears flew from her face. "May your memory be for a blessing!"

Sophie was winded and wheezing by the time she reached Zugstrasse, the street that led to the station. At the sight of white smoke billowing into the sky, she felt another flicker of hope. Maybe everyone was being deported. Maybe Germany had decided to banish Jews, and they could all go find friendlier places to live. Did such places exist?

When she reached the station, Sophie stopped abruptly when she saw a dozen bodies lying on the field next to the tracks, blood staining the ground beneath their heads. Frantically, Sophie checked each one to make sure none of them were Giddy or Golda. When she found they weren't, she turned her attention to the train.

A freight train.

Sophie looked down the line and counted twenty-five cars behind the engine. The entire population of the ghetto couldn't be on this train, Sophie told herself. Or could it? There would have to be a hundred — at least a hundred — people stuffed into each car. And there were no windows. How could they even breathe? Sophie ran to the closest car and stopped cold.

The keening sounds coming from inside punched her in the chest.

But she had to find Giddy.

Sophie ran along the tracks, screaming, "Giddy! Giddy!" But of course, no one could hear her. She grabbed the handle on a car's sliding door and tried to pull it open, but it wouldn't budge. She tried another. It wouldn't budge either. So she ran on, uselessly, endlessly, calling Giddy's name.

When Sophie reached the engine car, a truck entered the station from Zugstrasse and parked in front of the depot building. A Nazi got out and began walking toward the engineer, who was waiting for him near the front of the train. Sophie hurried to listen.

The Nazi shot out his arm: "Heil Hitler."

The engineer shot out his arm: "Heil Hitler."

"Total cargo?"

"Three thousand ninety-one."

"Loading time?"

"Last night. Midnight."

"Midnight?" Sophie cried. "Everyone has been locked inside those cars since midnight?"

"And I will not be held responsible?" the engineer asked nervously, "if the entire cargo does not arrive... undamaged?"

"Of course not," the Nazi replied. "What arrives will be sorted for usefulness."

"Ah, okay, good," said the engineer, loosening up. "Very good."

"But I warn you," said the Nazi, "the commandant is not in a good way. He recently lost his only child to tuberculosis, and his wife is inconsolable. She will not let him sleep. He is very irritable. I would not arrive late, if I were you."

"I'm ready to go."

"Guard in place?"

"Yes, sir, he's in there." Sophie turned and noticed that attached to the back of one of the middle cars was a guard booth that arched above the train.

"Fine, good," said the Nazi. "You are cleared to depart. Heil Hitler."

"Heil Hitler."

When the Nazi turned away, Sophie reached down and picked up a rock at her feet and threw it, hitting him squarely between the shoulder blades.

He spun back, enraged, drawing his gun.

The engineer, horrified, had his hands up. "I, I...," he stuttered, looking around, behind him, above him.

The Nazi, fuming, stomped over and pressed his gun to the engineer's forehead.

"I didn't!" the engineer swore. "I didn't!"

"I would kill you right here and now," the Nazi hissed, "if you didn't have a job to do that reflected on the job I have to do." Instead of shooting the engineer, he struck him across the face with the butt of his gun. When the engineer fell to the ground, he turned and walked away.

The engineer got to his feet, wiping blood from his cheek.

Sophie was thinking.

While the engineer, shaking his head, headed back to the train, Sophie approached the car with the booth attached. It was sitting atop two angled metal ladders on a platform. She climbed up, pressing her back against the side of the freight car as the train began to move.

For the next few hours, the train carried Sophie across the countryside then up into forested hills and low mountains. Despite being whipped by roaring, cold winds, all she could think about was Giddy suffering with her people.

It was dusk when the train came to a stop at a concrete platform in front of a red brick building topped with evenly spaced towers. Nazis with rifles stood in each one, ready to shoot. Sophie, sore from the journey, climbed off the booth's platform. It was a windy, overcast day. The sky was a looming shadow.

The platform was swarming with Nazis wielding guns and

truncheons and whips, some with frightening German Shepherds on leashes. They were spread out in formation, making a series of rows and columns.

A Nazi slid open the door of the first train car. Sophie ran over to it, telling herself that Giddy would get out.

Instead, a mass of bodies fell onto the ground, landing in gruesome positions. When the air rushed into the car, everyone alive cried out. Then came a mad push for more. A pair of Nazis stepped in front of the door and screamed for everyone to stay where they were. One fired his gun into the air to get everyone to settle down.

"One at a time!" a Nazi shouted through a megaphone. "Leave your belongings in the car! They will be delivered to your quarters! I repeat, leave your belongings in the car! One at a time!"

"How will you know what belongs to whom?" someone called, but he was ignored.

After Nazis hauled the dead bodies out of the way, they pointed to one person at a time to get out of the freight car via a small set of steps. No soldiers made any effort to help anyone disembark, and many people, especially older ones, fell. Those who could not get up again were dragged by an arm or an ankle to where the dead bodies lay and left there.

When the car was finally empty, everyone was ordered to go stand in line in front of another Nazi on the platform. People cried, and they would not move until Nazis started clubbing some of them in the head. A young man, after ducking a club, ran down the platform, although it was not clear where he thought he was going. The Nazi who'd failed to bludgeon him took out his gun and aimed. He let the young man take a few more strides, then shot him in the back.

Cowed, everyone began to move. When they reached the designated Nazi, he immediately began directing women and children into one line and men and older boys into another. Sophie, terrified, ran frantically between the two lines, scanning for Giddy and Golda. But they had not been in this car.

Nazis positioned at the other cars were about to open their doors when a whistle sounded. It was blown by a much more authoritative-looking, older Nazi. He was carrying a clipboard and walking toward the second car, looking over the newly formed line of women and children as he passed. When he reached the train car, the Nazis gave salute. He was a tall, sharp-nosed man with a full head of hair that was just turning silver. His face was puffy. His eyes were tired and set deeply above dark, heavy bags.

"Yes, commandant, sir!" one of the Nazis cried.

"When you unload these cars —" the commandant said, "I'm looking for a child. A boy. Perhaps eight years old. A boy who looks... pleasant. Find some and bring them to me. Bring their mothers or fathers as well if they are with them."

"Yes, sir!" the Nazis replied, and then one of them unlocked the freight car door and slid it open, again letting a mass of bodies fall to the ground. The commandant walked by each of the cars and, it seemed, relayed the same message.

The scene repeated itself with each car: corpses fell, survivors cried and begged, beatings ensued, someone was shot to show that the Nazis meant business, and finally, the defeated ultimately rushed over to their assigned line further down the platform. Sophie, growing increasingly frenzied, ran along the tracks, searching for Giddy and Golda.

She could not find them.

Sophie looked back to the platform; had she missed them? It was then that she spotted a growing cluster of parents and young boys forming around the commandant. A Nazi was leading more to him when the commandant waved them off.

Finally, the last car was unloaded, and to Sophie's infinite relief, Giddy and Golda stepped out. Giddy did not look as bad as Sophie had expected. Golda, though, looked frail, possibly sick. Her eyes didn't seem to blink. Sophie remembered the vials of medicine she'd successfully stolen, but after feeling her pockets, realized they'd all fallen out on the train.

Golda and Giddy followed the crowd sullenly to the now very long lines. Sophie saw the commandant sending away some of the parents and sons that had been taken to him.

Sophie ran.

The commandant was kneeling to talk to a small boy, and he'd set his clipboard on the ground so he could turn the boy around to inspect him. When Sophie reached them, she tore the top page from the commandant's clipboard and ran with all her might, waving it above her head in the wind.

The commandant rose and called out. Nazis chased Sophie from all directions, or the flying paper, anyway. She raced straight to Giddy and wedged it under his foot. Two Nazis were there a moment later, as was the commandant, who retrieved his paper himself.

"And what do we have here?" he said, observing Giddy's relatively healthy appearance. He took Giddy's chin in his hand and turned his face side to side. Golda reached for him but was pulled back by a Nazi. "How old are you?" the commandant asked.

Giddy, visibly shaking, said, "I'm ten, sir."

"Hmmm," muttered the commandant. "But you look eight. And cute as a button, too." He grabbed Giddy by his pitcher ears and twisted them playfully. Giddy grimaced. Then the commandant stood up and addressed Golda, who looked on the verge of disintegrating where she stood.

"Ma'am," said the commandant, "I'm going to make you an offer. I'm going to offer it once and only once. Your son will not survive here, but I can take him away... to someone who will protect him. I can assure you, he will be well cared for. I'm going to give you ten seconds to think about this offer."

The commandant looked at Giddy and said, "Son, your mother is strong. She can work to earn her freedom, but she will not be able to look after you here. If your mother approves, I am going to take you somewhere safe until she is free."

Giddy burst into tears and turned to his mother. Golda's face was a mask that looked to Sophie like death itself. Golda nodded without looking at the commandant; her eyes were riveted to her feet. Her lip trembled, but she did not speak.

Nor did she look at the commandant when he said to a Nazi, "Take him to my house." And she didn't once look at Giddy as he was dragged away, sobbing, twisting round and crying, "Mama! No! Mama! No!"

Sophie's stomach churned. The sight of Golda turning, expressionless, back to her line, was almost too much to bear. But for the first time in a long time, she felt she'd achieved something. Giddy would be safe — she'd make sure of it. And Golda would work in this place, whatever it was, and she would survive. Sophie would make sure of that too. The three of them would outlast these Nazi bastards.

As the line progressed sluggishly, Golda moved like a machine. She showed no outward sign that she'd just consented to her son being taken away. Just imagining what Golda could be thinking gnawed at Sophie. She decided then and there to bring proof of

Giddy's wellbeing to Golda whenever she could.

As Golda neared the end of the line, there was another Nazi, this one older than the commandant. He had long graying sideburns and wore glasses. He'd been waving the younger women off to a different line to his right, and the older women and youngest children to one on his left. He was looking into some of the women's mouths now and feeling around their necks. "Don't worry, I'm a doctor," he told them.

When Golda reached this supposed doctor, the commandant suddenly appeared. He whispered something to the doctor and walked away with his clipboard. Without examining her, the doctor waved Golda to the left.

"No!" Sophie cried when Golda complied without protest. "No!" she cried again. "To the right! To the right! She is not old!" She thought about dragging Golda out of the line, but the commandant was standing nearby, watching.

Sophie looked around, panicked, trying to figure out what was happening and what to do about it. The Nazi at the head of Golda's new line blew a whistle and ordered everyone to walk through the arch in the depot building. Once they passed through, they came to a gate. This gate, and the fences that extended from both sides of it, were much more imposing than those around the ghetto.

The gate opened, and Golda's line was directed toward a blockish concrete building with two chimneys. Lines of younger men and women were being led through the gate behind them and directed toward an array of long, windowless wood structures. Golda's line was halted, and at that moment, someone cried out from behind them. Everyone turned to see a woman running much like the man who'd been shot earlier on the platform.

The gate was now blocked by half a dozen Nazis, so the woman veered away and headed for the nearby fence. Strangely, no one shot at her. The Nazis just watched, smiling cruelly. The other prisoners in their lines looked on with fear and fascination in their eyes.

The woman jumped onto the fence. There was a spark and a snap, and she was thrown backwards onto the ground. Her body went rigid and — horrendously — it began to smoke.

The soldiers laughed, but only until the commandant approached them. Apparently, he didn't find it funny. Sophie couldn't hear what he told them, but he made his displeasure more than clear to the men, who stood at attention, nodding vigorously. Sophie dared to hope the commandant was a decent human being.

"Move!" shouted the Nazi now holding the door open at the building with chimneys. Golda's group obeyed his gestures to file inside. "Everyone must remove their clothes in the vestibule!" he shouted. "You will be given showers to sanitize yourselves!"

Sophie felt a wave of relief. A uniformed female Nazi was there — a rare sight that momentarily confused her. She was directing the line through a door into a vestibule for the women and children.

Sophie followed the women into it and watched everyone, quietly, with downcast eyes, remove their clothes. They all stood there, shivering in the cold room — maybe two hundred older women with arms across their chests and hands between their legs. Young boys and girls stood at their knees, naked and afraid.

In the crowd of bodies, Sophie recognized Roz Rosenstein and Selma Brenner. She also saw that they noticed Golda, and then looked away.

The female Nazi came into the vestibule and ordered everyone to file into the shower room, which was behind a metal door that she pulled open. Sophie could see a large empty room behind it with pipes crossing the ceiling in lines. Shower heads hung from each, spaced a few feet apart.

Golda shuffled in along with the rest of the crowd. Her expression hadn't changed since Giddy had been taken away.

Sophie sensed that she'd made a catastrophic mistake in judgement when the female Nazi shut the metal door behind the prisoners and pulled a heavy bar across to lock it. The woman slid open a small window in the door and put her face up to it. Moments later, Sophie heard a hissing sound from the shower room and smelled something like bitter almonds. And then she heard shrieking. And then banging. And then desperate clawing at the door.

Sophie threw herself at the Nazi. She was a stout woman, but the surprise of being struck by something she couldn't see, made her fall back enough for Sophie to grab for the bolt. Sophie opened it a few inches, but then froze when Golda Goldfarb's face smashed itself into the little window. Her eyes were bloodshot and bulging. Her face was blue.

The female Nazi rushed back to the door, knocking Sophie aside, and the bolt slid closed again.

"Help!" the female Nazi called when Sophie, recovered, tried to jerk it back. "Help!"

In just a few seconds, three other Nazis were in the vestibule.

"The door!" the female Nazi cried. "The lock won't stay!"

Sophie had no choice but to draw back.

Golda's lifeless face slid down the window until, finally, it was out of sight.

PART THREE
THE CAMP

Sophie Siegel — April, 1944

Frau Kruger tucked Giddy into his bed, an intricately carved four-post canopy heaped with lacy blankets. She was an attractive, if harsh-looking, woman with an angular face, penetrating eyes, and a posture that made her always seem ready to pounce. But with Giddy, she was as tender as could be. Lightly gripping his ears the way she often did, she kissed him all over his face, then crossed the room. Facing the bed, there was a wall of shelves containing dozens of brightly colored wind-up toys: fire engines, trains, autobuses, cars, and motorcycle men. Sophie, standing over Giddy like an imaginary friend he'd forgotten about, often watched him polishing the toys with a rag, only to return them directly to their perches without ever having played with them. He kept his room immaculate. Sometimes Frau Kruger, who maintained a tidy house, had to make him stop cleaning it after she deemed it spotless.

Frau Kruger closed the lacy drapes — the house was drowning in lace, all of which she had sewn herself. Then she walked to the door and paused to say, "Good night, Hans, darling." When Giddy said, "Goodnight, Mama," she smiled, then headed downstairs.

Sophie stood next to the bed, waiting for Giddy's silent tears. He'd cried like clockwork every night for the past year, the second the stairs stopped creaking under Frau Kruger's heels. Sophie knelt down and whispered, "Giddy Goldfarb, you are my light and my life, the reason I go out in the morning and come home at night." She held his hand gently, which he always flung over the side of the bed, and massaged it until he fell asleep. Why he didn't consider the ritual remarkable, she didn't know.

Sophie took a blanket out of Giddy's closet and carried it over to the cushioned window seat. She separated the drapes just enough so that she'd wake at first light. That is, if she ever fell asleep in the first place. She lay down, closed her eyes, and waited for the image of Golda at the window of the gas chamber door to materialize in the darkness behind her eyes. It always did. The faces of her parents rarely haunted Sophie anymore — they'd faded into the mists of her memory of another time, another age, another life. Another world, in which she was another person. But Golda's blue skin and bloodshot eyes would rarely leave Sophie alone. That happened here, in this world. Now. Sophie was haunted by her failure to act:

she might have gotten the door open had that suffocating face not paralyzed her for those crucial few moments. That, and Golda was only in that chamber of death because she, Sophie Siegel, had gotten her separated from Giddy.

Almost nightly, Sophie relived the horror of seeing the prisoners in striped uniforms drag the corpses out of the gas chamber. Stupefied, she had watched them cut off the dead women's hair and wrench out their gold teeth before lugging the corpses, one by one, to another room where they were burned in a row of ovens. It seemed her memories would punish her forever.

A few hours after Golda's murder, Sophie tried to sabotage the gassing by breaking every showerhead in both the men's and women's chambers. The following morning, expecting triumph, she watched a group of women and children enter the chamber. When the women saw the broken heads, they began to complain, but the door was locked behind them anyway, and they all died the same horrific, suffocating death as those before them had.

It turned out that the gas didn't go through the showerheads. Rather, pellets were dropped through the ceiling by a Nazi wearing a gas mask. Sophie continued her sabotage anyway, hoping just one group of prisoners would see the broken showerheads, realize the sham and so fight to stay alive. But she knew it was no use. The only people who reacted to the damaged fixtures were the Nazis. Before long, rotating guards were stationed in front of the building around the clock, and they remained there for a month, until their presence seemed to scare off the supposed saboteur. Sophie had been thwarted, but in her mind, only temporarily. She decided to go nowhere near that building again, not until she could think of a way to shut it down forever.

Sophie lay on Giddy's window seat, fighting off these excruciating memories, until finally, at some unknown dark hour, she fell into a fitful sleep.

When the sunlight woke her, Sophie sat up and peered through the curtains. Giddy's second-floor window provided an expansive view of the forest that surrounded the house. Just below her window was a wrap-around front porch and the driveway that snaked onto the property from a road leading to the forest. To the right was the red-roofed barn where the commandant kept his hunting dogs. Everything gleamed; it looked to be a hot day.

After carefully folding her blanket and returning it to the closet, Sophie went into Giddy's washroom. She splashed some water on her face; it was amazing how much better she felt having been able to sleep, such as she could, in a comfortable place. Being clean made her feel better too. Little things were not so little after all.

Sophie's most recent outfit, swiped from Frau Kruger's charity box, was in poor shape. She headed down to the first-floor closet, where the box was kept, and swapped it for a blue summer dress with two deep pockets, hemmed with lace, of course. Upon trying to slide the box back into place, Sophie found that it wouldn't budge.

Pushing aside the hanging clothes, Sophie discovered another box was in the way. Thinking maybe it had more dresses to choose from, she pulled it out and opened it. Inside was extra lace, but under it were photographs, hundreds of them. All were of a little boy — the real Hans. She was stunned to see that the little blond haired, blue-eyed, cherub had the same jug-ears as Giddy. However, this little boy's face was spattered with freckles. Sophie sorted through the pictures and found many taken on a beach; she could see that his entire body was a tapestry of tiny brown flecks.

Sophie could hear Frau Kruger tossing and turning under the canopy of lace that encased her enormous bed as she sneaked past the master bedroom. After tiptoeing downstairs and into the kitchen, she helped herself to an egg and a few loose slices of salami from the icebox.

The front door was unlocked — the commandant had already gone out to the barn to feed his dogs. He and Frau Kruger never locked their house. What did they have to fear in this world?

Sophie settled into the back of the commandant's big black boat of a car, the top of which he kept down in good weather. Fifteen minutes later, the commandant climbed into the driver's seat, turned on the ignition, and steered the car away from the house.

Sophie was on her way to the camp.

Thirty minutes later, the car came to a stop in its usual spot by the administration building. Upon climbing out, Sophie saw that it was going to be a bad day. Black smoke disgorged into the clear blue sky from the crematorium. There'd been a gassing overnight.

While the commandant headed inside to relax with his coffee, Sophie walked onto the campgrounds with her head down, trying to keep her breath as shallow as possible to avoid inhaling any of the smoke, the ashes of her people. She passed through the many rows of barracks that occupied the main part of the camp, abashed at how she once thought nothing could be worse than life in the ghetto. Inside each of the wooden cabins, as many as forty prisoners slept on planks, six or seven per, stacked three levels high.

The camp was normally quiet at this time. Roll call was at sunrise, well before Sophie arrived each morning. Afterwards, prisoners were given a few minutes to take care of "necessities" and drink the foul "tea" they were given for breakfast. Sophie tried it once and spat it right out. It was lukewarm water that tasted like dirt. She was fairly certain it *was* dirt. From there, everyone was marched out of camp to their work details: chopping wood, building walls, clearing fields, digging mass graves, or whatever other backbreaking jobs they were required to do that day. Given the smoke this morning, there was obviously a group of prisoners assigned to burn the bodies from last night's mass murder.

"A23210! You have sixty seconds!"

Sophie's heart sank when she heard these words echo through the camp. She looked toward the last row of barracks and saw a group of maybe thirty prisoners lined up.

"A23210! You have fifty seconds!"

When she reached the barracks, Sophie saw a Nazi — an overgrown man-child with blond peach fuzz on his cheeks — pointing his gun at the line of prisoners, whose knees knocked as they held one another's hands. The man-child's uniform, green pants and a green belted jacket with two large pockets on the front, was in pristine condition. His cap had the Nazi eagle above a skull and crossbones. Most of the Nazis running the camp wore the same.

The prisoners were a group of men, bald and skeletal in their striped uniforms. Those who weren't gassed upon arrival had their heads shaved before being deloused with a caustic solution that scorched their scalps. And then their names were replaced with numbers, which were not only sewn onto their jackets, but also burned or tattooed onto their arms. These particular men all wore yellow stars, for Jews were not the only people the Nazis wanted to exterminate. There were homosexuals in the camp, and gypsies, and political prisoners, each with a different patch. These few distinguishing marks aside, Sophie had come to understand that any semblance of individuality that survived the journey here was to be erased.

"A23210!" the man-child shouted, "You have twenty seconds!"

Sophie knew that prisoners often couldn't or wouldn't do what they were told, and nothing would make them. Every few days, someone snapped. There was usually no obvious trigger or last straw — people just broke. They might refuse to go to their worksite. They might just lie down and not get up. They might not come to roll call in the morning. These prisoners were almost always beaten savagely, although at times the guards got more creative with their punishments.

"Please, sir, let me get him," said a prisoner standing to the side of the line. His name was Hershel, and he was the kapo, the prisoner in charge of this barracks. He was a tall man in his early twenties, and in comparison to his charges, a strong man. He was given extra rations to make sure the prisoners he was responsible for remained obedient at all times. To assure this, he regularly harassed them. Slapping was Hershel's preferred motivation technique: quick, sharp slaps to the face. Many of the kapos abused their fellow prisoners. It infuriated Sophie, especially when she saw them escalate such behavior when Nazis were present. She knew they did it to keep their privileges, one of which was being allowed to continue living.

"No," snarled the man-child. "Get in line."

"But —" Hershel gasped, "I'm the kapo!"

"I said get in line!"

Hershel's mouth dropped open — he knew that stepping into line might mean the end of his life. Terrified, Sophie ran into the barracks. There was a prisoner lying on a bottom bunk, and she stopped short when she saw who it was: Pepi Schenkel. She'd lost track of him in the ghetto for a second time after seeing him on the stage of the empty theater. He was blinking at the bunk above him, talking to himself yet again. "Gone," he said. "They're gone. Gone! All gone. They'll come back. Don't be stupid. They're gone."

"Fifteen seconds!"

"One might make an impression by arriving to the party fashionably late," Pepi said, "but I saw someone else with the same ensemble, and haircut too, if you can believe it. So, it's simply out of the ques —"

Sophie grabbed Pepi by the wrists and pulled him off the bunk. His eyes spiraled with confusion as he resisted, but he was skin and bones and she had him on his feet easily.

"Ten seconds!"

Sophie pushed Pepi, like a gangly, life-sized puppet, out of the barracks. She stood him up against the outside wall, at the end of the line.

"Well, well, well," said the man-child. "Thank you for gracing us with your presence this morning."

"The pleasure is all mine," Pepi said, but he seemed to still be grappling with how he'd gotten there. Everyone in line relaxed a bit, dropping one another's hands.

"But since we're already here," said the man-child. "I'm thinking it would be a pity to waste a good decimation."

This was met with silence. No one knew what that meant.

"Which means I am going to shoot someone to pay for your crime."

Hands clasped again. The men, dirty-faced, bony, and brittle, stood together, shaking. They all had distended bellies, something Sophie now knew was a strange effect of starvation.

"But I'm the kapo!" Hershel exclaimed. No one had taken his hand.

"Shut up or it's you," said the man-child, pointing his gun at Hershel, who shut up.

"Shoot me," Pepi said. "This is my fault." His eyes were clear. He was absolutely serious.

"It *is* your fault," said the man-child. "Shooting you would certainly teach you a lesson."

"Yes, good," said Pepi. "We Jews value education very much. There's never a bad time for a good lesson."

Sophie shook her head. That sounded like Pepi. But what was he doing? She couldn't let him get shot!

"Although," said the man-child. "What would it teach everyone else?"

"To follow orders, presumably, lest you get shot," Pepi replied. "If I read the situation correctly."

"You do not read the situation correctly," said the man-child.

"No doubt," Pepi admitted.

"If I were to shoot you," the man-child explained, waxing philosophical, "it would confirm a direct correlation between cause and effect. You commit a crime, you get shot. Am I right?"

"I expect you are," Pepi replied.

"In other words, it would establish a system of justice on which a Jew might depend."

"This," Pepi said, "is something I do not think you need to fear."

The man-child wasn't listening. "So," he continued, "if you won't get up in the morning, *maybe* you get shot. Or maybe someone else gets shot. Maybe no one gets shot? Who's to know? Am I right? This is a system without a system. This is how the world must be for the Jew."

"Please! Shoot me!" Pepi begged, no longer able to carry on the absurd conversation. "I got up yesterday," he said, "and the day before, and the day before, and the day before, for one reason only. Because I am a playwright. I wrote a play, but they burned my manuscript. I get up every day to repeat the lines so that one day I will be able to write them down again. Today, I woke up and they were gone. Shoot me. Please. Shoot me. Poetic justice is my due."

"A playwright?" the man-child mused. "I have some good news for you then: new material! Real life drama! I'm going to start a count with you, actually, not you, and shoot the tenth person down the line. And if you don't get up tomorrow, we'll do it again. And we'll do it again the day after that. Or maybe we won't. It's impossible to know. The plot, as they say, might twist."

"No!" Pepi cried.

The man-child pointed his gun at the man standing next to Pepi and counted, "One," then pointed to the man next to him and said, "two." Then, over Pepi's repeated cries of "No!", he continued down the line.

When he got to ten, he pulled the trigger.

The prisoners all cried out, but the bullet went well over the barracks and into the sky.

Sophie had lifted the man-child's arm.

"What the hell?" he said.

He pointed and fired again, this time into the ground.

The man-child scowled at his gun as if it had betrayed him. Embarrassed, he looked around to see if any of his fellow Nazis had witnessed his ineptitude. Then — thank goodness — it seemed he didn't want to risk it happening again. "Kapo!" he screamed. "Get everyone to the crematorium for your clean-up shift! Now!"

Sophie knew this was far from over. The man-child would make these prisoners pay in some way for his failure. But not here and not now. She'd learned to take victories whenever she could get them.

"Move!" Hershel screamed, even though everyone was already heading in the direction of their destination. He started slapping them randomly on the back of their heads to make them move faster. The man-child nodded, approvingly.

Sophie walked with the group, just to make sure nothing else went wrong.

Which, of course, it did.

When the group cleared all the barracks, Pepi bolted.

"Stop!" the man-child cried. He leveled his gun at Pepi's back but seemed to think the better of trying to fire it again. Instead, he ran after Pepi.

Sophie ran too. She knew what he was doing: running for the fence.

The man-child kept shouting to stop, but Pepi kept running.

"No, Pepi, no!" Sophie cried, but Pepi kept running.

When he was just a few yards from the fence, a Nazi in the tower shot him.

Pepi's body whipped around, and he fell to the ground on his back, holding his shoulder. Sophie thought about the commandant upbraiding the guards who'd let that woman electrocute herself when she'd first gotten to the camp — she remembered hoping it meant he was a good man. But now she understood why. You weren't even allowed to kill yourself here.

"Whoa! Whoa!" the man-child called, waving at the tower. "No more!" he shouted. "I will handle this!" His face was red and throbbing. He unholstered his gun, but then put it back, deciding on another course of action.

After grabbing Pepi by the wrists, the man-child began dragging him across the hard ground. Pepi, bleeding from the shoulder, did not resist. His eyes stared, unblinking, up at the smoky sky above.

"No!" Sophie screamed, seeing where they were headed. She ran to Pepi and grabbed his ankles. This momentarily brought the man-child to a stop. His eyes screwed up, but then he yanked Pepi hard, pulling his feet right out of Sophie's grip, leaving the rags he'd been wearing for shoes in her hands.

Sophie dropped the rags and tried to get hold of Pepi's ankles again, but the man-child dragged him too quickly, all the way to the doors of the gas chamber building, where the prisoners now stood. Sophie knew they cared. She knew they wanted to do something. But she also knew they were too defeated and demoralized to do anything but watch with empty eyes the horror unfolding before them.

"Kapo!" the man-child raged. "Open the door!"

Hershel did as he was told, and the man-child easily hauled Pepi inside the building.

Sophie ran in after them, but it was too late. The man-child had Pepi off the floor, braced against his hip, like a piece of broken furniture. Pepi continued to offer no resistance, making it all the easier to maneuver him into the crematorium.

Then the man-child pushed past another troop of prisoners finishing their shift and jammed Pepi Schenkel, headfirst and alive, into an open red-hot oven. He slammed the door shut on Pepi's ungodly screams.

Sophie spent the next two days holed up in one of the commandant's guest rooms, the one nearest Giddy's bedroom. She didn't leave it for any reason other than to get food or to use the toilet.

Why Sophie was so distraught at Pepi Schenkel's death, she didn't know. It wasn't only the pain he must have endured being burned alive, or even the fact that she was quite certain she'd seen him tuck his arms against his sides to make it easier for the man-child to shove him into the oven. It was true that it was the worst, most abominably cruel murder she'd seen yet, and she'd seen too many to count. But... Pepi wasn't family. He wasn't even a neighbor. And he had definitely become deranged. Regardless, his death felt — was it because he was the only source of humor she'd seen since this ordeal began? — like a terminal blow. It made no sense. Unable to sleep, unable to think about anything else, Sophie wept continuously for nearly forty-eight hours.

But on the third morning, she discovered that the grief, if that's what it was, had diminished just enough to let her go check on Giddy. It receded altogether when she saw him.

Giddy looked wonderful. He hadn't grown much in the past year, but he'd put on weight, all that he'd lost and then some. Seeing him in his shorts and short sleeves, it was clear that he'd developed some muscles too. His face had regained its pre-ghetto proportions and his cheeks had actual color in them. His hair, cut short, had shine. His jug-ears were as adorable as ever.

Giddy, it dawned on Sophie, was thriving.

Sophie never really wondered what Giddy did all day. It had been enough to know that he was safe. But now she realized what a great life he had. Frau Kruger was an odd woman, there was no doubt about that. She smoked one cigarette after another all day long, and the fact that she called Giddy by the name of her dead son was creepy in the extreme — but otherwise, she seemed to be a more than good mother. The woman doted on Giddy in a way a child might only dream of, plying him with snacks and treats and constantly asking him what he needed to be comfortable. As far as Sophie could tell, the only conflict they had was over Giddy's obsessive cleaning of his room.

Frau Kruger seemed content to spend most of her day sewing lacy garments in the living room where Giddy studied with a series of tutors: one for mathematics, one for literature, one for science, and one for piano. Every time he did something well, she exclaimed, "Very good, Hans! Very, very good!" Which was frequent because Giddy was a fast learner. He never complained, even when his math instructor asked him to determine how long it would take to rid Germany of half a million Jewish cockroaches if half of them were exterminated every day. Sophie wanted to throw the lace-covered furniture around, but Giddy showed no signs of being bothered in the least. He simply worked the problem out in his head, and quickly.

All that before lunch, which Frau Kruger made and brought in to Giddy — cooked sausage and bread, some of which Sophie ate off his plate. Much to Sophie's delight, Frau Kruger was tickled to see what she thought was Giddy's hearty appetite, and so she kept his plate full all afternoon.

A fifth teacher came after lunch and took Giddy into the woods to get exercise and learn about nature. Sophie decided not to go along, opting instead to observe how Frau Kruger spent her free time. First, she cleaned — vigorously, which explained the absence of a maid in the house. Frau Kruger clearly enjoyed the work, unlike Giddy, who seemed to clean almost violently.

When Frau Kruger was done, she retired to the library, a sumptuous room on the ground floor with rich wooden shelves running along the walls. They went up so high that ladders were installed, which ran along rails to provide access to the upper shelves. Frau Kruger put a record on the large phonograph, Mozart. Then she took a book from one of the shelves, *Mein Kampf,* by Adolf Hitler, and sat down to read.

Sophie stood there, mesmerized by the books. There were hundreds upon hundreds of them. She thought about Rabbi Hasendahl's sad little library in Ortschaft and how much she'd loved it. She remembered tottering around with Giddy on her shoulders shouting *Stomp!* every time she took a step. She'd promised to be his golem, to protect him. And that's what she'd done. And that's what she would never stop doing.

Sophie went upstairs to take a rare nap but decided to explore Frau Kruger's room instead. She was immediately attracted to an elaborate vanity visible from inside a closet. The closet was bigger than any bedroom Sophie had ever had, and it was jam-packed with racks and racks of dresses, like at a clothing store. Open packages with foreign-looking stamps littered the floor. The vanity's shelves were chock full of fascinating vials and tubes and containers. There was a stack of magazines on its tabletop, and Sophie couldn't help but page through some of them. The German ones were filled with pictures of Eva Braun, Hitler's girlfriend. The foreign ones overflowed with alluring, exotic women with names like Greta Garbo and Jean Harlow and Katharine Hepburn.

This room, these dresses, the pictures — they filled Sophie with both longing and resentment. She used to spend great lengths of time sitting at her Papa-made humble vanity, in front of her small mirror, contemplating her looks. But since she'd vanished, she'd thought very little about her appearance. Sophie looked into Frau Kruger's mirror and saw nothing. She ran her hand through her hair, which now fell halfway down her back. She cupped her breasts, which had grown without her noticing. But what did it matter? It would never matter what she looked like for the rest of her life. It occurred to Sophie that she hadn't even noticed missing her last few birthdays. Rather than flinging the dresses to the floor and tearing up the magazines, she went and took that nap.

Giddy was back for dinner, which Frau Kruger served in the formal dining room with formal dinnerware, even though the commandant would not be home until dark. While she and Giddy ate the beef stew and potato pancakes she prepared, she quizzed him on various things he'd learned during the day. He responded to every question correctly. It all seemed too good to be true. But then Sophie finally saw Giddy break this facade, and she caught a glimpse of the damaged child she knew he still had to be.

"Is my —?" he started to say, but then seemed to choke on his words. "Is she —?" he tried again, looking at his lap.

"She is doing wonderfully well!" said Frau Kruger, smiling brightly. "Working hard every day to earn her freedom."

Giddy nodded but did not look at Frau Kruger. Sophie did, though, and it was at that moment she realized the commandant had only pretended to give Golda a choice in giving him away. Of course he only pretended! If Giddy thought his mother had willingly handed him over, and that she was working to get him back, he would be... exactly as pliable as he'd been.

"Now go wash up for the night, my dear Hans," said Frau Kruger, "and meet me in my room for story time. Then it's off to bed with you."

At this simple instruction, Giddy started to cry.

"Now, Hans, darling," said Frau Kruger. "None of that nonsense. The commandant will not want to hear that you cried about such a silly thing."

At this, Giddy promptly pulled himself together. He got up from the table and said, "Thank you, Mama, for dinner. I'll be in your room shortly."

Sophie skipped story time, electing to clean up in Giddy's washroom more thoroughly than she usually got the chance to do. When he returned, she held his hand while he cried and told him he was the reason she went out in the morning and came home at night.

When Sophie lay down on the window bench, it was with profound relief. Knowing how Giddy spent his days filled her with a deep and abiding sense of satisfaction that made every atrocity at the camp recede in her mind, even Pepi Schenkel. No matter how little help she provided there, she was performing a miracle here every single day, even if it was hard on Giddy. Though the question remained: how was she to make a bigger impact at the camp — and without triggering retribution worse than whatever evil she might prevent, or more realistically, stall? It was a daily dilemma, but Sophie was determined to solve it.

That night — miracle of miracles — she slept soundly.

Sophie's newfound optimism died the very next morning. As did another piece of her soul.

As usual, the commandant pulled his car through the gates. However, today, he did not head for the administration building. Instead, he drove around the perimeter of the camp, to the far end, and parked there. Curious, Sophie got out to see what could have altered his normal routine.

There was a new building, evidently built in just the past few days. It was, like the barracks, basically a wooden box, but it was much sturdier and had a metal roof. The commandant walked part way around both sides, inspecting the new construction. Then he opened its large and heavy wooden door.

That's when Sophie heard the howling. She thought she'd heard all possible expressions of pain, but this was something else, something worse even than Pepi Schenkel. This was coming from children.

Sophie ran into the building behind the commandant. It took a few moments to comprehend what she saw. First, she was puzzled by the dark curtains, thick heavy curtains, that were hung along all four walls. They turned the building into a cave. A soundproof one, Sophie realized.

She was then confused by the rows of cots and the tables and racks full of medical equipment. Was this a new infirmary? Sophie had visited the camp's infirmary many times, and it was always full of patients dying, though mostly quietly. Were they operating on someone? The ferocity and sheer volume of the screaming made it almost impossible to think. It was coming from behind a partition.

The commandant walked casually toward it, seemingly unperturbed by the hellish noise. Sophie, afraid of what she would discover, followed on shaking legs.

Of all the heinous things Sophie had witnessed, this was by far the worst. There were two cots. A boy was strapped down to each one. They were maybe ten years old and obviously identical twins, a pair of stubbly-headed skeletons with big brown eyes protruding in their delirium and pain. Both boys had their right arms gruesomely severed. Belts were cinched around their stumps, which continued to bleed. The bloody detached arms lay on a metal table between the cots. And between the arms rested a saw, a saw Sophie's Papa would have used to cut logs, dripping with blood.

The contents of Sophie's stomach began to rise into her throat. She covered her mouth with her hands and wretched. The boys continued to scream.

A man — the older man with glasses and silver sideburns that had directed Giddy's mother to her death in the gas chamber, the man who told the women whose mouths he was inspecting that he was a doctor — stood next to the table, wearing a long white laboratory coat. With a gory gloved hand, he picked up the arm nearest the boy on the left cot and began testing its fit onto the stump of the boy on the right. The boys' caterwauling was relentless, piercing, and all-consuming, yet the old man acted as though he were working in silence.

"I'll leave you to your work!" said the commandant, raising his voice to be heard. Even he looked green.

Sophie, her hands still clamped over her mouth, frantically looked around for a way to help.

The doctor, if that's what he was, looked up in surprise, having been so absorbed in his work. "Oh!" he shouted. "Commandant! Thank you for checking in on me. I expect you wish to know if this new arrangement is satisfactory. I can assure you that it is!" He set the severed arm back down.

"I'm pleased to hear it!" the commandant shouted. "But don't let me take you away from —!"

"Oh, these two?" the monster of a doctor said. "They'll be dead in an hour! I'm just noodling around. Say! While you're here, I would like to discuss a matter."

The commandant waved the doctor over to him and led him out of the building, so that they might actually hear each other.

When the door closed behind them, Sophie went to the boy on the left, who was howling so hysterically, she thought his eyes were going to explode. She leaned over him, and he seemed to see her.

"May your memory be for a blessing," Sophie said softly and kissed him on the forehead. Then, looking deeply into the boy's petrified eyes, she pinched his nose shut with one hand and covered his mouth with the other. He stopped screaming. Then, he stopped breathing. His body relaxed.

Sophie did the same for the boy's brother, telling herself while his soul departed that it was a blessing to be released from such agony. Rabbi Hasendahl's voice spoke inside her head from the cave of his classroom, reminding her that it was also a blessing to be a blessing. But she wasn't sure she believed it anymore.

After getting Giddy to sleep that night, Sophie lay on his window bench, staring at the ceiling, trying her best not to let the vision of the boys' faces join the others that haunted her. She succeeded, but only because she was consumed by the fact that, with her own hands, she had taken life, even if it was for reasons of mercy and grace. She was now not only failing to keep people alive, she was making them dead.

Sophie Siegel, she thought, *angel of death.*

Over the next four weeks, the minute the commandant parked his car at the administration building, Sophie climbed out and headed straight across the camp to what she considered the torture chamber.

It was always twins. They were culled from the selection lines and who knows where else. The monster was an early riser, so most days Sophie arrived to find he'd already been well at work: performing amputations or injecting children with substances that sent them into unbearable convulsions. One day, she found him stabbing a little girl with a long needle all over her body to see if her sister felt any of the pain.

The screaming in that building — the screaming never ended. Until it did. Each day, while the monster was preoccupied with one of his victims, Sophie gently put the others, one by one, out of their misery.

As the weeks passed, the monster grew increasingly frustrated with the "fragility of the local specimens" and complained about it every time the commandant visited. Finally, after the inexplicably premature demise of the eighteenth set of twins, he told the commandant that the pool of subjects available at his camp was unsuitable, and that he would have to run his experiments elsewhere.

The morning the monster declared his intentions to depart, he was packing his equipment into various boxes. Sophie found the long needle he'd stabbed the little girl with and stood behind him with it trembling in her hand.

When he bent down to arrange some of his tools in a box, she raised it over her head, zeroing in on a birthmark on the back of his neck.

But then she lowered the needle.

And the Monster stood up.

Sophie couldn't bring herself to do it.

She despised herself for her weakness.

The next day Sophie went back to the camp, but she didn't know what to do with herself. She felt no sense of victory at having rid the camp of the monster. Everything seemed pointless. Her efforts felt like a waste of time.

After climbing out of the commandant's car, merely out of her previous habit, she headed for the kitchen, yet another wooden box of a building in the center of the camp. The workers were already inside, standing at six long tables, peeling potatoes. They'd be standing there until dusk.

Sophie watched them work. Every one of them was eating vegetable peels. And no one was murdering them for it. It was a mystery to Sophie why the usual rules didn't apply here, although she knew their regular rations would be curtailed to cancel the benefits of this boon. It couldn't be that the Nazis wanted the workers to keep their energy up — that wasn't the case anywhere else work was performed. If someone fell down dead on the job, that meant only that they were no longer of use.

There was only one Nazi in the kitchen. Sophie pondered the meaning of this unusual arrangement. Even if he tried his best — and he didn't try at all — he couldn't stop twenty some odd people from sneaking a peel into their mouths every so often. They'd have to have a guard standing by each worker, watching them all day to prevent such a thing. That was impractical — and so Sophie understood. The Nazis were never impractical. They wouldn't make a rule they couldn't enforce. If a half-dead prisoner barely able to stand on her feet put a forbidden potato peel into her mouth — next she might dream of rebellion.

In the back of the kitchen was a long stove with many burners. Each had a large pot sitting on top, filled with already boiling water. One of the prisoners, the "cook," was in charge of putting bits of rotting potatoes and rutabaga into the pots, along with some kind of flour. At lunch, prisoners carried the pots out to the various work sites. New arrivals could rarely stomach the stuff until they'd forced it down a few times, which they always managed when faced with the alternative of dropping dead.

There was a separate stove in the back for cooking the meals for the Nazis, and a separate table as well, where the lone Nazi guard peeled and chopped fresh vegetables: carrots, celery, beans, and more. This station, of course, he watched when he was not working. Although not *that* closely. Sophie walked to the table and, when he wasn't looking, stuffed her pockets full.

Sophie knew where all the worksites were outside the camp. Her routine had been well established before her stint as an angel of death. Each day, she'd head to the gate, wait for it to open to allow Nazis in trucks or jeeps to come or go, then travel to each location to drop the fresh vegetables into the prisoners' soup. But as she headed to the gate this morning, she heard shouting coming from behind the last row of barracks.

With her heart already heavy, Sophie reluctantly headed toward the uproar. There she found, in a field beyond the barracks, Pepi's former group. The very same bunch that witnessed his end and just barely escaped their own. Hershel, the kapo, was doing the shouting this time. No Nazi was present.

There were holes all around the field, small but deep. It was a field of holes now, and Sophie thought about the field of unmarked graves in the ghetto. Twenty-two prisoners had dug them, and now they seemed to be filling them in.

"Faster, you vermin!" Hershel railed. "Faster! It's your own fault we're doing this! Do you hear me? Your own fault!"

Suddenly, Sophie understood. They were digging holes with the sole purpose of filling them back up. And from the looks of it, they'd probably been doing this for weeks as punishment for seeing the man-child fail to shoot one of them.

"Degenerate, disgusting, sub-human vermin!" Hershel spat.

Sophie reckoned he believed what he was saying about his fellow Jews — that they were subhuman, that they'd brought everything that happened to them upon themselves. How else could he explain to himself how he treated them? She turned away from the scene, disgusted, and walked to the main gate.

Perfect timing. Just as she got there, it opened for a truck.

After taking only a few steps toward the woods that bordered the camp to the south — there was a work detail clearing trees to make space for more barracks, a planned camp expansion — Sophie heard an explosion that made her clutch her heart. She was easily startled lately, by any sudden noise, even soft ones.

The explosion had come from the hills to the north. And then there came a second one. This wasn't a sound like she'd heard in or around the camp before. Not gunshots. These were detonations. Sophie watched a smoky plume rise into the sky, then set off in its direction, nervous to discover what was happening there.

Sophie found the worksite by following the plumes of smoke and debris. There was an explosion every ten minutes. After nearly an hour of climbing through the rising hills, she found herself on a dirt road, which she followed for another seeming eternity. Abruptly, it dead-ended near a steep and rocky slope. A truck was parked at its termination.

There were half a dozen Nazis and maybe two dozen prisoners. Most were clambering unsteadily down the hillside, clutching rocks of various sizes to their sunken, striped chests. Men and women alike had their heads shaved, and since all were so ill-fed, it was difficult to tell them apart. Two prisoners close by were not working. One man was lying on the ground with his shirt off and blood dripping down his back. The other, a woman, sat beside him, picking rocks out of his skin.

Sophie approached the truck where five Nazis were clustered and listened to them talk. Their task was to blast the hillside in preparation for an underground factory for airplane parts. Apparently, their above ground facilities were getting bombed too often. This news cheered Sophie immensely. She had no idea how the war was going and never thought about whether or when it might finally end.

One prisoner on the slope was not hauling rocks. Rather, she was squatting on a ledge, well up the hillside, working some kind of tool on the stone: a hand drill. Sophie climbed up, wanting to get a closer look. The prisoner's name was Fanny Cohen. A sixth Nazi was standing well above her, keeping a safe distance, Sophie assumed. She squinted up at him, a dark figure in the bright sunlight.

"Time!" he called, and everyone carrying rocks down the hill dropped them and blundered with reckless abandon down to the road.

The Nazi dropped something that landed at Fanny's feet, a stick of dynamite. "Light it, A38019!" he shouted.

Fanny set the dynamite into the hole she'd drilled.

"Light it!" the Nazi ordered, tossing down a match.

Fanny found the match and struck it on a rock. She lit the fuse.

"Run, Fanny!" Sophie shouted, ready herself, to do exactly that. But the woman simply stood where she was as sweat poured down her face.

"Run!" Sophie cried.

Sophie grabbed Fanny by the arm and at that moment, the Nazi shouted, "Run, dog!"

They ran.

Fanny was in no shape to move with any speed or agility, so Sophie pulled her as best she could, stumbling along the way.

The dynamite exploded, spewing debris up into the air and down the hill. It swept past Sophie and Fanny in a spreading cloud, sending them onto their faces. Fortunately, they'd reached the road. It seemed neither of them suffered more than superficial scratches.

The Nazis at the truck let out a round of boos. Sophie, back on her feet and blistering mad, saw one of them handing money over to another.

A whistle sounded from the ledge above, and Sophie's heart nearly stopped. There was no mistaking that sound. That rich, beautiful tone. She shielded her eyes to see the ledge and the Nazi on it. But she didn't need to.

It was Dieter Wolf.

At nine o'clock that night, Sophie was standing at Hershel's barracks, watching him conduct the nightly headcount. The prisoners stood grimly before him. Hershel called twenty-two numbers, and twenty-two "yes, sirs" were shouted in return. Satisfied, he sent everyone to bed with a slap in the face.

When the last prisoner went inside, Sophie tapped on the side of the building, attracting Hershel's attention. She tapped again but moved along the wooden planks as she did so, until she turned the corner behind the barracks.

"Who is that?" Hershel demanded, following the noise. "You're going to get it if I find you out here!"

When he turned the corner, Sophie grabbed him by the wrists and slapped him across the face with his own right hand. He yelped. She slapped him again with his left hand. Then again and again, with both hands, until he doubled over, choking, "I'm sorry! I'm sorry! I'm sorry."

When she let go, Hershel sank to his knees, crying like a child.

Sophie walked away. The commandant would be heading

home soon.

Sophie had been going to the camp seven days a week, every week, because that's what the commandant did. But he took the next day off to go hunting with his dogs, and that's when Sophie made the troubling discovery that Giddy spent half of his Sundays with Frau Kruger at church.

To see what Giddy was being subjected to, as well as to stop herself from plotting a thousand ways to kill Dieter Wolf, Sophie went with him. She knew she'd have to deal with the man who murdered her parents, but she also knew she wouldn't think of any practical way to do so until she calmed down. Perhaps being kept away for a day was a good thing.

Sophie decided that, under no circumstances, would she allow the Nazis to destroy what was left of her humanity. She'd come to terms with not having killed the monster. She wasn't going to punish a Nazi by becoming a Nazi. Not even Dieter Wolf.

Giddy had to get up early, scrub himself to perfection, and dress. Sophie was appalled to see him come downstairs in a child-size Nazi uniform, complete with a little black tie and cap that had the eagle carrying a swastika pin on it. The cap was a bit too large and fell over his ears. Frau Kruger wore a tight-waisted black and white dress and a wide-brimmed hat, like the ones in her French fashion magazines. Sophie heard the commandant tell her once that such fashions were now considered un-German, but she paid him no mind.

After breakfast, a Nazi from the camp showed up at the house in the fanciest automobile Sophie had ever seen. It was long and black with a little red Nazi flag on each of its swooping fenders. It had big lights mounted on the front. The black top glimmered in the sun.

Sophie climbed in behind Giddy and sat next to him on the long and luxuriously soft backseat. While they drove through the countryside, the driver attempted nervous, cough-riddled conversation with Frau Kruger, who smoked continuously. Giddy looked out the window without speaking, and Sophie spent the entire ride thinking black thoughts about Dieter Wolf. She worried that he wouldn't be at the camp tomorrow. She worried that he would be. What could she do about him? Since the moment her world turned upside down, Sophie, with perhaps the exception of the moment she almost murdered the monster, had thought about helping people, not dispensing justice. But now, despite her recent resolutions, she was thinking about it. She was thinking about it hard.

Sophie Siegel, she thought, *angel of vengeance.*

After a thirty-minute ride, they parked at a rustic stone church topped with a wooden spire and a cross. Fancy cars filled the lot, which told Sophie this was a place for rich people, as did all the expensive dresses she saw on the women getting out of them. The men, all military it seemed, were in uniforms decorated with pins and patches.

Sophie knew she couldn't sit with Giddy, so she made her way to the back of the church and watched the service from there. There was a lot of standing and sitting and singing and chanting about things which meant nothing to her. And then the priest gave his sermon.

He was a wisp of a man in layered black robes, over which hung a huge and intricate wooden cross on a chain around his neck. He wore glasses and had stripes of thinning hair combed over a pink skull. From behind a marble pulpit that was as wide as three or four podiums, he read a prepared speech about the coming thousand-year Reich and Hitler's grand mission to rid Germany of the parasitic scourge of sub-humans, especially the Jews, who were a pestilence upon the land. He said Jews were devils with actual horns, horns they shaved down to pass among humans. He said they were demons who drank the blood of Christian children when they could catch them. He said they were irredeemable Christ-killers with a lust for evil in their dark hearts. He said Jewish men were animals who lay with beasts and Jewish women were whores with teeth in their private parts who could seduce anyone but an upstanding Aryan man. He said it was every good German's duty to do everything they possibly could to support the Führer.

Sophie's blood boiled. She stared at the back of Giddy's head in his pew, worrying herself sick about what he might be thinking. She didn't care what they said about Jews anymore — to *her* — but the idea of Giddy's mind being poisoned filled her with a fury that made her grind her teeth. What if he came to believe it? What if he forgot who he was? What if she'd done the wrong thing getting him to the Krugers?

No, of course it wasn't the wrong thing. Anything was better than the camp. Absolutely anything.

The priest was still going on about diabolical Jews when Sophie, overcome with rage, found herself walking up the long aisle to the stage he was standing on. She climbed up the steps, walked to his pulpit, and stood right next to him. He said the Jewish problem had only one solution.

Sophie kicked him in the calf. When he grunted and doubled over behind the pulpit, she tore the glasses off his face and dropped them at his feet. Then she stomped on them, hard. A commotion broke out among the congregants as everyone stood to see what was the matter. When the priest got down on his knees to feel around for his glasses, Sophie yanked the chain off his neck, threw down the cross, and cracked it in half with her heel.

Then she went back to her seat.

Without his glasses, the priest could not continue reading his speech, so he made it up as he went along. Fortunately, he was boring on his own. Unfortunately, the service droned on all morning.

When it finally did end, the priest walked with his congregation out of the church. Just inside the front doors was a huge font full of water, nearly big enough to bathe in.

When the priest reached the font, Sophie shoved his head down into it, and for extra measure, while his arms flailed, she picked up his feet and dunked him in entirely.

Once the sopping wet and completely confused priest was helped back to his private rooms, Frau Kruger spent an hour outside talking with a group of other women. They expressed some concern for the priest, but their conversation mostly revolved around how bothersome the shortages were becoming because they couldn't get their favorite cuts of meat and jellies and beauty supplies. Frau Kruger showed Giddy off to everyone like he was a prize hog. No one batted an eye at her calling him Hans.

Meanwhile, Sophie tried to come up with a way to keep Giddy from ever being brought here again, but she couldn't think of anything other than setting it on fire.

When Frau Kruger was finally ready to go home, Sophie got back in the car feeling defeated by everything she couldn't do anything about. The elation she'd experienced at having given that priest what he deserved was long gone.

But then Giddy got in. And when the driver went to open the door for Frau Kruger, he slyly reached under his oversized cap and took two bits of something — sausage! — out of his ears, then dropped them casually out his open window.

Sophie had never been so proud of anyone in her life.

But when they got back to the house, she was nearly mauled.

The commandant had returned from his hunt and was herding his dogs, about a dozen of the bearded beasts, back into the barn. The gate in the fence running alongside the driveway was open. The second Sophie stepped out of the car, the largest dog of the pack broke away and bounded toward her.

The commandant shouted at the dog to stop. Frau Kruger cried out, snatching Giddy up from the ground, then turning her back to the onrushing animal. The driver stepped in front of them both. But Sophie knew the dog was after her. The back door of the car was still open, so she jumped on the back seat and scrambled her way onto the roof, hoping the dog would have trouble getting up there too. It didn't. It leapt right onto the hood of the car and was poised to leap over the windshield to kill her, when a shot was fired.

The dog let out a squeal and then slid off the hood onto the ground, leaving a smear of blood.

The commandant, having reached the car, said, "I simply can't imagine what got into him."

Frau Kruger was furious, too furious it seemed, to speak to her husband. She set Giddy on his feet, lit a cigarette with an unsteady hand, and said, "I'm going to lie down. You two are on your own for lunch and dinner." Then she walked toward the porch. "Hans," she added without looking back, "I'll see you for story time tonight." Giddy's shoulders slumped as he walked behind her.

While Frau Kruger and Giddy went back into the house, Sophie climbed off the car, quivering and cold.

"I really hate to lose such a good hunter," the commandant said, looking at the dead dog. "What was he doing?" he asked. Without waiting for an answer, he went over to look at the car's roof and ran his hand over it, feeling what must have been a dent. "The dog didn't get up here, did it?" he asked.

"No, sir," said the driver. "You got him on the hood. Outstanding shot, sir."

"Very strange," said the commandant. "Very strange." Then he said, "That'll be all."

"Yes, sir," said the driver, who got back into the car and left.

With her heart still hammering, Sophie followed the commandant into the house, where Frau Kruger — who hadn't gone to lie down — was waiting for him.

"Reinhard," she said tersely, puffing madly on her cigarette. She was pale and still shaken. "It could have killed Hans."

Sophie hadn't known the commandant was called Reinhard and disliked the fact that he even had a name. He nodded to concede his wife's point. "My deepest apologies, dear," he said. "That particular dog was given to me by a junior officer who raises hunters. He assured me it was the best he'd ever seen. But I consider that an act of sabotage, even if it was unintentional, not to mention unsuccessful. Tomorrow, he will find his career taking an unexpected turn for the worse."

"Good," said Frau Kruger, who turned and headed upstairs.

The commandant watched her ascend, then went into the library.

Sophie went upstairs and spent the rest of the afternoon and evening in the guest room so she could think. She came out to swipe some snacks around dinnertime, but, once again, skipped out on Giddy's story time. Sophie guessed he was being subjected to tales about evil Jewish boogeymen and couldn't plug his ears against them. She'd had enough of that today. Instead, she went to bed early. A plan was taking shape in her mind.

Tomorrow was going to be a big day.

At the blast site the next day, Dieter Wolf was having a new kind of fun. He'd evidently been disciplined for his previous game — too many of his workers couldn't haul rocks with shrapnel in their backs. Today, after each explosion, when prisoners were carrying debris down the hill, he had one of them stand next to him on the ledge, throwing fist-sized rocks. He offered extra rations if they hit someone hard enough to make them fall. Fortunately, most of the prisoners made halfhearted attempts, although it seemed to Sophie that one or two tried their best.

Unfortunately, this prompted Dieter Wolf to throw rocks himself, and he had terrific aim.

After dropping fresh vegetables into the prisoners' bowls of soup that afternoon, Sophie went to the back of the Nazis' truck and took a single stick of dynamite, putting it in her pocket. Then she walked away.

Back at the camp, Sophie discovered that another prisoner had managed to commit suicide on the electric fence: Hershel, the kapo. Had she not had that stick of dynamite, and a plan — and Giddy — Sophie suspected the news might have induced her to do the same.

Nine days later, Sophie had collected ten sticks of dynamite, all with very long fuses. Exactly how many she needed, she didn't know, but she was fairly sure she had enough.

When it was dark, Sophie walked into the gas chamber/crematorium building, which had remained unguarded since she'd stopped breaking showerheads. She went through the women's vestibule, entered the showers, set three sticks of dynamite on the floor, and lit them. Then she made haste to the men's shower and lit three more.

Sophie proceeded quickly to the ovens. There were five of them. She lit the fuses on the last three sticks and scattered them throughout the room.

Then she made a run for it.

The explosion was not as spectacular as Sophie imagined it would be, but the dynamite was more than effective. She was safely across the camp when she heard it go off. There was a series of loud and rapid bangs and flashes of light in the night. The building did not burst into powder as she hoped it might, but the walls broke apart and the roof fell in.

Sirens wailed.

Lights from all the towers swung toward the scene.

Nazis were running.

Prisoners were shouting.

Sophie was smiling.

The commandant did not return to his house that evening, but rather spent the night issuing irate orders for headcounts and searches. Sophie slept in the back of his car, reveling in the destruction she'd wrought — but also drenched with fear about the consequences it might bring.

When she entered the administration building the next morning, Sophie found the commandant still shouting at his staff. He was demanding that they make sure the camp was in perfect order.

Prisoners, who'd been confined to their barracks after the explosion, were still locked down. Someone important was coming. No doubt, because word had already spread about what happened. For several hours, Nazis rushed in and out, reporting on the status of the barracks, the kitchen, the infirmary, the grounds, the fence, and the work sites.

At noon, everything seemed to be ready, including a tray of bread and lunch meats, but no visitor arrived. The commandant paced around the administration building as he waited, seeming somehow both calm and ready to explode.

Finally, in the late afternoon while the prisoners were still confined to their barracks, an elegant black car arrived. An important-looking Nazi got out of the back, a Colonel Lindemann, whose lapel buttons had something like a hybrid of a branch and a sword on them. He was a distinguished older man with a weathered face and intense eyes. His uniform was even fancier than the commandant's, who hurriedly strode out to meet him. Together, they walked back into the administration building.

Although Colonel Lindemann didn't raise his voice, he was obviously upset. "You better have an explanation," he said, as the commandant led him to a table draped in fine linen. "Your job depends on it."

"Please, Colonel," said the commandant, gesturing for him to have a seat. "Have some refreshments." He nodded to a Nazi holding the tray, who hurried over. Another delivered a steaming cup of coffee.

The Colonel, glowering but apparently hungry, sat down and made himself a sandwich.

"I have answers for you, sir," said the commandant, taking a seat himself.

Sophie sat down in an empty chair by the table, eager to see if the second part of her plan would work out as well as the first.

"I hope to God you aren't about to tell me that partisans breached your camp, commandant," said Colonel Lindemann. "If such is the case, this is your last day here."

Sophie didn't know who or what partisans were, but she was shaken to realize that she hadn't considered the possible repercussions of her plan on the commandant. What if he was transferred? She would go with him, that's all. But what if he was fired? And If he was no longer able to provide a comfortable home for Giddy?

"No, sir," said the commandant, coolly and calmly. "I am aware that there are terrorists prowling through the woods all over Germany, attacking our people and resources like cowards. But not here. I assure you that we are constantly monitoring our perimeter. This morning we conducted a thorough inspection of the fence. There are no breaches."

"Then it was a Jew," said Colonel Lindemann. "Obviously one from the work detail at the blast site. Am I to understand, then, that you have no control over either your prisoners or your supplies and equipment?"

"I can assure you, Colonel," said the unflappable commandant, "that every single prisoner was accounted for well before the blast. It was not a prisoner."

"You are not suggesting..."

"The prisoners on that detail were interrogated overnight. One of them claimed a Sergeant Wolf, on occasion made... irregular use of explosives."

The Colonel set down his sandwich.

The commandant nodded to one of his assistants, who stepped to the table and laid a stick of dynamite on it. "This was found in the men's barracks," the commandant said. "Under Sergeant Wolf's mattress. And this... was found on his person," he added, sliding something across the table.

It was Papa's whistle.

The Colonel took the whistle and examined it closely. After turning it over a few times, he said, "These are Hebrew letters."

The commandant nodded.

"And where is Sergeant Wolf now?" the Colonel asked.

"In a cell," said the commandant.

The Colonel stood up, drained his coffee, then said, "Assemble the camp."

"What?" Sophie jumped to her feet. But of course she was not noticed.

Thirty minutes later, all the prisoners — Sophie estimated there were nearly a thousand — stood in the field of holes. A post had been erected at the far end, and Dieter Wolf was tied to it, naked. His hands were bound behind the post and his feet in front of it. He was shouting, but his words were not audible, even in the silence of the still warm evening. A guard stood next to him, at attention.

Sophie smiled to see Dieter Wolf humiliated this way. It was only fair.

The commandant stepped onto a small platform, brought out for the occasion, and addressed the assembly through a megaphone. "You are here to witness what happens to a traitor," he shouted, "to a saboteur, to a Jew-lover." Then he added, "In many ways, he is far worse than a Jew, because he chose, of his own free will, to be one of them." The commandant turned and signaled to the guard standing stiffly next to Dieter, who was flailing against his restraints.

Sophie didn't know what was going to happen, but she wanted to see the look on Dieter's face when his punishment was announced. Perhaps now he would have his head shaved and be given a number. Maybe he'd be forced to put on striped pajamas and join the prisoners he so delighted in tormenting. Sophie hurried across the field to watch her revenge up close.

She immediately regretted having wished such things, even upon Dieter Wolf, and then stopped dead in her tracks. All thoughts of guilt and vengeance dissolved into dread. She'd gotten close enough to see what the punishment actually was. The guard was holding a stick of dynamite, the tenth stick that Sophie had stolen, the stick that had been found under Dieter's bed... and now he was lighting its fuse. He dropped it at Dieter's feet and ran.

"Nooooooo!" Sophie screamed, backpedaling wildly. She put her hands out, as if to stop time itself.

The explosion blew chunks of Dieter Wolf all over the field. Sophie was thrown on to her back, his blood covering her face, her front, the palms of her hands.

Lying in the dirt, Sophie heard Colonel Lindemann shout, "Where is prisoner A38019?"

Sophie sat up, her wide and wild eyes white upon her blood-streaked face.

No one moved, but then a kapo emerged, pushing a sobbing woman through the ranks of ragged prisoners up to the platform. Frantic and disoriented, Sophie rose to her feet. It was Fanny Cohen.

What *now?*

"And this is what happens," the commandant declared, "to any Jew impudent enough to inform on an Aryan." He nodded and two Nazis stepped forward to grab hold of Fanny.

"Oh, God," Sophie said. "Oh, God, no!"

The Nazis shoved Fanny into the closest hole, then began shoveling dirt into it. Fanny stood up, but the moment her head was visible, one of them kicked her in the face. She fell back into the hole and did not get up again.

They buried her alive.

Colonel Lindemann left when the last shovelful of dirt was dumped into the hole. Then, the commandant had all the prisoners form a line and ordered every single one of them to stand on Fanny Cohen's grave before returning to their barracks. They were told they'd be confined without rations until tomorrow.

The commandant, evidently satisfied that he'd saved his job and restored order to his camp, decided to head home early. Sophie, a filthy, blood-caked automaton, walked behind him back to the administration building, wondering whether being painted red made her visible. She didn't care. She rode home lying in the back of the commandant's car, her eyes open but unseeing. Dieter Wolf's blood stained the seats, but Sophie didn't care about that either.

She did not feel good about destroying the gas chamber. It would be rebuilt.

She did not feel good about destroying Dieter Wolf. There were a million Dieter Wolfs.

Sophie realized that protecting Giddy was the only thing she was good at.

She was done with the camp.

Dusk was coming on when they got back to the commandant's house. Sophie, numb, climbed out of the car. The commandant didn't head into the house but rather headed through the gate, no doubt to see to his dogs.

Sophie walked up the porch steps and tried the door; as usual, it was unlocked. She could smell the ham that must have been for dinner as she walked past the dining room and into the kitchen. There she found some thick slices of rye in the bread box. She devoured them ravenously as she headed upstairs for a bath and a change of clothes.

But when she passed by Frau Kruger's room, she heard Giddy whimpering, "Please no story time tonight, Mama. Please not tonight."

Curious, Sophie eased open the door.

Giddy, his pajama top pushed up to his shoulders, lay across Frau Kruger's lap. They were on the bed, under its lace canopy. Sophie could not tell exactly what was happening, but a sick feeling in her gut told her it was not good.

"Once upon a time," said Frau Kruger, "there was the most wonderful boy in the whole world. His name was Hans." She was holding a cigarette, glowing orange at its tip. Then she said, "He had big eyes and even bigger ears, and freckles *alllll* over his body."

Then Frau Kruger pressed her cigarette into Giddy's back. Giddy shuddered violently but did not make a sound.

Sophie launched herself through the canopy at Frau Kruger, who cried out as she was knocked onto her back. While she scrambled to find her cigarette, Sophie reached for Giddy, but he was tangled in the canopy, which had been torn down in the scuffle. Sophie clawed at it, until she managed to drag him off the bed. They both fell to the floor.

"Help!" Frau Kruger cried, thrashing to get free of the lace she'd gotten tangled in. Then she went still and stared, horror-struck, at the bloodstains Sophie had left behind on her white sheets.

Giddy was lying on the floor with his face down, covering his head. Sophie went to help him, but she froze at the sight of his back. His shirt was still up around his shoulders.

There were small burn marks, new ones and obviously older ones, all over his skin.

Frau Kruger began struggling with the canopy again, now calling desperately for her husband.

Before Sophie could decide what to do next, the bed went up in flames.

Frau Kruger screamed, thrashing in the burning lace. She rolled off the bed, setting the rug on fire in the back of the room. Fire raced up the curtains. Sophie stared at them, mesmerized for a moment, thinking of Pepi Schenkel.

Giddy whimpered on the floor at Sophie's feet, bringing her back to her senses. The fire was coming across the rug now, and quickly. Sophie lifted Giddy to his feet, then hurried him into the hall, down the stairs, and out of the house.

With her chest heaving, Sophie stood on the porch. It was getting dark. Her time in the camp was over, and now her time in the house was too. The car! The commandant always left his keys in it. Could she drive it? No way. Could she and Giddy hide in the back until the commandant drove away? Not a chance.

"Katrina!"

The commandant!

He'd come out of the barn and was sprinting madly toward the house. A dozen dogs ran behind him, barking ferociously.

Sophie looked at the house. The upper stories were engulfed in flames.

She didn't know what to do.

If they ran, the commandant would see Giddy. If they stayed, the commandant would see Giddy.

Paralyzed, Sophie did nothing.

The commandant ripped open the fence gate, fortunately kicking it shut before the dogs could get through it behind him. Shouting for his wife, he ran up the path to the porch and didn't seem to see Giddy until he got to the door. When he did, he stopped and grabbed Giddy by the arm. His eyes were pools of fear. "What have you done, you little Jewish pig?!" he screamed in Giddy's face. "I'll feed you to the dogs! I'll gas you like I did your mother!" Then he let go and ran into the house.

Sophie decided she would have to drive the car. Giddy would just have to think... it didn't matter what he would think! Who knew what he thought about anything? He hadn't reacted in any way to the commandant telling him his mother was dead. But the decision was taken out of Sophie's hands when Giddy stepped into the house and grabbed his boots from their cubby by the door. He came back out on the porch and put them on, looking disturbingly calm.

"Katrina! No, Katrina!" the commandant cried from upstairs.

Giddy stood up, drew in a deep breath, and took off. He ran straight down the porch path, past the commandant's car, making a beeline for the woods.

Sophie ran after him.

Sophie could barely keep up. Giddy ran like a track star, his arms pumping at his sides. Under the forest canopy, it was significantly darker. The woods were thick with undergrowth, but Giddy found room to run between the tree trunks through a maze of towering shadows. Deeper into the woods, they wouldn't be able to see at all, but Giddy ran onward. Gasping, Sophie followed, running like a lunatic, terrified that she'd lose him and hellbent not to.

Ten minutes later, Giddy stopped in a clearing. He didn't seem winded, but Sophie was grateful for the rest. She bent over with her hands on her knees, trying to catch her breath.

That's when they heard the dogs.

They sounded far away, but they were coming.

And Sophie was covered in blood.

Jolted, Giddy took off again. He fell over a branch, got up, and kept going. "Stop!" Sophie cried. She was going to lose him for sure in the dark. But when Giddy reached the edge of the clearing, Sophie heard a terrible smack and the sound of his body crashing to the forest floor. He'd hit his head on a low branch.

"Giddy!" Sophie cried, rushing over to him. He lay still on the bed of leaves covering the ground. "Giddy!" she begged, shaking him by the shoulder. He was not unconscious, but woozy.

The barking was getting louder. And now the darkness had fully settled in.

Continuing to run was out of the question. Sophie got Giddy to his feet and lifted his wrists until his hands landed on the branch that had knocked him down. It was thick and sturdy. He seemed to understand what his own hands were leading him to do and gripped it. Sophie lifted him by the waist and Giddy, regaining his faculties, swung a leg over the branch and got himself balanced.

The dogs were close now. Sophie could hear them tearing through the brush, breaking through shrubs, following their scent. Giddy, hearing this as well, reached up for another large branch and hoisted himself further into the tree. Sophie heaved herself onto the first branch and had just barely gotten herself onto Giddy's, when the first dog burst into the clearing.

It shot like an arrow, straight to their tree. Bloodthirsty and baying, the dog attempted to climb the trunk, but failed.

"Help!" Giddy cried. "Help! Help!"

The rest of the dogs tore into the clearing and surrounded them.

Sophie waved her hand over her head. There were no more sturdy branches within reach.

All the dogs were at the base of the tree now, lunging and drooling.

Another leapt onto the tree trunk and dug its claws in. This time it stuck.

"Help!" Giddy cried. "Please don't eat me. Please don't eat me. Please don't eat me!"

The dog was clawing its way up the trunk, and now other dogs were leaping and latching themselves onto it too.

The first dog made it onto the branch.

Sophie was between the beast and Giddy. When it attacked, she was going to grab it and take it to the ground.

It would be the last thing she ever did.

The dog, growling ominously, tested its balance on the branch. But the moment it positioned itself to pounce, a shot rang out. It fell out of the tree, dead.

Flashlights were suddenly wheeling around the clearing.

More shots were fired until the dogs barked no more.

A few minutes later, the commandant was marched into the clearing, in nothing but his underwear, by partisans who'd intercepted him running behind his dogs. One of them had his uniform folded up under an arm. All the flashlights landed on his stony face.

After helping Giddy down, the partisans tied the commandant to the very same tree. In the glare of their flashlights, he raged at Giddy. "Jewish dog!" he spewed. "Jewish pig! I should never have given in and brought one home. You killed my wife! You burned down my house!"

This provoked a round of cheers for Giddy. The partisans — it seemed there were five of them — patted him on the back.

"Bravo, young man!" said one of the partisans, a shadow behind his light. "I believe we have a new recruit!" Then, to the commandant, he said, "Condolences on the loss of your no-doubt better half. But this boy has done us quite the service. It just so happens that we were on our way to burn down your house!"

"You think you can bring the German war machine to its knees with ragtag troops of starvelings?" the commandant mocked.

"Ah," said the partisan. "You misunderstand our mission completely. We have no hopes of any such thing. We seek only to bring Nazis to their knees, one at a time if necessary."

"As the Jews always say," said another partisan, "one is not obligated to complete the work, but neither is one free to desist from it."

"Jewish scum," the commandant snarled, absurdly sure of himself, "you will all die."

"Perhaps so," said the first partisan. "But not tonight. Tonight, commandant, that is your job." He raised a gun he'd pulled from the waistband of his trousers, and before the commandant could get another word out, shot him between the eyes.

PART FOUR
THE WOODS

Sophie Siegel — September, 1944

Sophie lay on the pine and spruce needles under a ring of tightly packed trees encircling the troop's latest refuge. The sky was a mosaic of blue shards arranged by a fraying tarp of fall-colored leaves. Four of the five partisans, plus Giddy, were also resting in the refuge, lying on their blankets, contemplating the treetops. The troop's leader, Max Kleinman, was somewhere nearby, keeping watch. This is how they spent their days: doing absolutely nothing but staying quiet and hidden. And alive.

Sophie breathed in and out. The forest breathed in and out too, pulsing with silence, a living silence that felt like the embrace of strong arms. She closed her eyes and focused on the fog inside her mind, casting about for her parents. The best part of being in the woods was that Sophie finally had time to remember what she had lost. The worst part was that she couldn't picture any of it. She couldn't remember what Judenstrasse looked like. She couldn't remember what her house looked like. She couldn't remember what her room looked like. But what was hurting her most was that she couldn't remember what her parents looked like.

Sophie breathed in and out again, concentrating on conjuring up their faces. But they wouldn't come. She had lost them.

It wasn't that life in the woods was without danger or stress, not remotely. Food was exceedingly scarce, so everyone was always hungry, and until the troop happened to come upon a stream, they all stank to high heaven. And they couldn't stay anywhere for long, so there was no settling into any kind of routine — other than sleeping the days away and scrounging for food where they could. That, and living in a permanent state of paranoia; they had to be ready to run at any moment, day or night. Twice, they'd fled from armed peasants hunting for Jews with pitchforks and spades. Once they had to run for their lives under artillery fire shot indiscriminately from outside the forest.

But Sophie was no longer forced to witness cruelty and depravity and death on a daily basis. Nor was she continually confronted with how little she'd managed to help anyone but Giddy.

She'd come to a conclusion: one person, even a person with an extraordinary advantage, was too insignificant to make a difference in a world overrun by evil. Now, more than ever, Giddy was her priority, and it was going to stay that way.

Every night, when darkness fell, the troop risked their lives by venturing out of their refuge. They stole food, weapons and tools, and perpetrated acts of sabotage. They slashed tires and wrecked the engines of Nazi vehicles. They burned down the farms of peasants who were Nazi sympathizers or anti-partisan. They'd even blown up a small but important bridge.

Luckily, Sophie didn't have to worry about Giddy during these missions because the troop wouldn't allow him to join them, despite his relentless campaign of pleading, wheedling, and pestering. Giddy insisted he could help because he was a fast runner, had a stellar sense of direction, could make use of his small hands in situations that required them, and he wasn't scared of anything.

The partisans, who were all amused by Giddy's passionate pleas, might have been persuaded had the troop's sole female member, Gitla Feiner, not reproached them.

"How dare you even consider endangering the life of this innocent child," she scolded her fellow partisans. "A shanda! You idiots should be ashamed of yourselves!" Gitla was a sinewy woman in her late thirties who used to be a nurse in the City. She kept her hair shaved close to her skull for hygiene's sake, but otherwise had soft features that gave her a girlish look, when she wasn't unleashing scorn on someone, anyway. She sprayed insults like machine gunfire, Yiddish machine gunfire.

"I'm twelve years old! " Giddy cried.

"If you are twelve years old, you little pisher," Gitla told him, "I'm Sleeping Beauty."

"That's quite the coincidence," said Shmuly Shechter, the troop's ace thief and chief agitator. He not only didn't fear Gitla's temper, he enjoyed it. "I'm a prince!" he declared. "Shall I wake you up?"

Gitla, whose hard shell rarely cracked, flushed every time Shmuly pretended to flirt with her, even though he was a decade and a half younger than she was and possessed a badly scarred face — courtesy of the thugs who'd left him alive inadvertently after dragging his entire family out of their home on The Night of Broken Glass and beating his parents and three brothers to death. Gitla responded every time he got fresh with a flurry of curses. "If you came near me, you good-for-nothing momzer, I wouldn't bother getting up alive."

"But I really am twelve!" Giddy cried, ignoring or oblivious to the adult banter. "I'm just small!"

Benjy Grossman, a compact, jowly man in his forties who'd had his bakery in the City set on fire by neighboring gentile merchants, said to Giddy, "As the Jews always say, 'If you sit at home, you won't wear out your boots!'" Benjy was always saying 'as the Jews always say.' It seemed he could produce the perfect Jewish proverb any time he wanted.

"But my boots are already worn out!" Giddy protested.

"It's okay, because you're not at home," said Juda Eisen, the troop's slow-thinking but good-hearted muscleman. He was in his fifties, well over six-feet tall and, despite the deprivations of life in the woods, a powerful man. His face was flat and his jaw was square, but there was something about the gentle giant that made him less intimidating than he might otherwise be, at least to his friends. In the City he'd been a janitor in a synagogue before it was desecrated and the rabbi was murdered. He always tried to explain Benjy's sayings to Giddy, and always explained them incorrectly. No one in the troop had much luck hunting, but if anyone got their hands on a pheasant or a quail or a hare, it was Juda.

Max, Shmuly, Gitla, and Juda had been randomly tasked with sabotaging a munitions factory by partisan leadership in the City. The four strangers inserted wrenches into every machine inside and switched them on, successfully crippling the entire operation. Deemed to be a good team, they were shortly thereafter dispatched to the woods.

"I'll protect the boychick on our missions," said Juda.

Gitla turned her sizzling eyes on him. "And then who will protect you from me?" she asked.

"Yes, ma'am," said Juda, who was afraid of Gitla.

And so Giddy had to remain in the refuge when the troop went out at night. Though not alone, for someone always stayed behind with him. As far as Sophie could tell, no one ever minded, and not because it was safer or easier work — it was that they'd all fallen in love with him. No matter how filthy, foul-smelling, miserable, or indignant Giddy might be at times, he was still the goofy, jug-eared kid who made people smile whether he wanted to or not.

Sophie had reason to hope Giddy would soon be saved altogether. The troop generally took advantage of whatever sabotage opportunities arose, but at times they were given specific assignments delivered by a man called Itzy Perlman, who'd appear out of the blue. Itzy was one of many runners who delivered orders from partisan leadership in the City to groups like theirs in the woods all over Germany. There were thousands of partisans in the forests of Eastern Europe, some with hundreds of members. This news filled Sophie with hope. How Itzy found their little group baffled her, but when they heard his owl-hooting signal, they knew he was close.

A few days after the commandant was executed, Itzy had found the troop. He'd given them a few sticks of dynamite and the location of the bridge they later destroyed. He'd been taken by Giddy's story — and by Giddy himself, of course. So when Gitla rather forcefully suggested that he help "the poor pisher," Itzy said he had contacts in the City who forged papers to help get people out of Germany, especially children, and promised to make inquiries the next time he was there. Gitla made him swear to God, and he did, most likely to be spared her wrath. Then he left, taking the commandant's uniform with him.

Every day since then, Sophie hoped for Itzy's return. Whatever plan he set in motion, she would make sure it worked. Giddy would finally leave this wretched existence behind. And then...

Well, Sophie wasn't ready to think about that yet.

But Giddy wasn't taking his confinement well. Every night he objected furiously to being left behind. Max, who was a clever, levelheaded man in his forties with heaps of curly hair on his head — he'd been a university professor — had a solution. He told Giddy he could only take part in partisan missions if he was an official partisan, and that he could only become an official partisan after he was officially trained. A system was thus devised whereby whomever remained behind with Giddy gave him lessons in their particular expertise. And each had the power to decide when Giddy had learned all they had to teach.

Shmuly took Giddy out into the pitch-black woods to teach him tricks of the thieving trade, including ways to sneak around silently and how to stand perfectly still for great lengths of time. The thugs who'd murdered Shmuly's family had stolen his house, so he'd been forced to learn such things to survive on the streets. Max taught Giddy about the history of anti-Semitism, a topic about which it seemed he could talk forever. Gitla, using embarrassingly explicit terms, was teaching Giddy about the human body, but also medicine and how to treat injuries. Benjy, silly as it seemed in the current circumstances, was teaching Giddy how to bake. Last but not least, when Juda stayed behind, he taught Giddy how to fight with bare hands and how to use unconventional things as weapons, like dirt, belts, and the hardest spot on one's forehead.

Giddy seemed to like the tutors who came to the commandant's house well enough, but he loved these new teachers. He threw his whole being into his role as partisan-in-training. But it was all a ploy. Sophie had heard Max telling Shmuly and Gitla that they'd teach him forever if that's how long it took for Itzy to get him out of there.

"It's not going to be easy," Shmuly had responded, "because that little shit is a sponge. I'm already making up half of what I teach him."

"Thank goodness you're a natural born schmeggege," Gitla remarked.

"If you are not careful," Shmuly replied, "I will steal a kiss." He produced a wink, eliciting a scowl from Gitla, along with an invitation to do something foul to himself.

Sophie made no effort to learn anything Giddy was taught, even when his lessons were delivered just a few feet away. Instead, she lay there looking up through the trees, trying to find her parents.

One morning, just before dawn, the troop returned from a mission in particularly good spirits. As usual, the first order of business was debriefing Giddy on what they'd accomplished — in painstaking detail. They informed him that, using wooden poles fashioned from small trees as levers, they'd successfully caused a landslide that blocked a supply route not far from their refuge. Furthermore, they'd come across a kindhearted farmer on their way back, who'd given them a handful of turnips — although they were almost too hard to chew and too bitter to swallow.

Benjy told everyone that, as the Jews always say, one who eats slowly lives long. Gitla told him, as the Jews always say, he should shove a turnip up his ass. And when Shmuly told Gitla that was no kind of talk for a princess, she told him that, as the Jews always say, he should eat the turnip Benjy shoved up his ass because he was a tuches lecker. Juda told Giddy not to eat a tuches turnip because it would make him sick. Giddy said, 'tuches turnip,' and broke into a fit of hysterics so loud the others had to calm him down lest he get them all killed. Sophie hadn't heard the sound of his laughter since the day she carried him around the rabbi's library on her shoulders. It made her so happy, she cried.

In the end, everyone ate their turnip. And after the meal, it was time again to sleep for the day.

A week later, in the middle of the night, Sophie was lying wide awake in another refuge when the troop came back from a mission. She could tell something was wrong. They typically returned in one of three distinct moods: disappointment at having achieved nothing worthwhile, excitement at having done something great, and/or relief at having survived a close call. Sophie couldn't see anyone's face in the dark, but all the same, the air hung heavy. Gitla, who had remained in the refuge with Giddy that night, seemed to sense it too; she immediately asked what was wrong.

"The damnedest thing," Max said. "The absolute damnedest thing."

"Tell us," Giddy said, as everyone assumed their sleeping spots.

When Max found his blanket, he shared the story: "We were walking along an isolated road and saw some lights in what looked like an overgrown cemetery. We heard shouting and insults of the sort we all know well, so we went for a closer look. It was a cemetery, a Jewish one. There was a work crew there with sledgehammers, crushing headstones and loading the rubble into a truck."

"Why would they do that?" Giddy asked.

"The stone," said Max, "they will use it to make roads."

"But using Jews to destroy a Jewish cemetery," Shmuly added, "that part is just for fun."

"Leeches should drink them dry," said Gitla.

"It wasn't right," said Juda.

"What happened?" Giddy asked.

"There were only two guards with them," Max told him. Then, in a matter-of-fact way that made Sophie feel sick to her stomach, he said, "so we grabbed extra hammers from the back of their truck and split their heads open."

"Oh," said Giddy.

"That's the good part of the story," Shmuly said.

"How do you think the prisoners reacted?" Max asked Giddy. "There were six of them."

"They were very happy?" Giddy guessed.

"They were very unhappy," Max replied.

"Unhappy?"

"Very."

"But... why?"

"Not only were they very unhappy," Max said, "they were very angry. At us. For causing them trouble. We told them we were partisans. We invited them to join us. Or to go find other groups in the woods. Or to just go wherever the hell they wanted."

"But they wouldn't," Giddy said.

"Indeed, they wouldn't."

"What did they do?"

"You won't believe what they did. Or tried to do."

"Tell me."

"They wanted to get back in the truck and return to their camp," said Gitla, sounding like she'd been there.

"They wanted to get back in the truck and return to their camp," said Max.

"But, of course, you couldn't allow that," said Gitla. "Please tell me you didn't kill them."

"We didn't kill them," Max said. "Anyway, they got to the guards' guns before we did, so it wasn't an option. They didn't want to shoot us, so we killed the truck. They killed themselves."

"With the guns?" Giddy asked.

"Not with the guns. The prisoners said they would finish their work, then walk back to the camp, ten miles away. So we left them breaking tombstones."

"They'll tell on you when they get back," Giddy said. "But no one will believe them. And they'll be punished."

Silence met the end of the story. But then Giddy finally said, "But... why?"

"Giddy," Max said. "Let this be a lesson to you. If you take away a man's livelihood, then brand him with a mark of shame, then steal his possessions and remove him from his home and family — if you then replace his name with a number and make him live like an animal... slowly but surely, you will have created an animal. The entire process is planned and predictable."

"As the Jews always say," said Benjy, "against stupidity, God is helpless."

"Which means," said Juda to Giddy, "that God helps stupid people, but less than smart ones."

"Thanks, Juda," said Giddy.

"Animals are stupid, boychick," said Max. "Never let them turn you into an animal."

"How can I help it?" Giddy asked.

"Stay human."

"How do I do that?"

"By learning lessons like this."

Sophie wished she could share the other ways to lose one's humanity. She wondered if she'd ever get hers back.

Another week went by, and Sophie was once again lying on her back, trying to picture her parents' faces from yet another new refuge as the sun went down. This particular somewhere took a full day of walking to reach. She'd been making no attempt to understand where they went or why. Everything looked the same anyway: trees, leaves, and an increasing number of needles on the ground each day. The troop had returned in a good mood an hour earlier, having found an abandoned storehouse that had some dried meat left in it, enough to last for several days — and heavier blankets, which everyone was thrilled to have as the nights were growing colder.

But at the sound of five sharp whistle blows from Juda, whose turn it was at the lookout point, everyone sat up, instantly ready for fight or flight. After a pause, there was a long whistle, which meant that the troop wasn't under attack, but should be ready for anything. Everyone had their weapon in hand. Shmuly and Gitla had spears made from branches. Benjy had a shotgun. Max had his pistol. Neither had bullets in them, because they'd all been used up killing the commandant and his dogs. Sophie guessed Max was regretting not having taken the guns from the prisoners in the cemetery.

Another signal came that sounded like the hoot of an owl.

Everyone relaxed, then filled with excitement.

Moments later, there was the sound of crackling leaves, and then two shadows stepped into the refuge, Juda... and Itzy Perlman.

Hugs were exchanged, then, eager to hear news of the war, the troop gathered around Itzy. He was a bearded man in his thirties, and when the starlight revealed him well-enough, one could see that he was light-haired and fair-skinned. He looked haggard but hardened against the elements, wearing what looked like mixed and matched parts of different military uniforms.

"Hitler is planning to launch a major offensive on the Western front," Itzy said. "He wants to take the port of Antwerp and split the Allied lines. The plan is to surround the Allied armies and force a surrender or peace treaty that signals their defeat."

As everyone took this in, Sophie could feel the distress among them ratchet up.

"What is our mission?" Max asked, revealing, in words anyway, neither doubt nor pessimism.

"Powerlines," said Itzy. "The partisans have declared all-out war on the German communication infrastructure. There are plans to attack communication centers and power stations around the country. We need everyone in the woods to travel the countryside, cutting every single powerline possible before the snows come. It's likely you have only a few weeks before you'll have to hunker down."

Solemn nods met these words. The troop was ready to do their part.

"I'm helping," said Giddy, attempting to lower his still boyish voice.

Instead of addressing the remark, Itzy answered the question everyone was about to ask. "I spoke to my contact," he said.

"And he will help with papers?" Gitla asked, sounding hopeful in a very un-Gitla-like way.

Sophie felt her heart leap into her throat.

"Unfortunately," said Itzy. "His help is no longer free."

"A bribe?" Shmuly asked. "Of course, a bribe."

"A payment will be required," Itzy confirmed.

"How much?" Max asked.

"Ten thousand Reichsmarks."

"Goniff," Gitla said, then spit on the ground. "He should crap blood and pus."

"As the Jews always say," said Benjy, "bribes blind the clear-sighted and upset the pleas of the just."

"That means blind people get upset if you try to bribe them," Juda explained to Giddy. "And that it's clear one should just say please."

"Thanks, Juda," said Giddy.

"I must go," Itzy told the troop. "I will appeal to him again when

I return to the City. May God protect you all."

And with that, Itzy Perlman faded back into the forest.

The next day, Sophie left Giddy with Gitla in the refuge and went along on her first mission, although she had her own goal in mind. Giddy was outraged to be, once again, kept behind. He declared that he had the right, moreover the duty, to earn any possible papers that got him out of Germany, and that he would refuse to accept any such papers if he hadn't earned them himself. But not one of the partisans would say he'd learned enough from them yet. They promised he was coming along, though. He was left seething, albeit adorably.

After an hour's walk, the troop descended on an isolated farmhouse. They'd headed out before dark this time, hoping to find some more peasants willing to spare them food and clothing, some tools, and maybe a few bullets too, if they were lucky.

The troop found a farmer and his wife raking leaves in front of their dilapidated home. Sophie thought it was a waste of time to ask for help from people who looked like they had nothing to give, but Max, as if sensing that everyone was thinking the same thing, said, "Sometimes the poorest people are the most generous. Let's see what happens."

When the older, sickly-looking couple saw the partisans coming down the dirt path to their property, they didn't seem alarmed. In fact, the farmer waved and nodded, so the troop picked up their pace. Of course, Max had his pistol sticking out of his trousers, and Shmuly had the shotgun in his hand, pointed at the ground. The couple couldn't know they were both unloaded.

"We're sorry to bother you," Max said once they reached the house. "But can we trouble you for some food? Winter is coming, so we could use some warmer clothes as well. And we would be eternally grateful for a two-man saw." He sounded very agreeable.

The farmer, who was wearing coveralls that hung loosely on his skinny frame, nodded toward his even skinnier wife, who was wearing a heavy apron and a kerchief over her hair. "We can't spare much," he said, "but Olga will see to some food and clothing."

Olga, saying nothing, walked back toward the house. Sophie saw the roof was sagging in the middle, surely leaking.

"I do have a saw in the shed over here," the farmer added, "but it might take some digging to find it. Follow me. We do not approve of what they're doing to you people."

"Thank you," said Max, visibly relaxing. "We appreciate your generosity."

Sophie was relieved that there wasn't going to be violence and felt reassured to find good people still existed in the world. Although, that was going to complicate her mission.

The partisans followed the farmer into a long, narrow shed overflowing with tools. It was getting dark, so everyone sorted through the clutter urgently. Sophie stayed outside, looking around the property, all of which showed signs of falling on hard times. The barn was in the worst condition; it looked ready to collapse. Sophie noticed a small field ran alongside it, so she decided to see if there was anything growing there. Upon getting closer, she saw that whatever crop had once grown there had since been burned.

Feeling apprehensive, Sophie turned to see that the farmer's wife had come out onto the wilting front porch of the house holding a very large basket overflowing with clothes. "Uwe!" she shouted, coming down the steps.

Then she did something peculiar. Rather than walking directly to the shed, she came down the steps and made a looping arc to the left, stopping in a specific spot on the leafy ground. Uwe came out of the shed, followed by Max, Shmuley, Benjy, and Juda, who was holding a two man saw almost as tall as he was.

"Here you are," said Olga, setting the basket at her feet. She smiled, but to Sophie's eye, it required great effort.

Excited, the troop walked toward her, but Uwe remained still.

"Stop!" Sophie cried, sprinting to cut them off, but she'd wandered too far away to reach them in time. When the four partisans got a few feet from the basket, the ground beneath their feet gave way and they fell into the earth.

When Sophie reached the pit, she saw it was deep, far too deep to climb out of. Max, Shmuley, Benjy, and Juda, all stunned, were trying to recover from the fall. They seemed to have landed on... a body? There was definitely another body down there, a dead one.

Uwe was kicking leaves on the ground next to the pit, uncovering a large metal plate. He lifted it at one end and dragged it toward the pit. He was going to cover them. He was going to inter the partisans.

"Filthy fucking Jews," Olga shouted as her husband struggled with the plate. She spat down into the pit.

She was leaning over to do it again when Sophie pushed her in.

"A ladder please," said Max, holding his empty pistol to Olga's head.

Uwe did not protest. He walked to the shed, went inside, then came out with a ladder, which he lowered into the pit. Shmuly put the barrel of the empty shotgun into the small of Olga's back and held it there while Max ascended the ladder. Once he was up and out, he aimed his pistol at Uwe while the other partisans climbed out after him, leaving Olga down below.

"That dead man down there," Benjy said. "When did he fall in?"

"Three days ago," Uwe told him. "Now let my wife up and take what you came for."

Max, Shmuly, and Benjy exchanged glances.

"You were going to leave us down there until we starved to death," Shmuly said.

"It's better than you deserve."

"Right," said Max. "Down you go. You can use the ladder or Juda here can toss you in."

"As the Jews always say," said Benjy as Uwe climbed down to his wife, "Woe to the wicked man, for he shall fare ill. As his hands have dealt, so shall it be done to him."

While Olga spewed insults about Jews, Juda lifted the metal plate and slid it over the pit.

The four partisans walked to the house, then in through the still open door, immediately covering their noses and mouths. The smell was an assault on their senses.

When they saw what was inside, all four vomited at their feet.

Sophie ran out of the house to throw up where it wouldn't be seen. But then she made herself go back in.

There were four dead people — they had to be partisans — lying on the living room floor, shoulder to shoulder, two young men and two slightly older women. All four were naked and at varying stages of decomposition. Even worse, their bodies had long bands of skin peeled off their arms, torsos, and legs.

The troop stood there for a long time, trying to understand what new form of barbarity they had come upon. Eventually, they turned their attention to the wood burning stove, on top of which sat a frying pan, containing what appeared to be curled remnants of cooked skin.

No one spoke for a long minute. Sophie refused to look any longer. She stood, nose pinched, eyes closed, trying to will herself out of this world entirely.

"Shmuly and Juda," Sophie heard Max finally say, "take these bodies outside and bury them in that pit."

"Those two down there will eat them," Shmuly said.

"Found this," said Benjy. Sophie opened her eyes and saw that he'd picked up a shotgun that had been leaning against the wall by the door. After breaking it open to look inside, he said, "Two rounds."

Max nodded.

Juda and Shmuly carried the first body outside into the dark, then came back for the others. Meanwhile, Max and Benjy began ransacking the house. They gathered up trousers and shirts and found coats and blankets. They were all tattered and patched but would more than do.

That reminded Sophie why she'd come along in the first place. She came for money. She was determined to find, if not on this mission then another, ten thousand Reichsmarks. She was going to drop them at Itzy's feet the next time he showed up.

Sophie attacked drawers and shelves and closets but found nothing.

Two gunshots sounded outside.

She kept looking.

"There's no food here!" Benjy complained from the kitchen.

Sophie, in the bedroom, found one crumpled Reichsmark under the mattress: her reward for subjecting herself to yet another atrocity she could scarcely endure.

But this money was probably stolen from Jews who'd been — Sophie couldn't even finish the thought. She tore the bill to shreds and decided her mission days were done.

No one said a word on the long walk back to the refuge. The troop never spoke while moving through the forest, but tonight, as they traveled among the indifferent Beaches and Oaks and Spruces and Pines, the silence felt like yet another burden to bear.

In the following days, no one mentioned — perhaps they hadn't even registered it — how lucky they'd been that Olga fell into the pit.

It was just before dark when Giddy declared that he was going along on the night's mission to cut power lines, and no one could stop him unless they tied him to a tree. A tree which he would then cut down with his teeth, which would show how he could also cut power lines down. It had been two weeks since the farm; the troop was in a refuge many miles away from it.

No one knew how to respond. Sophie had a feeling that Max was debating whether to tell Giddy about the cannibals, a detail he'd chosen to leave out when retelling the adventure. Everyone was amused by Giddy's threats, but they did their best to hide it.

Finally, Max said, "But boychick, you have not yet been initiated."

"Then initiate me!" Giddy cried. "I've learned everything you've all taught me. I even know how to bake schnecken!"

"Oh, I want some!" said Juda. "Please make me some!"

"I don't have an oven," Giddy informed him, but kindly. "Or the ingredients with me. Otherwise, I'd make you a million. Sorry, Juda."

"It's okay. I don't think I could eat a million, though."

"Oy vey iz mir," sighed Gitla, restraining herself. She never insulted Juda, although sometimes it was clearly difficult for her to resist.

"You don't know everything," Shmuly said to Giddy. "There is one last skill you must master."

"What is it?" Giddy asked.

Shmuly removed six lockpicks from the little leather bag he always carried, then he laid them across his blanket, alongside a dozen locks he'd liberated from Uwe's shed. Some locks were as large as an adult's open hand, others small enough to hide in a fist.

"What do you see?" Shmuly asked, regarding Giddy with his dark eyes. Giddy didn't answer at first. He just stood there, staring at the picks and locks, trying, Sophie could tell, to figure out the answer Shmuly was looking for. The other partisans looked on skeptically, but with interest.

"Let's go slow," Shmuly said. "What are these?" he asked, pointing to the locks.

"Locks," said Giddy.

"Not locks, boychick," said Shmuly. "These are problems. And what are these?" he asked, pointing to the picks.

"Solutions?" Giddy said.

"A fine guess," said Shmuly. "Very logical. But no. They are simply tools. Here's the thing, boychick — if the problem is a lock without a key, the solution is not a tool."

"It's not?" said Giddy.

"It's not."

"Oy," said Gitla, "listen to Rabbi Schecter over here."

"I don't think Shmuly is a rabbi," said Juda.

"You can say that again," Gitla told him.

"I don't think Shmuly is a rabbi," said Juda.

"Oy vey iz mir."

"Boychick," said Shmuly, undaunted. "Solutions don't come from tools. They come from people. And so, for a master thief, these picks are not tools. They are, or must become, part of your person. They must become highly sensitive extensions of your body. They are fingers. They are ears. Am I making sense to you?"

Giddy nodded eagerly. He had clearly forgotten about his plan to join the mission that night. Max looked impressed.

"And the locks?" said Giddy. "Are they part of me too?"

"No," said Shmuly. "They are part of someone else. They are complications, like the heart of a woman. Not so easy to unlock, yes, Gitla? I should know."

"A schlump like you couldn't unlock a woman's heart if she handed you the key," Gitla said.

"Sadly," Shmuly said, giving in this time, "she is right. A woman's heart is not a good comparison, as some problems are beyond a man like me. But these locks, boychick, I can coax them open. And so can you."

Although it wasn't Shmuly's turn to stay back with Giddy, he did, and in the dark that night he worked with his pupil, teaching him how to insert the picks in order to plumb the inner workings of a lock. He wouldn't demonstrate, though. This was the type of skill one could only learn by doing.

Giddy worked at the locks all night. Sophie stayed with him, curious to see if he'd lose interest. He didn't. In fact, he worked on them all the next day, well into the following night. Shmuly skipped five missions in a row, coaching, encouraging, and praising Giddy's indefatigable efforts.

On the fifth night, while Giddy was again fiddling in the dark, there came the distinct sound of a mechanism snapping open.

Giddy gasped.

"Boychick," said Shmuly from his blanket. "Was that what I think it was?"

"It was what you think it was," Giddy replied.

Then came the sound of Shmuly scrambling up from his blanket and rushing over the needles and leaves to Giddy, then scooping him up into his arms. "Mazel Tov, you thieving little pisher!" he whispered, spinning Giddy round. "You are not a problem! You are a solution!"

While Shmuly and Giddy celebrated, Sophie realized that her refusal to go on the missions was self-defeating. What did it matter where the money came from? What dead Jew wouldn't rather have their stolen money save a child than to have it remain in the hands of their murderers? How else was she going to get Giddy away from the evils of this world without exposing herself to them?

When the others returned at dawn, Shmuly informed them of Giddy's triumph. Mazel Tovs and backslaps rained down on the boychick, who tried and failed to control his goofy grin. After that, Giddy said he was good to practice on his own, so Shmuly rejoined the missions.

Sophie did too.

Having downed all the power lines in the area, the troop was obliged to move on. The first night they ventured out from a new refuge some days' hike away, they watched as patrols cruised the backroads at night, the ones with power lines running along them. The Nazis had apparently caught on to the partisans' antics, immediately combing through the surrounding woods when they encountered cut lines. As a result, the troop rarely stopped anywhere for more than one night. They'd sleep the days away, saw down poles at night, then move on in the dark.

While Giddy plied his locks, Sophie joined every mission in the hope of finding money. But the troop chose their targets wisely, so they never came across anything but the occasional military vehicle. Sophie grew increasingly worried about Itzy returning before she had his bribe, but she didn't know what she could do about it.

In late October, the troop decided they'd done all they could. The nights were freezing and snow was on the way. They hadn't seen nor heard anything from Itzy, so they slogged into an especially secluded part of the forest, found a hillside that wasn't frozen yet, and began to build a dugout.

The process took days. With only one shovel, which they'd taken from the cannibals, they dug for hours and hours. The dirt had to be carried away on blankets and spread in the forest inconspicuously. Everyone helped, including Giddy, although he had to be pried away from his picks and locks.

Shmuly stole some planks off the side of a decrepit nearby barn, some of which the troop used as support beams. They used others to create a roof that sat at just about ground level; one had to crawl in order to enter. The last plank was used for a shelf along the back wall to store their gear. When everyone agreed that the shelter was structurally sound, they set to work camouflaging it with leaves and branches and bush.

The same day the dugout was finished, the snow came. It fell endlessly for days. It fell in clumps and sheets. It fell like the end of the world.

Sophie Siegel — January, 1945

The winter months were brutal.

After the first blizzard, it snowed intermittently over the next eight weeks. But what was worse than any precipitation was the awful, bone-crushing, spirit-breaking cold. The troop spent virtually all their time in the dugout, huddled together; that is everyone but Sophie, who made the gear shelf her home. She spent most of her time with her back to the troop, making sure no one saw the condensation of her breath and plumbing her mind for her parents' faces. Every day, she grew more certain that they were lost to her forever. Whenever she looked at Giddy, he was working his locks, which he seemed to be doing, in part, to keep his fingers warm.

The troop managed to keep a fire going, without which they would have frozen to death. But they had to keep it small, both out of fear of giving themselves away and of asphyxiating. Everyone was constantly encrusted with soot. No one left the dugout unless to relieve themselves, to collect more fuel to burn, to steal or beg for food in the nearest villages, or simply because they were otherwise going to lose their mind.

No one knew what the date was because they were living through an endless white nightmare. The only light was the flickering flames of the sad fire. Everyone just lay in silence: filthy, cramped, hungry, and frigid. Even Giddy was too cold to practice lockpicking, his fingers finally too stiff. To no one in particular, he said, "What makes you so brave?"

No one answered for a second, but then Max said, "I'm brave because I want to show the Nazis that we Jews are stronger than they are."

Gitla said, "You are a yutz, is why you are brave."

"That does help," Max told her.

"What about you, Shmuly?" Giddy asked.

Shmuly said, "I'm brave because every time I get the chance to rob those evil bastards, they know Jews are smarter than they are. Sorry for the language, boychick."

"You are a schmo, is why you are brave," said Gitla.

"Thank you, princess," said Shmuly.

"As the Jews always say," said Benjy, "When you have no choice, mobilize the spirit of courage."

"Schnook," said Gitla.

"What about you?" Giddy asked her.

After a few, long moments, she said, "I am brave so I can survive to have children one day. That is the best revenge. I will have one hundred children. Maybe two."

"Then what are we waiting for?" Shmuly asked.

"Freedom," was Gitla's unexpectedly straight answer. "Not to mention finding out if I will ever bleed again after this prolonged malnourishment."

The men ignored this comment, but it shook Sophie. Her mother had told her about how women bleed, how it was part of being a woman. But it hadn't happened to her. Was it because she was malnourished too? Or was it because she was not a real person anymore?

"I don't think you can have a hundred children, Gitla," said Juda. "Even if you started right now."

"You'll be the death of me, Juda," Gitla said.

"I'd never hurt you," Juda told her.

"Oy vey iz mir."

"And what about you, Juda?" Giddy asked.

With no hesitation, Juda replied, "I am brave so my friends can get what they want."

"And the pisher?" Gitla said. "What about you? Will you tell us, why are you brave?"

"I am brave for my best friend."

Sophie, who was lying on the shelf under five layers of trousers and tops, rolled over to look at Giddy's grimy face in the light of the fire.

"Will you tell us about him?" Gitla asked.

"The Nazis," Giddy said. "They killed her parents when I was little. But she got away. She got away because she is an angel and she is smarter and braver and stronger than all those evil bastards put together."

At his use of profanity, the whole troop burst out laughing, but Giddy wasn't finished. "She watches over me," he said, "when she isn't stomping on the enemies of the Jewish people."

The laughter was gone, replaced by a respectful silence.

Then Max said, "May God bless your angel."

No one said anything else about the matter, and soon enough everyone fell asleep, everyone but Sophie, who spent another night of her life sobbing.

Several weeks later, the troop awakened to the sound of distant gunfire. No one moved; they only listened, frozen with closed eyes and held breath. No one prayed, at least not out loud. Sophie, meanwhile, screamed, *Go away!* until her voice went hoarse.

It worked; the gunshots stopped.

Some days later, Shmuly burned his shin. He was sitting too close to the fire and didn't notice his trouser leg was in flames until Gitla dove at him and put it out.

He was badly burned.

Gitla ordered everyone to get a handful of snow and to melt it in their hands. She pulled away what trouser material she could around the burn and had them all drip cold water onto it.

"This must be covered," Gitla said, when she was satisfied the wound had been cooled. "Find me the cleanest garment in here," she ordered. The best they came up with was a sooty blouse. Gitla said a soiled shmata was good enough for a klutz like Shmuly and dressed his wound.

Shmuly bore Gitla's ministrations stoically, boasting that the burn didn't even hurt.

"It will, you nudnik," Gitla told him.

"As the Jews always say," Benjy said, "Awful things come to those who wait."

And it did.

In the middle of the night, Shmuly began to cry out. Gitla tried to comfort him, but to no avail. His moaning grew so loud and constant that the others had no choice but to tie a shirt over his mouth, as if he were a hostage. But even muffled, Shmuly's moans were so woeful that everyone had to take turns the rest of the night standing in the cold for short stretches to get away from them.

The next morning, a raw, red streak was visible along Shmuly's shin. Though the pain was more bearable, he still couldn't do much of anything but groan. Gitla had everyone continuously cleanse the burn with melted snow, but Sophie suspected she was doing so mostly to keep them busy.

The following day, Shmuly's leg was worse. It was swollen,

hot to the touch, and pus oozed from the wound, soaking through the makeshift blouse bandage. The smell was noxious and over-whelming — it was the smell of hell.

Gitla confirmed that the wound was infected and declared that Shmuly was in danger of going into sepsis. She warned that he may soon become delirious, although it might be hard to tell what with all the fakakta things he was always saying.

Gitla's joke seemed to make Shmuly laugh despite his increasing pain.

Over night, Shmuly's entire leg had ballooned and turned nauseating colors. The wound was ceaselessly suppurating. Gitla told Shmuly that the only way he might survive was if they used the two-man saw to amputate his leg. But even if they managed to sterilize the saw, she warned, they'd be hard pressed to control the resulting bleeding. And that it was fairly likely that the stump would get infected even if they did.

Shmuly, his eyes fluttering, did not respond for a minute; it seemed he was too far gone to process how critical his condition had become. But then he opened his eyes and said very clearly, "No, princess. I won't put you all through that. I'll see you in Heaven."

"Jews don't really believe in Heaven," said Benjy.

"As if God would let a schmendrick like you in, even if we did," said Gitla.

"He won't have to," Shmuly said, smiling weakly. "I will pick the lock. Am I right, pisher?"

"You're right," said Giddy. "As the Jews always say, easy as schnecken."

"Nice one, boychick," said Benjy.

"Schnecken?" said Juda.

"No schnecken," said Giddy. "Sorry."

"Although," Shmuly said, again quite lucidly. "This might be a good time, boychick, to confess my sins."

"Jews don't confess their sins," said Benjy.

"Boychick," Shmuly said anyway, "I have no idea how to pick locks. I break them. I carry the picks around to make me feel like a thief."

"You lousy ligner," Gitla said. "God love you."

A few hours later, Shmuly began to rave. His words were mostly unintelligible, with the exception of names, perhaps family members Sophie guessed — Mama and Papa were among them. Time was running out as everyone gathered around and took one of Shmuly's hands or placed one of their own upon his chest.

"As the Jews always say," Benjy said softly, "the only truly dead are those who are forgotten."

Shmuly stopped his raving and said, stoically, "The only truly dead are those who are forgotten." And then again: "The only truly dead are those who are forgotten."

The partisans sitting around Shmuly began to say it with him. "The only truly dead are those who are forgotten. The only truly dead are those who are forgotten. The only truly dead are those who are forgotten."

Shmuly went quiet; the partisans did too.

But then Giddy blurted, "Shmuly Schechter, we will remember you!"

"The only truly dead are those who are forgotten," Shmuly said. His eyes were closed now.

"Shmuly Schechter, we will remember you," the partisans told him. Everyone was weeping.

"The only truly dead are those who are forgotten," Shmuly whispered.

"Shmuly Schechter, we will remember you!"

Shmuly spoke no more. He was gone.

Without warning, Giddy began to beat on Shmuly's chest. "You're a putz!" he cried. "You're a schmuck! You're a shnorrer!"

Gitla pulled Giddy off Shmuly and told the others to get the corpse out of the dugout immediately. Max, Benjy, and Juda wrestled Shmuly's body out into the cold, leaving Gitla to console Giddy, who continued to scream his pain at the now dead man. Sophie couldn't bear to watch, so she went outside.

The men dug a pit in the snow a few hundred yards away from the dugout, working slowly and somberly. Finally, Gitla and Giddy joined them to pay their last respects. Giddy was calm now, but his face reminded Sophie of his mother's on the day the commandant took him away from her.

"May your memory be for a blessing," they each said when it was their turn to shovel some snow into Shmuly's frozen grave.

As the days dragged on, Sophie began to worry about the troop. They weren't an overly communicative bunch to begin with, but now it was rare that anyone spoke at all. Maybe they were losing hope of making it through the winter. It particularly frightened So-phie that Gitla wasn't insulting anyone. She just lay on her back, staring at the roof of the dugout. The only sign of life among them was Giddy working at his locks. The clicking of his picks probing their metallic innards never ceased, except when the locks popped open, which was happening with increasing regularity, although no one, not even Giddy, made mention of it.

They were out of food again, so Max ventured out in a snow-storm to avoid leaving tracks. He returned with a treasure more valuable than gold: a massive sack of beans, enough to feed them for weeks. Even so, everyone guarded their rations closely — ev-eryone but Giddy, who was too busy picking locks. Sophie had no choice but to take some from his allotment, though he never seemed to notice. All the weight he'd gained at the commandant's house was long gone. No one bothered to ask Max how he'd gotten the beans, and Max didn't bother to explain.

An indeterminate number of days later, the troop woke up to find Gitla gone. At first, everyone assumed that she was out reliev-ing herself, but as time passed and she did not return, the troop grew concerned. Max climbed out of the dugout and everyone fol-lowed suit. The partisans looked like a crew of rag-clad skeletons, filthy beyond recognition. Outside, the cold cut like a knife.

The forest was blanketed in a pristine layer of pure white snow with no footprints to follow.

"Let's walk," said Max.

The troop circled the dugout, expanding their circuit as they went further out into the woods.

"We shouldn't be out here in the daylight leaving footprints," Max said while continuing to leave them.

With still no sign of Gitla, and it now being too cold and too unwise to continue, the troop headed back toward the dugout. Just as Benjy was about to say something about what the Jews always say, they saw their shovel sticking out of the snow where they'd buried Shmuly.

"Oh, no," said Max. He grabbed the shovel and began excavat-ing the grave. "Oh, God," he said after quickly uncovering Shmuly's frozen corpse.

Gitla lay next to it.

Juda put his hands over Giddy's eyes, but Giddy pushed them off.

"Why?" was all Giddy had to say.

"As the Jews always say," said Benjy, "one is only certain of death."

"As the Jews always say," said Juda, "she wanted to tell Shmuly off forever and have a million kids with him in Heaven."

Everyone turned to look at him.

"That's exactly right," said Max. He walked to Juda and hugged him. "That's exactly goddamn right."

"Thank you," said Juda, hugging Max back.

Max began to rebury the bodies with the freshly fallen snow.

"May your memory be for a blessing," everyone said when he was done.

Days later — maybe it was weeks — what was left of the troop woke up to find the world warm. They crawled out of the dugout, ecstatic to see the snow gone at last. The sun was shining. Everyone stood, breathing in the first smells of spring. Max cried at the realization that they'd survived the winter. They found Gitla's and Shmuly's bodies and gave them a proper burial. It was time to discuss what was next.

"First," said Giddy, "food. But not beans. I'm sick of smelling everyone's farts."

This made everyone smile.

"Agreed," said Max.

"Then what?" Benjy asked. "More power lines?"

"What if the war is over?" Giddy asked. "What if Germany won?"

"No food," Juda explained.

"What if Hitler surrendered?" asked Benjy.

"Lots of food," Juda explained.

"We need Itzy," said Max.

"Today's my initiation," Giddy said. "I'm ready to show you what I can do."

"Shit," everyone said.

Giddy laid out the locks on the forest floor. "Count," he said to Max.

Max started counting. "One. Two. Three..."

Giddy worked with great calm and even greater confidence. He chose one of Shmuly's picks, inserted it into a lock, fiddled a bit, and it opened. He used two picks at the same time on the next one, which also popped right open. He moved from lock to lock, and not one of them put up the slightest resistance. When the last one surrendered, Giddy looked up at Max.

"Thirty," said Max. "God in Heaven, thirty."

"That's," Benjy said, "that's —"

"Our pisher," said Juda.

Max promised on his mother's grave that, once they got a handle on how the war was faring, they'd "perform the final ritual," making Giddy an official partisan. Sophie could tell by the glance Max and Benjy exchanged that there was no such ritual. Giddy agreed to this final stipulation.

"Meanwhile," Max said, "tonight we'll dismantle the dugout, find a stream to bathe in, then get moving. Food will be our top priority. But our first concern is the people we've robbed these past few months. They just might decide it's worth coming into the woods to murder us now. It would be wise to create some distance."

By nightfall, all traces of the dugout were gone, everyone had washed away the hardened grime coating their bodies, and they were on the move. Hungry and weak, all were exhausted after only a few hours' trek. Luckily, they came across a bag of nuts inside the hollow of a tree; they were left there, no doubt, by peasants who really did want to help the Jews. Unless they were poisoned, of course. The partisans took their chances and ate them, and upon finding themselves still alive, they found the strength to walk for another few hours.

Max decided to stop; they'd spied a village in a valley beyond the edge of the woods, a promising source of provisions. No one had the energy for any kind of raid, though, and there was a full moon and starry sky. It was not a good night for sneaking about, so Max decided they'd camp there for a day and give it a go tomorrow night. The troop found a spot hidden by especially thick undergrowth, laid out their blankets, and all fell into a deep sleep.

Sophie slept close to Giddy again now that they were out of the dugout, and so he accidently kicked her when he got up in the dark. She figured he was going to pee, but then heard the clinking of Shmuly's bag of lock picks in his pocket. They were his now —

but before going to sleep, he had laid the bag next to his blanket. Why was he carrying them around in the middle of the night?

Speaking of peeing, Sophie heard the unmistakable sound of Juda relieving himself nearby. Somehow, no matter how little he ate or drank, he urinated like a horse. Upon this seeming cue, Giddy walked stealthily away from the camp in the other direction.

Worried, Sophie followed.

Giddy walked for forty-five minutes until he reached the edge of the forest. There, he stopped to look down at the village at the base of the hills. It had maybe a dozen structures. Past the main cluster of buildings, a mile or so it seemed, was a large farmhouse surrounded by orchards. It was even larger and more impressive than the commandant's house. Giddy stepped back into the safety of the woods and walked along the tree line in its direction.

"Don't do this," Sophie said, walking behind Giddy. She didn't know exactly what he was doing, but she was pretty sure she knew why he was doing it. He'd finally realized that he was never going to be initiated as an "official partisan," and he wanted to prove himself worthy in a way that no one could ignore. He was going to initiate himself. "Don't do this," Sophie repeated. "Don't do this. Don't do this." She thought maybe he might somehow hear her and mistake her voice for his inner one. But he kept walking.

Sophie stood behind Giddy as he squatted at the farmhouse door, working its lock with a pick. She scanned the dark windows of the house for any sign of movement, then turned around to check the orchards. She heard nothing but the fearful pounding of her heart.

But then there was a click, and then the sound of Giddy spitting on hinges. At last, the door silently swung open. Although there was a light on in the house, no one seemed to be around. Giddy quietly crept inside, leaving the door slightly ajar.

Like the commandant's, this house had a grand entrance and grand staircase. It also had a carpeted sitting room with plush couches and a piano. But the living room here was otherwise very different. There were folding tables set up all over, stacked with military equipment, mostly big metal boxes with dials and handles and antennae. As Giddy investigated, he came upon a small device that looked like a miniature metal briefcase with a cloth handle on top. A pair of large headphones sat next to it. Some kind of radio?

When Giddy picked it up, Sophie finally understood what he

was up to. Max had promised to initiate him as soon as the partisans got news of the war. So Giddy had gone out to get it for them. He did still believe they'd make him one of them after all. Of course he did.

Suddenly a voice boomed from upstairs: "I SMELL A JEW!"

Giddy bolted for the door with the radio.

Sophie bolted to the banister running along the stairs.

Legs in black pajamas and feet in fur-lined slippers appeared at the top of the steps. They belonged to a red-faced older man with a bulbous nose. He had a shotgun, which he was trying to aim while rushing down the stairs. When he came close enough, Sophie stuck a hand through the spindles and tripped him.

The man went head over heels, firing his gun into the ceiling as he tumbled down the steps. He crashed to the floor at the bottom, landing face down with a thud and a grunt. After that, he didn't move.

Sophie ran to the door and saw Giddy sprinting away into the night.

Sophie was about to run after Giddy, but hesitated. She turned back inside to see if anyone else would come down. No one did. Judging by the set up in the sitting room, she suspected there was no Mrs. in the house.

Sophie tentatively approached the man on the floor. Crouching down, she put her hand under his nose and determined that he was unconscious but breathing. A nasty knot was raised on his forehead.

She didn't know how much time she had before he came to, so Sophie quickly found what looked like an office and began rifling through the desk drawers.

In the bottom drawer, she found a wad of 100 Reichsmark notes in a silver clip emblazoned with a swastika. She tossed the clip aside and counted the notes with greedy fingers.

There were fifteen thousand Reichsmarks — more than she needed! Sophie couldn't believe her luck.

Back in the foyer, Sophie saw the man on the floor trying to lift his head, so she stuffed the money into her pocket and rushed out of the house. Under the shining moon and stars, her heart pounding now with hope — genuine hope that this would all soon be over — she ran all the way back to the refuge.

When she crawled back toward Giddy's blanket in the dark and found he wasn't there, Sophie's insides turned to gelatin. He'd left that house well before she did, and he ran far better than she did. Something must have happened to him on the way back. Maybe he was ambushed. Or maybe he'd fallen and fractured his ankle. Or worse. Why hadn't she come across him on her way back? She'd retraced her path perfectly.

Sophie could do nothing but sit and wait, trying her best not to fall apart, all the way through to sunrise.

At first light, she was nearly out of her mind. She stood up on rubbery legs, her vision swimming. Why didn't she go out and search for Giddy?

"Well, look what we have here," Juda called from somewhere. "Boychick!"

Max and Benjy opened their eyes and sat up. There was no slow coming-to when you were a partisan.

Into the refuge came Juda and a grinning Giddy, carrying his radio.

"You guys won't believe what the little pisher pulled off," Juda said, smiling ear-to-ear.

"Good god," said Benjy. "Is that a radio?"

"What did you do, Gideon?" Max asked. He took the radio from Giddy and began inspecting it. He opened a skinny vertical door on one of its sides, revealing gauges and inputs.

"You said you would do the ritual after we got news of the war," Giddy said. "So I went down to the village, and I found a fancy house, and I picked the lock and snuck in and took the radio, so now we can get news of the war. It was easy as pie."

"You stole pie?" Juda asked.

"Sorry, Juda," Giddy said. "No pie. But I can make you some one day. Benjy taught me how."

"That was foolish," said Max. "You could have been caught. You could be dead, and we would never have known what happened to you."

"But I'm not," said Giddy.

"But he's not," said Juda.

"Stop defending him!" Max cried.

"Yes, sir," said Juda, but he winked at Giddy, who tried not to smile.

"We're all impressed," said Benjy. "As the Jews always say, all new beginnings require that you unlock a new door."

"Stop already with what the Jews always say!" Max complained. "It's enough to make me convert so I can hear what the Christians always say."

"We know what the Christians always say," was Benjy's reply.

Max turned to Giddy and said, "Can I assume you covered your tracks?"

"I came back a different way," Giddy told him.

Sophie's face went burning hot. The relief she felt washing over her ceased as a molten pit opened in her stomach.

"Sometimes I walked backwards," Giddy promised, "and I doubled back a bunch. I brushed my tracks in places, and I walked in a stream for a long time too. It took me forever."

Max looked at his fellow partisans and sighed. He'd finally been bested. He put out his hand and said, "Welcome to the troop, Private Goldfarb. Well done. Very well done."

"But, what about the ritual?" Giddy asked.

Max looked around, then went over and picked up a long stick.

"On your knee, soldier," he said.

Giddy got down on a knee.

Max raised the stick over his head and waved it around, like it was part sword and part magic wand. "Gideon Goldfarb," he said, "little pisher, big thief. I hereby —"

A gunshot shattered the quiet of the morning.

A red flower bloomed on Max's chest.

And then he fell on the needles next to Giddy, dead.

Giddy's mouth dropped open and stayed that way.

There was another shot and Benjy cried out. He clutched his chest, fell to his knees, then tipped over, dead.

Giddy had not moved. He'd remained on his knee. Sophie knocked him to the forest floor, then draped herself over him.

Juda stepped in front of them.

There was a man there, a man in black pajamas with an ugly knot on his head. He had a shotgun pointed at Juda's heart. Juda put his hands up.

"Thought I smelled dirty Jews," the man said. And Sophie knew she would never forgive herself.

"We aren't dirty anymore," Juda said. "We had baths."

The man came closer to Juda, looking at him, curiously. "What are you, stupid?" he asked.

"Jews are smart," said Juda. "I won't let you hurt the boychick."

"You are stupid."

Sophie felt Giddy's body trembling beneath her own.

"As the Jews always say," Juda started to say, but the man shot him.

Juda doubled over, but he did not fall.

"You won't hurt the boychick," he said, straightening up.

"Jesus," said the man. "You may be stupid, but you're tough for a Jew."

Sophie heard him reloading his gun.

"Jews are tough," said Juda.

The gun fired again.

"Jews are brave."

"Jesus," said the man.

The gun fired again.

Juda's body fell over Sophie and Giddy's, at last dead.

"You must be the filthy little urchin who stole my radio," the man said. "And... looky here." Sophie heard footsteps approach. The man bent down and picked something up. She looked. "My money too," he said.

It must have fallen out of her pocket.

"I know you aren't dead, you little cockroach," the man said. "It's time to go to your cockroach heaven."

Sophie, realizing that lying there was suicide, leapt up when she heard the shotgun cocked. She grabbed Giddy by the wrists and began dragging him away on his back.

"What in holy hell is this?" said the man.

Sophie, hyperventilating, dragged Giddy across the clearing, but the man chased after them. Just before she got in amongst the trees, he brought a foot down on Giddy's chest, pinning him to the ground. When the man leaned down and pressed the barrel of his rifle into Giddy's forehead, Sophie grabbed the gun.

They struggled, but Sophie was no match. The man hurled her across the clearing with the gun, then again, put the end of it back to Giddy's forehead.

Sophie screamed.

Another shot rang out.

And the man in the black pajamas with a knot on his head fell down dead.

Itzy Perlman came into the clearing. "Are you okay, Gideon?" he asked, kneeling to inspect him where he lay. "Are you okay?"

Giddy's eyes were open, but vacant. He was in shock.

"You are alive, son," Itzy said, getting him to his feet. "You are okay. You are a survivor." He went around the clearing to look at Max and Benjy and Juda. He whispered a prayer for each.

When he finished, he came back to Giddy, who hadn't moved from where he stood. "I'm afraid we cannot take the time to bury our brothers-in-arms," he said. "It is time for the partisans to leave the woods. Follow me."

Itzy walked directly out of the clearing, but Giddy remained where he stood. Sophie, once again, took him by the hand and tried to lead him where he needed to go. Giddy resisted, forcefully. Before Sophie tried again, he said, "Max Kleinman, Benjy Grossman, and especially Juda Eisen, may your memories be for a blessing."

It was only then, with his hand in Sophie's, that he began to walk.

PART FIVE
THE CITY

Sophie Siegel — March, 1945

"You'll be glad to hear this," Itzy said. "The last time I saw you, we feared the German offensive on the Western front would destroy the Allied armies. It was initially effective; we thought the end had come. But… it didn't. The Nazis were eventually pushed back, and more importantly, they sustained heavy losses. Now the Allies are pressing in on all fronts. The Russians are a hundred miles from the City. The Americans are crossing the Rhine. The war is going badly for Germany. Very, very badly."

Itzy glanced over at Giddy to see his reaction, but there was none. Nothing he'd said over the last few hours had gotten any kind of response, and Itzy was looking discouraged. He returned his focus to the road; they were heading toward the City in a military flatbed truck he'd recently stolen.

The drive had begun in mournful silence, but about an hour into it, Itzy asked how Giddy was feeling. Giddy ignored the question. A while later, Itzy prodded further, asking point blank, what exactly happened. Sophie was quite prepared to hurl herself out onto the road if Giddy blamed himself for the massacre of his friends, but he ignored that question too. After another prolonged silence, Itzy, persisting, asked how the troop had managed to survive the winter. Once again: nothing. Finally, he gave up. That is, until he, in a last ditch effort, shared the news about the war.

Giddy continued to stare out the window, watching the countryside roll by. They passed forests and fields and farms, some of which were nothing but debris-strewn craters left by the bombs that destroyed them. Along certain stretches, the road had been blasted away too. None of it phased him. It appeared to Sophie that Giddy was, at last, broken.

But Sophie also felt a strange surge of hope. If the Nazis were losing, even if it wasn't for long, surely they'd have bigger things to worry about than chasing Jews around. Surely, they'd be too distracted to notice a single jug-eared Jewish boy sailing off for America.

And that's when that molten pit opened once again in Sophie's stomach. She'd completely forgotten that the man in the black pajamas found his stolen money on the forest floor. And that she could have easily taken it back when he was dead.

The means to save Giddy had been within reach, and she let it slip away. She'd failed him.

"The problem," Itzy continued, "is that because he's losing the war, Hitler is becoming increasingly desperate, which makes him increasingly unpredictable and dangerous. There are rumors that the Nazis have nearly readied a functioning nuclear bomb — and the means to deliver it as far as America."

Sophie fell back into her seat. The worst possible news, of course. Even if she hadn't lost the money, what would be the point of going to America — or anywhere else — if Hitler could destroy it? What would be the point of anything she'd done? Had she kept Giddy alive, made him suffer through one hell after another, for absolutely nothing?

Sophie screamed.

She screamed and screamed, thrashing her now waist-length hair wildly about her head, raging like a child who discovers the world is indifferent to her wishes.

When Sophie finally stopped to breathe, she heard Itzy say, "Of course the resistance is working to make sure this doesn't happen."

"How?" asked Giddy, and Sophie felt another surge of hope. Giddy had responded in a voice that seemed nearly dead, but he had responded.

"By killing Hitler," Itzy said.

Giddy, suddenly revived, turned to Itzy and said, "I want to help."

"I'm sure you do," said Itzy. "Let me ask you something. Have you killed anyone before?"

"They wouldn't let me," Giddy said.

"Listen, Gideon," Itzy said. "How old are you now?"

"A million."

Itzy nodded. "Yes, I am too," he said. "But how —?"

"Twelve."

"You don't look —"

"I'm twelve."

"Okay," Itzy conceded. "You are a million and you are twelve. Either way, you know that there are people who must be killed if we are to survive."

"Lots of people," said Giddy, and a chill ran down Sophie's spine. She was fifteen. A million and fifteen.

"Indeed," Itzy agreed. "But what I'm trying to tell you is that, once you kill a person, you are not the person you were before."

"I'm already not the person I was before."

"I understand, Giddy. But there are many people you can become. All I'm saying is choose wisely."

"I want to help."

"You don't have some kind of death wish, do you?" Itzy asked. "I've seen it many times. People who have lost everything just want to go out and take some Nazis with them. It's understandable, and they can be very useful. But they don't last long."

"I can't die," Giddy said.

"You *can't* die?"

"I have to live. I have to find my friend, Sophie Siegel."

"Good," said Itzy. "That's very good. People who have something to live for are the ones most likely to survive. Tell me about this Sophie Siegel."

"She is the best person in the world. She was born here, in the City."

"Perhaps I may be able to make inquiries about her whereabouts."

Giddy nodded but said nothing. Promises, Sophie could tell, no longer moved him.

"Your friends will curse me from the grave if I get you killed," Itzy said. "I feel obligated to get you travel documents. There's a lot of chaos just now, which helps us operate more freely, but it also means there are hordes of people attempting to flee. The price for counterfeit papers is astronomical. We'd need perhaps fifty thousand to get you safely out of Germany right now. The Reichsmark grows increasingly worthless every day. Jewelry is the preferred currency right now."

"I won't go without Sophie."

"Listen," said Itzy. "Let me see what I can find out about her. Sophie Siegel. Let's make a deal: if I find out she somehow left the country, will you agree to go wherever she went?"

"Yes," said Giddy.

"Very well. Let's get you somewhere safe in the City for now. I have some people who will take you in. They'll get you cleaned up and fed. You are traumatized. You are grieving. You are starving. You need to eat, and you need to rest."

Giddy didn't respond. He turned back to the window, back to watching the world pass by.

After an hour of silence, Itzy turned to Giddy again and said, "I noticed that Gitla and Shmuly were not present."

"Dead."

Itzy nodded and said no more.

Eventually, as the countryside fell behind them, they entered the City. Sophie could not believe her eyes.

The City was unrecognizable, obliterated. As far as the eye could see were broken buildings and rubble-strewn streets. It looked to Sophie as if the giant she and Giddy had once read about had stomped everything to smithereens.

It certainly seemed as if the Nazis were losing, and that was good. That was beyond good. But Sophie wept for her first home anyway because, much like her and Giddy, it was in ruins.

Itzy drove through the shattered streets, where demolished buildings lay next to others still standing, untouched. The City appeared to be deserted, a ghost town, sad and surreal. They eventually passed into the outskirts, which appeared more intact, then entered a neighborhood of what looked to Sophie like small castles. The homes, if that's what they were, were stately stone structures, all square, with columns standing beside arched doors. Rows of square windows wrapped around them three stories high. Every one was festooned with Nazi flags and banners.

Itzy parked in the driveway of one of the homes, the one with the biggest flags. Then he turned to Giddy, who was looking up at the house with his big eyes, and said, "The elderly couple who live here are powerful figures in the Nazi party, in its propaganda program. But they are allies. Since the start of the war, they have been operating as a nexus for spies. They are no longer rich, despite appearances, but they are well prepared. They filled their basement with preserved foods and other supplies *years* ago in anticipation of... all this. They are very busy — they never sleep — so do not disturb them unless it's absolutely necessary.

"How do you know they'll let me in?" Giddy asked.

"Because they are my parents."

Itzy Perlman was not Itzy Perlman. He was Erich Alberg. He used the Jewish-sounding name so as not to raise suspicions among the partisans, and also because his parents arranged to have his real name added to the passenger list of a plane that had crashed in Bavaria in 1941. As far as the government was concerned, he was dead.

Before taking him into the house, Erich told Giddy that it might be a while before they saw each other again, but he promised to bring back information about his friend, Sophie Siegel. "On my honor, man-to-man," he said.

The Albergs were small, white-haired, and withered, but they were dressed in the finest of apparel — Frau Alberg wore an ornate burgundy dress and matching heels but had no jewelry on. Herr Alberg wore a dark suit, but under his cuff Sophie got a glimpse of a gold watch. But of course she would never steal from the very people protecting Giddy. The Albergs were full of vim and vigor and offered no hint of protest when Erich asked them to take Giddy in.

After hurried hugs and even quicker goodbyes, the door closed behind Erich. After a moment, Herr Alberg said, "Welcome, Gideon. Please do not take offense that we will have little or no time to interact with you. We are working every minute to hasten the downfall of Adolf Hitler."

"I understand," said Giddy. "Thank you for letting me stay in your home."

"You are very welcome here," said Frau Alberg. "Please, let me show you the way down to the basement. There you can bathe, find new clothes, eat, and rest. It will be best that you remain below, as we have frequent visitors here, some trustworthy and some decidedly not."

"You can trust me," said Giddy.

Frau Alberg offered a thin-lipped smile at this and said, "I have no doubt about that." She put out a hand for him, but Giddy did not take it. Frau Alberg did not seem offended in the least. Sophie followed as she led Giddy into an opulent sitting room, approached a bookshelf, and pulled on a particular volume. There was a click, and the entire shelf opened like a door.

It was, in fact, a door, behind which was a set of steps.

"I think you'll find everything you'll need," Frau Alberg said.

Giddy nodded and headed down the stairs.

Sophie passed through the secret door behind him.

The basement was not like any Sophie had ever seen. It was a maze of rooms with polished stone floors and dark wood paneling along the walls. Most of the rooms were pantries full of cans and jars of food. Without even looking at what he was grabbing, Giddy immediately took four cans off the shelves in one of them and carried them to a small kitchen. After finding a can opener, he proceeded to gorge on all of the contents without bothering to chew: plums, peaches, beans, and peas.

Then he threw up in the sink.

So he tried again, this time actually eating his food rather than inhaling it.

Satisfied, Giddy wandered through the rooms until he found one filled with shelves of clothes neatly folded in stacks. Giddy picked out new underwear, black shorts, and a black shirt, then carried them into a washroom, where he found a bathtub. Giddy gasped when, after turning on the spigot and letting the water run, he saw actual steam. When he began getting undressed, Sophie went to find some food for herself. She snacked a bit from various jars with lids she could unscrew: nuts, raisins, and pears. After watching Giddy, she thought it wise to pace herself.

Sophie heard the water draining from Giddy's bath. He'd been in there for a very long time. When he finally reappeared, Sophie couldn't believe it: he looked transformed, almost reborn. Despite everything, after all he'd gone through, there, standing before her, was the bright-eyed little jug-eared boy who'd lived in the house attached to hers — or a starved version of him, anyway. Giddy looked ready to pass out, so it was no surprise that he proceeded to wander through the basement until he found a bedroom and then went straight to sleep.

Sophie was about to leave him to his rest when Giddy flopped his arm over the edge of the bed and opened his hand. Her heart stopped when he began flexing his fingers in a beckoning sort of way. She stood, frozen in fear and fascination. Did he do this every night?

Sophie went over and knelt beside the bed. She took Giddy's hand. But before she got the chance to speak, Giddy said, "Sophie Siegel, you are my light and my life, the reason I go out in the morning and come home at night." Fat tears rolled down Sophie's cheeks; she hadn't known he'd ever heard her father say that to her mother. Had she told him? Then Giddy said, "It stinks in here," and fell asleep.

Sophie, overflowing with happiness and sadness and elation and despair, went to find some new clothes and to take her own much needed hot bath. When she finished, she too found a bedroom and quickly fell asleep.

Sometime in the middle of the night, the bombs began to fall. Sophie shot up in her bed at the first explosion; it convulsed the entire house. She tossed off her sheets and was running to Giddy's room when the second one hit. The impact sent her flying down the hall. She heard cans and jars crash onto the floor from collapsing shelves.

When she made it to Giddy's room, Sophie thought he was gone — he wasn't on his bed. But at the third explosion, which thankfully sounded further away, she heard him. He was under the bed, reciting the Shema. She climbed under too and prayed with him.

Shema Yisroel...

A fourth explosion, nearby again, shook the room.

"Mama, Papa," Giddy whispered. "I will see you soon."

Sophie reached out and wrapped her arms around Giddy.

"I'm sorry, Sophie," Giddy croaked. "I'm sorry. I'm sorry. I'm sorry —"

And then a bomb hit the house.

There was one loud *BOOM!* And then the basement seemed to buckle. Debris showered down on the bed and the floor, choking Sophie and Giddy as it billowed around them. They heard cracking stone and breaking glass. It was as if the entire house was collapsing on top of them.

"I'm sorry, Giddy," Sophie croaked. "I'm sorry. I'm sorry. I'm sorry."

Then there was quiet.

Finally, Sophie climbed out from under the bed. Giddy was right behind her. The room was intact, although a long fissure now ran along the ceiling. Several surrounding rooms, including the washroom and three pantries also survived. But the rest of the basement had not. Enormous blocks of stone from the upper floors had crashed through the ceiling. Couches and desks and tables and rugs lay mangled in the debris.

There was a high-heeled foot sticking out of the rubble. Frau Alberg's foot. A few feet away, there was a hand with a gold watch.

Sophie watched as Giddy climbed up over the wreckage toward the bodies. She was afraid they were still alive and that he'd try to rescue them. But when he got close enough, he said, "Itzy's, I mean Erich's, parents, may your memories be for a blessing."

Giddy reached a hand between two nearby slabs of stone. After some struggle, he pulled out a book, which he carefully wiped off.

He spent the next hour looking for more, and all the while Sophie stared at the watch, which she dared not take. It belonged to Erich now, and when he returned, he would do with it what he thought was best. When Giddy had a dozen books, he took them to his bedroom and stacked them on the table beside his bed.

Giddy then climbed through the ruins up into the first floor of the house, which was now the only floor: an anarchy of fallen stones and crushed furniture. No walls, no ceilings, just the night sky above. A million stars were visible as Giddy looked up and down the street. Standing there right next to him, Sophie did the same.

Not a single house was standing. Not one person was outside.

Giddy made his way down to the basement again, found his bedroom, and went back to sleep.

To Sophie's increasing consternation, every evening Giddy climbed up onto the highest point of the rubble that used to be the house and sat with a jar of fruit, watching planes roar across the sky, dropping bombs. This happened for six nights in a row. Sophie sat next to him nervously, watching the distant detonations and the fountains of debris that exploded into the sky.

The bombs started falling in the daytime as well, but Giddy spent those below, reading one of the books he'd salvaged: a hefty tome about world mythology. Sophie, for her part, spent her days combing through the rubble for anything valuable. Anything that might be worth fifty thousand Reichsmarks. If Itzy — Erich Alberg — was still alive somewhere in the City, she knew he'd come to check on his parents. And on Giddy. What other hope was left? When he came, she was going to be ready.

But she found nothing.

One day during the second week of bombing, Sophie left Giddy to his reading and investigated the wrecks of other houses on the block. They were all similarly leveled and difficult to navigate, but there had to be jewelry in some of them, she was sure of it. But she found only broken furniture, soot-covered clothing, and bodies.

This is what I've become, she thought. *Sophie Siegel, scavenger.*

When she finally gave up, she took Herr Alberg's watch off his wrist.

One night it rained. And when the sun came up, Giddy climbed outside. He seemed to have a set purpose, so Sophie followed him up onto the rubble, curious. For the first time, Giddy left the pile of wreckage, picking his way down toward the back of the house. Sophie was worried that he was aiming to leave, that he'd given up waiting for Erich. Instead, he stopped at what was left of the Alberg's garden, which was now a great mud patch.

Giddy sat down and started digging with his hands.

"Giddy!" Sophie involuntarily cried. "What are you doing?" Was he looking for fresh vegetables? Had he finally lost his mind?

Sophie thought about Rabbi Hasendahl's boys and wondered what had become of them. She thought about Rabbi Hasendahl's hanged body alongside those of the Jewish Council. She hadn't thought about them in a long time.

Giddy was scooping up clumps of mud, setting them on harder and dryer ground. Once he'd gathered enough, he started packing the clumps into a ball.

When he formed a neck, Sophie confirmed her suspicions: he was making a golem. She went back to his room below and found the mythology book lying open on his bed. The story he was reading was called "The Jewish Defender Made of Mud."

Sophie considered tearing the pages out. Surely he would know that meant she was with him. She considered finding a way to write him a message imploring him not to give up. But she didn't know what that would do to him — or to her — so she went back up through the rubble to do what she did best: watch over him.

Giddy worked feverishly for the next hour. The sun was out, and it was warm, so he had to hurry before his material dried out. He was working on the second leg when a voice called his name.

"Gideon?"

Giddy and Sophie both turned to see Erich Alberg climbing down the wreckage toward them. There were cuts and abrasions on his face, but he was wearing the uniform the partisans had taken from the commandant, and it was immaculate. Giddy looked up at him with big, wet eyes.

"I came as soon as I could," Erich said. And then, "My parents?"

Giddy shook his head.

Erich nodded.

Giddy took Erich's hand and led him over and down into what was left of the Albergs' home and showed him the bodies. Erich said a prayer to himself, moving his lips silently. When he turned around, he saw his father's watch sitting on a chunk of stone. Sophie had set it there while he prayed over his parents. Why had she thought it was okay to steal it in the first place? Did she think *she* was going to trade it for Giddy's papers? Perhaps she no longer knew right from wrong. Erich took his own watch off and put his father's on in its place.

"Gideon," said Erich. "Once again, I am sorry to say there is no time to mourn our loved ones. I'm on a mission of utmost importance. A mission that could save the world. Please, clean yourself up – you're coming with me."

Giddy went to clean up — luckily, water was still running in the basement washroom. He found another set of clothes, black shorts and shirt again. Erich was waiting for him in front of the house in a new car, a gleaming silver convertible with its top down. On the blighted street, it looked almost miraculous, like it had been driven there from Heaven. Giddy got into the passenger seat and Sophie climbed into the back.

Erich consulted his father's watch, then looked at Giddy. "The Russians have just about taken the City," he said, "but that does not mean we are safe. From them. They will get their hands on Hitler within days, if they can find him. But he must be found today. Today! We have reason to believe that he will be ordering the launch of nuclear weapons tonight."

"Are we all going to die?" Giddy asked.

"No," said Erich. "*Hitler* is going to die. We know where he is, and we are going to kill him."

They drove toward the heart of the City, maneuvering around massive craters in the streets, even driving through them when necessary. Only the odd military vehicle appeared occasionally, speeding down side streets. Explosions sounded in the distance.

Erich turned to Giddy and asked him if he knew that women sometimes "sold their... company for money."

"Of course I do," said Giddy, although Sophie had a feeling he did not.

"Well," said Erich, "we are going to a house where such women work, a house visited by many prominent Nazis, right in the middle of all this madness. We've learned that quite often these girls — they are very young — are taken to a secret bunker under the

Reich Chancellery, the seat of Hitler's government. That is where we believe he has been hiding with his top generals and staff since early January. We've received intelligence that a new group of girls will be taken there tonight. Or sooner."

"Are we going to sneak in with them?"

"That, I don't think is possible," Erich said. "Instead, we are going to talk to a particular girl in this house, one who is new there, a special girl, and ask for her help."

"Is she very beautiful?" Giddy asked.

"She is extraordinarily beautiful," Erich said. "But what makes her truly special is that she's Jewish."

The streets became nearly unnavigable. There were some people now, covered in dust, wandering aimlessly, like dirty ghosts. Just about everything had been blown to bits, with the exception of the rare, seemingly untouched house or building. It was almost as if they'd been protected by some kind of force field.

They entered a neighborhood of row houses that reminded Sophie of Judenstrasse, except these were made of stone and looked very fancy. The one in the middle had been destroyed, but the rest seemed unscathed. Six expensive vehicles were parked in front of the last house.

Erich parked alongside them, turned off the car, then looked at his father's watch again. "Stay here, Giddy," he said. "I may be a little while. Lie down in the back seat and wait for me to return. If all goes well, we will be free to find a way to get you out of Germany."

"You have enough money?"

"I don't," Erich admitted. "But I have hope."

"But what about —?"

"Oh! By the way," Erich said, cutting Giddy off. "I was able to get information about your friend, Sophie Siegel."

Stunned, Sophie, leaned forward.

"Her name was on a passenger manifest," Erich said, "for a ship that went to America. Two years ago now. New York City. The Big Apple."

Without responding, Giddy climbed into the back seat. Sophie saw that tears were in his eyes as she climbed out of the car. Erich got out as well, then headed up the steps onto the house's tiny front stoop. Sophie hurried behind him, blessing another good man for his lies.

Entering the house was like stepping into another dimension. It was not a world of devastation but instead, one dripping with luxury. They'd come into a lavish lounge area, lit with the soft light cast from lamps with glass shades made of many colors. Tapestries of dark purples and blacks adorned the walls. The floors were carpeted in crimson. There were silk clad tables and couches piled high with pillows. Two uniformed Nazis were seated at separate tables, the remains of their meals left on fine china. They had finished eating and since turned their attentions to the scantily dressed women on their laps, both cackling at their apparent charms.

An older woman with long black hair and bangs down to her eyes emerged from the glamorous gloom in a pleated dress with a glossy sheen. Like the younger women, she wore no jewelry. "Welcome!" she said, approaching Erich with hand extended. "Welcome," she repeated once more as he grudgingly took and kissed it. "My name is Ursula. What can I do for you?"

"I'm here to see the new girl," Erich said.

"Ah," said Ursula, pursing her bright red lips. "You are wise to come so early, when she is still free. But can you afford her? She is truly something to behold."

Erich slid his father's watch off his wrist and held it out. "Will this do?" he asked.

"Nicely," said Ursula, taking it from his hand. "Head right on up, my good sir. Room Four."

When Erich was halfway up the stairs, Ursula warned, in a very different tone, "You do know she's a Jew, right? I don't want you telling me later that your... business was... tainted."

Erich looked at Ursula long and hard, then said, "I've been duly warned," then continued up the steps. Sophie was, again, right behind him.

Erich pushed open the door. The room wasn't large, and what there was of it was dominated by a king-sized canopy bed, hung with pink and purple patterned silks. Between the bed and one wall was a vanity, where a young woman was seated, brushing her long, lustrous black hair, which was down over her face. When she heard Erich enter, she turned gracefully around, tossing her hair to the side.

Sophie's jaw dropped.

It was Lea Malka Mankowitz.

The prettiest girl she'd ever seen had become the most beautiful woman in the world.

Lea Malka was tall, really tall, maybe six-feet, Sophie thought. But she was also lean and lithe and glowing with vitality. Her hair fell past her shoulders in long, lush waves. It was obvious that she had never been sent to the ghetto and definitely had never spent a day in a camp or the woods. She was well-fed, groomed, and looked to Sophie, in the soft light of the lamps around her room, like some magnificent creature from a more marvelous world.

"Well, hello," cooed Lea Malka in a sultry voice as she rose from her stool. She was wearing a sheer, silvery gown that showed the shape of her undergarments beneath.

Erich shut the door behind him, then said, "Listen to me closely."

"What?" said Lea Malka, thrown by a manner she had not expected.

"My name is Itzy Perlman. I'm with the partisans."

A manicured hand shot over Lea Malka's mouth. "Is the war... over?" she asked. "Are... are you here to save me?"

"The war is not over," Erich told her. "And I am here so you can save me. So you can save you. So you can save us all."

"What — what can you possibly mean?" Lea Malka asked. Looking lightheaded, she moved to sit on the edge of her bed.

"Hitler is going to authorize the launch of nuclear weapons tonight. *Then* the war will be over. We will have lost. And we will all die. Even one so lovely as you."

"Do you think —?" Lea Malka said, standing up again like she'd been sprung from a trap. Her voice was not only stable but sharp. "Do you think because I am kept looking this way that I have had it easy? I have been a prisoner in places like this — one after another after another — for *years!* I am violated by these animals *every single day!* I cannot be saved, Mr. Perlman. However I may appear on the outside, I am dead inside. I've been dead for a long time."

"Then help us end this war," Erich said. "It is time to bite the hand that fed you." There was evidently no time to spare for expressions of sympathy.

"Tell me what I can do," Lea Malka asked. The anger that had flared in her eyes was gone. She'd made a decision.

"Sometime today," Erich told her, "transport will arrive at this very house, and the most desirable girls will be loaded into it. *You* will be loaded into it."

Lea Malka nodded, waiting to hear more.

"You will be taken to an underground bunker where the high-est-ranking Nazis are hiding. You will be there to... help raise their spirits."

"What do you want me to do?"

"I want you to find Hitler, and I want you to kill him."

Lea Malka seemed to accept this as a perfectly reasonable as-signment. "And how will I kill him?" she asked.

"With this," said Erich. He took out his wallet and carefully re-moved a razor blade, then handed it to Lea Malka. She gazed at her reflection in the shining piece of metal, perhaps seeing in her own eyes what Sophie saw: resolve.

"Let this be your deliverance from captivity," said Erich. "Let this be the end of your degradation. Let this be your retribution."

Lea Malka tucked the blade into a stocking, then looked at Erich and asked, "They will kill me after I kill him, yes?"

Erich nodded.

"Good."

"Ladies! Ladies!" Ursula called from the first floor. As she made her way up the stairs, the clicking of her heels reverberated through the hall. "Ladies!" she called again, "You must stop what you are doing! You must come down at once!"

The door to the room flew open.

"Oh, thank goodness!" Ursula sighed. "You aren't... busy. Downstairs," she ordered Lea Malka, "at once."

Lea Malka looked at Erich quickly as she passed him on her way out of the room, but said nothing.

"My apologies, sir," Ursula said to Erich. "This is a situation I cannot control," she added. "I'm ever so sorry. If I can ask for your patience, I will make it up to you with two girls at no extra charge."

Sophie saw that she no longer had the watch. Erich must ask for it back! She must find it!

"That won't be necessary," Erich said, surely forgetting about Giddy in the heat of the moment. He followed Ursula into the hall, where a dozen other young women were rushing along, pulling on heels, straightening dresses, and touching up makeup.

Sophie followed everyone downstairs. The men who were there earlier had since left, and there were now two new Nazis. Neither seemed particularly prominent, but both looked hostile.

"Line up!" one of them snarled. Perhaps in his thirties, he had a patch over one eye.

The girls were all downstairs now and did his bidding.

"Lights!" Patch Man shouted. "I want more light!"

Ursula went to a wall and flipped a switch, illuminating a chandelier.

"Better," said Patch Man, who was now openly ogling the girls in their tight dresses. Not one among them wore earrings, a necklace, or even a ring. Lea Malka, Sophie saw, was at the far end of the line, next to a piano. There were twenty girls, standing shoulder to shoulder.

Patch Man approached the first girl, at the other end of the room, and looked her up and down like she was meat on a hook in a market stall. She smiled at him and curtsied. He went along the line then, inspecting. He squeezed a breast. He patted a behind. He told a curvaceous young woman to turn in a circle for him. "You," he said to her, "what is your name?"

"Berta, sir," she said.

"Step over there."

"And you and you," he said to two others as he moved along. One was tall and long-limbed — her name was Sigrid — the other was dainty, no more than five feet tall — her name was Nina.

Patch Man moved on. "And you and you," he said to two more girls, who told him their names were Astrid and Lena. "That will do."

Sophie turned panicked eyes to Erich, who had drawn back to the now open front door. There was panic in his eyes too.

"*Ahem,*" said the other Nazi, who had not spoken yet. "Sir?"

"What?" Patch Man demanded.

The other Nazi pointed his chin to the end of the line. Patch Man turned and saw Lea Malka standing by the piano. He performed an almost comical double-take and walked toward her, looking her up and down. "My god," he said. Then he turned to Nina, the short girl he'd chosen, and said, "Not you, get back in line."

Nina's eyes darkened. Her face went hard. "But —" she said.

"*Nina,*" Ursula warned.

"I said get back in line!" Patch Man shouted, and Nina reluctantly obeyed. Then, to Lea Malka, he said, "You will come." To the five selected girls, he said, "You are receiving a great honor. You will spend the night with the finest men in Germany. The finest. Do you understand?"

The girls exchanged excited glances. Lea Malka, seeing this, pasted a happy expression on her face as well.

"You will not fail to please anyone who asks for the pleasure of your company. Do you understand?"

The girls nodded enthusiastically.

"If you do well, you may be retained for a number of days. If that is the case, we will send for your material needs. At the moment, we have no time for such things. Do you understand?"

More nods.

Sophie had a feeling these girls were meant to be rewards for winning the war.

"There is a truck outside," said Patch Man. "Go get into the back."

Sophie saw little Nina, back in the original line, trying to control a blackening mood. She was looking at Lea Malka with murder in her eyes.

Where was that watch!

"Ahem," someone said again. This time it was Ursula.

"What?" Patch Man demanded again.

"Our... agreement?"

"Yes, yes," he said, impatiently. He reached inside his jacket and came out with a fat envelope bursting with notes. "Here," he said, handing it carelessly over to a very pleased Ursula, who fanned quickly through it.

Sophie homed in on that envelope; she saw nothing else. Watch or no watch, jewelry or no jewelry, that had to be more than enough money to get Giddy out of Germany.

"Now," Patch Man said to the chosen girls, "get moving." He headed for the front door and the girls followed behind in a line. Erich was already outside. Sophie could see him standing by his car, watching. Parked next to his convertible was a long and menacing military green truck with no windows.

Sophie was torn: she needed to get outside, but she couldn't leave before she got that money!

Lea Malka, last in line, was about to step out over the threshold when a voice screeched, "No filthy Jew is taking my spot!"

Lea Malka turned around, clearly startled, to see who had insulted her. It was Nina, who was now galloping toward her with an expression so venomous that Lea Malka froze in place.

Without breaking stride, Nina snatched a knife from one of the dirty plates on a table as she darted by, screaming, "Filthy Jew!"

Sophie was too stunned to react. Ursula was too stunned to react. Everyone was too stunned to react, even Lea Malka. When Nina got close enough, she pounced on Lea Malka, stabbing the knife into her heart.

Pandemonium erupted.

Lea Malka's brown eyes goggled. Her mouth was petrified, an open O. Her legs crumpled as blood leaked from her chest.

The girls screamed.

Ursula ran to Lea Malka and dropped to her knees. She knew not to pull the knife out, so she pushed her hands into Lea Malka's chest, applying pressure to stop the bleeding. They were immediately covered in blood.

Then Nina tackled her.

Patch Man charged back into the house, demanding to know what was going on. Though he needn't have asked; he took one look at the scene and shouted, "I have no time for this!" After which he exited as quickly as he had entered. The four girls waiting outside wanted to know what was causing the uproar inside the house.

"Get into the truck!" Patch Man ordered them.

Sophie saw Erich, dismayed, get into his car. Giddy sat up in the back seat. She saw the envelope of money on the carpet where Nina and Ursula continued to struggle. So much money. More than enough money.

The rest of the girls in the house continued to scream and scramble about.

Meanwhile, Lea Malka's face had gone gray. She was dead.

Sophie dove into the confusion, scooped the envelope off the bloodstained carpet, then ran outside.

Patch Man and the other Nazi were still yelling at the girls to get into the truck, but they were not cooperating; they were still concerned about what was happening inside. Patch Man fired his gun into the air and that finally silenced them. They got into the truck.

Erich started up the convertible. Giddy was in the passenger seat.

Sophie stood, a statue between the two vehicles. One, with the money she'd stolen, would take Giddy out of Germany at last. The other was her opportunity to end the war, once and for all. Giddy would be safe, wherever he went. They all would. This was an opportunity only she could take, and only *right now.*

Only Sophie Siegel. No one else in the world.

Time stood still as Patch Man made sure the girls were all sitting down

Erich put his car into gear.

The world went silent.

Sophie's hands and feet went ice cold.

Her body shivered.

She couldn't move.

Erich backed out of his parking spot.

He moved the convertible alongside the truck and tipped his cap to Patch Man, who nodded back.

Sophie ran.

Erich's car was sitting next to the still-open rear doors of the truck when she reached the passenger side window. "I love you Giddy Goldfarb!" Sophie cried and threw the envelope onto his lap.

Sophie leapt into the back of the truck just before Patch Man closed its doors.

PART SIX
THE BUNKER

Sophie Siegel — April 30, 1945

Although the girls never discovered why chaos had erupted in the house, and despite being a bit unnerved by the Nazis' harsh treatment, they all seemed to forgive and forget rather quickly. None of them speculated why Lea Malka wasn't with them; they were too busy chattering about the men they would soon meet. Would they be young and dashing? Or wrinkled and fat? They speculated incessantly; that is, when explosions weren't causing the truck to swerve violently all over the road. The girls shrieked every time this happened, but as soon as the danger passed, they'd burst into laughter.

Sophie sat at the end of one of the two benches getting bashed repeatedly against the rear doors, crying her eyes out.

The truck slowed to a stop and the girls went quiet. Astrid squealed, "Oooh, this is so exciting!"

Berta said, "I get the Führer!" and the other girls fell into hysterics.

"If Eva Braun is around," said Sigrid, "I'll distract her for you." And another round of hilarity ensued.

The truck began to move, but at a snail's pace, down a precipitous decline. Then, again, it came to a stop. The engine was turned off and the rear doors were opened by another Nazi, a young and handsome man the girls made eyes at the moment they saw him. Sophie jumped out first.

"This way please," said the Nazi, who'd gone red in the face at the girls' leering. He opened a massive metal door after spinning a lock bigger than a steering wheel. Everyone followed him into a concrete cubicle of a room with nothing in it but another door.

"This way," the Nazi said again, leading the girls through the inner door, which led to a set of concrete steps, which they descended for a very long time. So long that the girls took their heels off along the way.

"Are we going to hell?" Lena asked, which caused more giggles.

The girls were starting to complain when they reached yet another door with a wheel on it. This led to another concrete cubicle, which led to yet another. Then they passed into a long concrete passageway lined with wooden doors placed at regular intervals.

Finally, they stopped at one.

"For you," the Nazi said to Sigrid, opening the door. Inside the room was a plain wooden dresser and a single bed with a sheet but no blanket on it. Sophie saw the displeasure on Sigrid's face when she saw this. "Someone will come for you soon," the Nazi told her, easing her inside by the shoulder. He shut her in, then showed the three other girls into rooms nearby.

The last girl to be deposited, Berta, stopped the door before it closed on her. "Sir?" she said, "May I ask if Fraulein Braun is here?"

"Frau Hitler is here, yes," the soldier told her.

"Frau Hitler?"

"Yes. She arrived recently. She and the Führer were married the night before last."

Berta's heavily made-up eyes widened with what looked like genuine disappointment. Sophie realized Berta really thought she could woo Adolf Hitler tonight, while bombs fell on the City and nuclear missiles were being readied to launch. Berta nodded, then closed herself into her room.

The Nazi departed. Sophie walked behind him.

He walked through the labyrinthine corridors, then down a short set of stairs into another concrete maze. He stopped and opened a door, a washroom. Just then, a cluster of women in smart skirts and blouses came around a corner. They were all crying. "I can't believe it," one said. "I won't believe it."

Curious, Sophie followed them.

The women wove through the halls until they reached a dining area where Nazis and women in business attire were seated. The men were mute. The women were unsuccessfully trying to hold back tears. They seemed to be waiting for something. Sophie sat down in an empty chair.

A few minutes later, Hitler entered the room and Sophie's body turned to ice.

She'd last seen his face on the film in Frau Volker's class. He'd been braying and blustering, and he had terrified her as the implacable embodiment of evil.

But this Hitler, in the flesh, was something very different. He was dressed in his fine uniform jacket over black pants, but he was much diminished. His eyes did not burn into Sophie like black coals the way they had from the newsreel. He looked thinner now, and his face was flaccid. The only thing that made her sure he was himself was that awful, awful little mustache.

Warmth spread back into Sophie's limbs.

The room was utterly silent.

Hitler looked everyone over and said, "Thank you for your dedicated service. But it is over. I am ending it now."

And then he turned and left the room.

Could he mean by launching the missiles? Sophie wondered. *But why is everyone crying?*

She hurried after the Führer.

Hitler walked through his secret bunker, making the occasional turn, before entering a room. Sophie stepped in behind him. It was a study. There was a small wooden desk in one corner. On top sat a row of leather-bound books, a marble ink blotter with two inkwells and a pen, a lamp, a wooden clock, a stamp, some sheets of blue paper, and a little dog figurine. A black grandfather clock stood by the door. On the floor was a rug patterned with dark floral shapes. In the middle of it all, sat a small wooden table surrounded on three sides by a couch and two brass chairs.

Sitting on the couch was Eva Braun, Hitler's much younger girlfriend that Frau Kruger, and seemingly all of Germany, was obsessed with. She was wearing a blue dress with white trim. She looked somber, but also pleasant with her slightly chubby cheeks. Her blond hair was short and curled on the sides of her head. She was holding a small but bulging paper bag on her lap, worrying its rolled-over top with fidgeting fingers.

Hitler produced a pistol from his jacket and set it on the table. "You don't want it?" he asked, looking at the paper bag. "It's your favorite."

"I just can't," Eva said, smiling sadly. She set the bag on the table. "But thank you, anyway."

Hitler nodded. "No tears," he said. "You first, then I will follow." He reached into his jacket pocket and removed something, which he held out on his open palm. A capsule.

Eva took it from his hand. "No tears," she said. "Me first, then you will follow." She put the capsule into her mouth and bit down on it.

Sophie smelled something familiar: bitter almonds.

Hitler took Eva's hand and looked into her eyes, which shortly began to roll back into her head. Her face contorted grotesquely as her body seized.

She slumped over on the couch.

Hitler let go of Eva's hand, then reached into his pocket again. He took out another capsule, which he set next to his gun. Then he turned to look at his dead wife. He looked at her for a very long time.

Sophie knew now that there were no nuclear bombs. The war was over.

Hitler was going to kill himself.

And she had let Giddy go. For money that was possibly useless.

But Hitler did not pick up the pill or the gun. Instead, he just sat there, continuing to look at his dead wife. After a long minute, he stood up and began pacing the little room. Sophie watched him warily.

"Darling, Eva," he said, "thank you. You know I don't trust these infernal pills. I don't trust Himmler, that turncoat. I don't trust anyone! So they worked on Blondi? Our dear sweet Blondi! My God, the sacrifices we must make for the Fatherland! But a dog is not a person! What does it do to a person? I trust no one. No one but you. Thank you, darling. Thank you for showing me that it will work when needed. You are safe now. Safe from the Russian dogs who would defile you. Safe from a world still infested with Jewish rats, despite our best efforts to exterminate them! But I'm well aware that if the dogs catch me, they might turn me over to the rats. Oh, how the Jews would love to get their filthy hands on Adolf Hitler. Oh, how'd they'd love to humiliate me. But it will not happen, Eva! You can trust me. It. Will. Not. Happen! No Jew will ever lay a finger on the Führer!"

The war was not over.

Hitler stopped pacing and turned to face his dead wife. "I'm sorry, dear, that I cannot take you with me. Gears are turning, as it were. Plans are arranged. I'm going to Argentina, and it will require beginning a new life. I will be in hiding, perhaps for years, and I am told hiding one is far easier than two. I'm sorry, darling. But I must go alone. One must die alone. And one must be reborn alone. In due time, the Thousand-Year Reich will rise from the ashes of this temporary setback. Fear not for your body, darling, for it will be incinerated in the garden outside the Chancellery." Then he added, "So, until we meet again, Frau Hitler. I bid you good-bye."

He turned and stepped toward the door.

Sophie shoved him back so hard that he fell over the table.

"What — what is this?" Hitler cried, struggling awkwardly to his feet, his pasty face now throbbing red. His eyes scanned the room, flustered and frantic. He stepped toward the door again, and Sophie shoved him again, and again he fell over the table and onto the floor. Then Sophie grabbed his lapels, pulled him to his feet, and pushed him down onto the couch next to his dead wife.

"What is happening?!" Hitler demanded. Sweat was dripping down his face. His hair was a mess; he looked almost as crazed as he had in that newsreel. Only this time he wasn't fulminating about wanting her and everyone like her dead. "I demand to know this very instant what is happening!" Hitler cried. "Who is here? Who is here? Who are you?"

Sophie lurched to the desk, snatched up the pen, and jammed it into the inkwell. Then she snatched up a sheet of blue paper, turned, and slapped it down on the table. Hitler looked incredulous.

"Who is here?" he asked, but with no ferocity left in his voice. He was afraid. "Who are you?" he begged.

Sophie drew a triangle on the paper, then a line cutting across it just below the top point. On that line she wrote: SOPHIE SIEGEL, TOP STUDENT.

Then Sophie used the top line she'd drawn to create a second, downward-facing triangle.

A Jewish star.

The instant Hitler's mouth dropped open in disbelief, Sophie seized the capsule from the table and shoved it inside. Then she gripped him by the top of the head and under his chin and forced his jaws closed. When his body began to seize, she picked up his gun and shot him in the temple.

Sophie pocketed the blue piece of paper, and then, on impulse, looked into the paper bag, which was still sitting where Eva had set it. Inside was a large piece of cream-filled, two-layered cake, drenched in honey.

Sophie stuffed the whole thing into her mouth.

PART SEVEN
THE BIG APPLE

Sophie Siegel — September, 1960

One cool and blustery fall evening, Sophie was sitting on a bench in Central Park, warm in her yellow cardigan and matching shawl. On the bench next to her, a man tossed breadcrumbs to a roiling mass of hungry pigeons at his feet. The leaves were turning, and the colors — rusts and apricots, crimsons and golds — enveloped her. It was beautiful. Sophie tried to notice beautiful things every single day. A steady stream of park-goers flowed past the bench in both directions. It was another day of people watching.

Sophie became a people watcher almost immediately after killing Adolf Hitler. While she was savoring the honey cake, a pair of Nazis entered the room, apparently expecting to escort Hitler elsewhere, only to be flabbergasted at the sight of their dead Führer. They argued at length about whether they'd misunderstood that his suicide was meant to be a ruse — if it wasn't, why was there a body of a man who looked like Hitler already prepared? Eventually, they summoned more Nazis, who evidently weren't in on the escape plan at all, leading to even more confusion. Eventually, both Hitler's and Eva Braun's bodies were carried out of the bunker to be burned in the garden. Sophie followed them out.

Russian soldiers were running wild on the streets as she walked away from the palatial Reich Chancellery. They were destroying everything and attacking anyone they could get their hands on, especially women. Sophie had no hope that things would be better with the Russians replacing the Nazis, but she didn't care at the moment. As she strode through the bedlam on the streets, she wasn't looking for goodness or peace. She was looking for Giddy Goldfarb.

It took three days of wandering to find the remains of the Albergs' house. Sophie lived in the basement for a week, hoping Erich would return and provide some sort of clue about Giddy. But he never came. Given that he was technically considered dead, Sophie knew she'd likely never see him again.

So Sophie started watching people. She watched people for an entire year in various Displaced Persons camps throughout Germany. She sat in the intake areas of former military barracks, converted summer camps, and hotels — all day every day. Very much the same way she now sat in a park halfway around the world. She often read through the lists of names of those processed through these centers, but never saw the name Gideon Goldfarb.

At the end of her rope, Sophie had no choice but to believe that Erich had used the money that had fallen into Giddy's lap to take him to America. It was then she decided to follow. But first, there were some things she needed to do.

Sophie scoured the City until she found her grandparents' neighborhood. Both couples had lived on the same street. All the homes there were abandoned; the windows had been broken and everything inside was gone. Some houses had been burned down completely.

Next, Sophie found her way back to Ortschaft. On Judenstrasse, she discovered all the homes were now occupied by gentiles, although she didn't recognize any of them. She went into her old house and found a family of four inside. A tall man, his short wife, and their beautiful twin daughters were sitting at Papa's blue table. The girls were coloring. Sophie stood there, staring at the table, feeling suddenly adrift, as if time were out of joint, feeling as if she'd been given one last glimpse into a vanished world — her vanished world.

When the dizziness passed, Sophie went into her bedroom and saw the hole in the wall with the little door still there. She went and opened it. The one on the other side was closed, but she was shocked to see an inscription on the back of hers. How had she not noticed it before? It said, "I love you, Angel, always and forever."

It was then that Sophie could see her Papa's face. His bushy brows. His prominent cheekbones. His nose. His strong chin.

And then she could see her Mama's face. Her soft lips. Her wide smile.

Sophie had her parents back.

The wardrobe and vanity were also still there. Now curious, she pulled each away from the wall enough to see. On the back of both, it said, "I love you, Angel, always and forever."

On her way out, Sophie lay down under the blue table and saw, above the girls' pink knees, the same inscription one last time: "I love you, Angel, always and forever."

It was time to go to America.

Sophie stowed away on a ship and journeyed to New York. At the end of the voyage, she stood on the deck with thousands of other travelers as they sailed into the harbor. Everyone wept when they saw the Statue of Liberty.

Sophie spent her first month in New York trying to establish a life for herself. She eventually settled on living in department stores, which had everything she needed, from washrooms to beds, to changes of clothing. She rotated which one she stayed in every few weeks, just in case, but Macy's was her favorite.

She spent the next year teaching herself English in the New York Public Library.

Once she had a basic command of the language, Sophie began her investigation. But there was no record of a Gideon Goldfarb in the New York telephone directory. Pretending to be a store manager, she wrote letters on Macy's stationery to Ellis Island and got a response saying they had no record of any such person. They cautioned her, though, that many people did not use their real names when they arrived in America, for all sorts of reasons. Sophie wrote to everyone and anyone who might be able to help her: Jewish settlement agencies, state governments — but nothing. No Gideon Goldfarb.

In a fever of hope and desperation, Sophie wrote letter after letter asking about every name she could remember. She wrote after her grandparents. She wrote after Levi Bernstein, Hirsh Finkel, and Joseph Dressler. She wrote after Ruben Linker and Israel Bokser and Moshe Epstein and Simon Horn and Arno Dallman and Gisela Hessler. She wrote after Hani Ferber and Solomon Posner and Jashel Lipmann and Mattias Kohler and Jakob Neuman. The replies were universally the same: nothing, nothing, and more nothing. She even remembered the boy Giddy had given that carrot to in the ghetto. His name was Leo. But she never knew his last name. That made her cry.

In the midst of her frenzied efforts, on impulse, Sophie checked for Bruna Muller in the phone directory. And there she was, right there. She lived in Manhattan. Sophie called the number from a phone in Macy's and when Bruna answered, she knew it was the same girl who'd accused her of cheating from her work all those years ago. Sophie vividly recalled looking into Bruna's blue eyes while she held her mother's hand, watching the Jews of Ortschaft get driven away in carts from Judenstrasse. That was the moment when their eyes seemed to lock.

After a long silence, Bruna, in a tremulous voice that was nothing like the haughty tone Sophie remembered, said, "If I was responsible for causing you pain at some time in my former life, I am so sorry. I have caused many innocent people much suffering. I want you to know that here, in America, I am a good person. I run a home for war orphans."

Sophie hung up.

Sophie had no choice but to accept that everyone from the life she wished to remember was lost to her, everyone but Giddy. So she dedicated her American life to people watching. One of them, one day, would be him. She'd watched people from her bench in the park every single day since. It had been thirteen years; she was turning thirty in a few months.

"No one sees us," said the man tossing breadcrumbs to feed the pigeons

Startled, Sophie turned to him.

"Walk right by us, they do. Every day. Like we don't even exist. Like we're invisible or something."

"Are — are you talking to me?" Sophie asked.

"Nothin' personal, I suppose. Can't see what they can't see. Doesn't mean it doesn't hurt. Did I fight the Nazis so they could walk right by me every day like I don't even exist?"

"Sir? Are you talking to me?"

"It is what it is, I guess."

He was talking to the pigeons.

"I see you, sir."

Sophie turned to see a young man in his early twenties, she guessed. He was tall and muscular, like an athlete; but he also wore a tweed jacket with patches on the elbows, like a college professor. On top of everything else, he wore a Dodgers cap, which made him look like a teenager. He had on leather gloves and held a briefcase in his left hand. Sophie thought of Giddy — the man had lovely long eyelashes — but she always thought of Giddy when she looked at a man in his twenties with even the slightest resemblance to what her memory had preserved.

"I appreciate that, son," said Pigeon Man. "Have yourself a wonderful evening."

"You as well," said the young man, who walked on.

Sophie watched the man as he headed down the path through the park and saw him do something curious: he reached his right hand outwards and flexed his fingers, leaving them splayed as he walked.

Like he was holding someone's hand.

Sophie found herself rushing after him, but her heart was pounding so hard, she could hardly walk straight. No matter. She trailed the man out of the park, resisting with all of her might the urge to put a hand on his shoulder and turn him round. She followed him onto a green and white public bus, which was so crowded that he had to stand, holding the overhead rail with his free hand. Sophie couldn't get a better look at his face because there were too many people standing around him. Could Giddy have grown so tall and strong? From what she'd seen of him at the park, he did not look like an older version of the Giddy she'd known. She told herself not to get too excited. She'd followed hundreds of men over the years. Every time ended in disappointment.

The man got off in Flatbush, Brooklyn and began walking through the neighborhood. The sun had gone down, and the streetlamps were on. Kids were playing kick the can on the street while their mothers were calling them inside.

Finally, the man approached a lovely two-story brownstone duplex. It had red and black bricks on its first story and yellow ones above. Parked in front of the house was a van painted with a business name: Big Apple Locksmith. The logo featured an apple with a keyhole in it.

Sophie took a deep breath and told herself — nothing, she told herself nothing. It was better that way.

The man opened a little gate on the left side of the duplex and went up a few steps, where he unlocked a yellow door with an oval window. Sophie exhaled and walked into the house behind him.

"Please," Sophie said to herself as the young man set his briefcase down by the door. "Please, please, please."

He took his gloves off and set them on a bench with a hall tree attached. Then he took off his jacket and hung it up.

And then he took off his hat.

Letting his jug ears flop free.

Sophie teetered on her feet as the air around her seemed to shimmer. She staggered backwards and dropped onto a couch in a small living room. She shivered as her limbs turned to icicles.

Sophie was not prepared for this. After waiting so long, she was simply not ready.

On the coffee table in front of her, Sophie saw a framed picture, black and white, severely wrinkled. It was a photograph of Erich Alberg in a suit and tie, standing with his parents in their home.

A woman came down the stairs at the back of the room, a dazzling woman with a long brown ponytail, wearing yellow capri pants and a floral blouse. She smiled broadly, showing clean, white, American teeth. With eyebrows raised, she said, "So? How did it go?"

"I passed with flying colors," Giddy said, unleashing his goofy grin.

"So, you are a professor now? It's official? No more locks and keys?"

"Oh, I don't know about that," Giddy said. "But maybe only on the side. As the Jews always say: Have a back-up plan."

The woman ran to Giddy and embraced him. "We will celebrate!" she said.

"I will make schnecken," Giddy told her. "And play piano for you."

"Yes!" said the woman. "But first, go up. She's almost asleep, but she heard you come in and wants to show you something. I left her lamp on."

Sophie could not comprehend what she was seeing. It was happening too fast. It had taken forever, millions of forevers, all the forevers, and now it was happening too fast. She felt flooded by emotions she could not control, and they were going to drown her.

Giddy was alive.

Giddy had a wife.

Giddy had a child.

Sophie was overjoyed.

And completely devastated to realize he no longer needed her.

"Of course," Giddy said, kissing the woman on the lips.

"She told me her teacher pulled her aside this morning," Giddy's wife told him when their lips parted, "to say she was going to grow up to be smarter than Albert Einstein. I'm telling you, Professor Siegel, we have our hands full with that little pisher."

Sophie willed herself off the couch and, on wobbling, frozen feet, followed Giddy upstairs. He opened a door to a child's bedroom painted in soft blue; there was a small lump under fluffy white covers on the bed. A little pink hand slipped its way out through the blankets and hung off the side, twitching expectantly.

Giddy walked over, got to his knees, and took the little hand into his own. "Sophie Siegel," he said, "you are my light and my life, the reason I go out in the morning and come home at night."

The hand disappeared back under the covers, then reemerged with a blue piece of paper. Giddy took the paper and held it under the lamp. Sophie could see it had a Jewish star drawn on it. The name Sophie Siegel was written in adult handwriting across the horizontal line below the top point.

"It's for doing good in class," a tiny voice said.

"You must be very proud of yourself," said Giddy.

The tiny voice said, "I love you, Daddy."

"I love you, too, Angel."

Sophie feared she was about to pass out. In a panic, she saw that little Sophie's closet was open and managed to stumble her way inside and sink to the floor. Sitting now and catching her breath, she closed the door.

She'd won. She'd failed and failed and failed. She'd caused pain and death and suffering. But in the end, she'd won.

"Story, Daddy," Sophie heard the tiny voice say, and so she opened the door just a crack and peeked into the room.

"Which one, Angel?" Giddy asked.

"My favorite!"

"Your favorite? Which one is your favorite?"

"You know, Daddy! You know!"

"I know, Angel, I know. Okay, here we go. Once upon a time, when Daddy was a boy, he lived in a very bad place in a faraway land full of monsters. And he was stuck there because he needed treasure to come to America, where he could be safe."

"Safe to have me!"

"Exactly. Safe to have you."

"And then what, Daddy?"

"Well, I was in a car."

"Uncle Itzy's car!

"Uncle Itzy's car. Right."

"Then what happened?"

"And then a miracle happened. Money, a whole lot of money, fell right into my lap."

"From the sky!"

"You know it didn't fall from the sky, Angel."

"The girls!"

"There was a truck with a group of girls, and one of them threw the money to me. I'll never know why."

"Because of Sophie, Daddy! My Sophie!"

"I like to think so, Angel. I really like to think so."

Sophie, her heart both bursting and breaking, stood up. Confused, she looked down to see she was wearing a frayed yellow nightgown that seemed five sizes too small. A trickle of blood was running down her leg. She reached into the pocket of the nightgown and found several pieces of folded paper, pages from a book. After giving them a look, Sophie tucked them back into her pocket.

Sophie quietly scratched the closet door. Then she tapped on it. Then she scratched it again. She had to say goodbye to Giddy.

The door whipped open.

Sophie met Dieter Wolf's eyes. He looked her up and down, then grinned, flashing broken teeth.

But Dieter's face faltered when Sophie smiled like someone who knew something vitally important that he did not.

What she knew was that this too shall pass.

"I have lived," Sophie said, "in a way that brought honor to my people. May my memory be for a blessing."

THE END

AUTHOR'S NOTE

It is acknowledged and respected that there are those who object to books about the Holocaust that take liberties with historical details — even though they may be explicitly works of fiction. Here, I have invented Sophie's town, her ghetto, her camp, her woods, and of course, her revenge — and I set the entire story, in service of efficient storytelling, in Germany. My goal was not to dramatize any specific historical records but, rather, to communicate in a unique way the emotional realities, as I imagine them, of life during Hitler's reign of terror. At the same time, I tried to depict only the kinds of events that actually happened.

I would regret causing anyone pain by having introduced *The Vanishing* into the world, but I stand with Neil Gaiman, who tells us that "it is easy to pretend that nobody can change anything," but that, in fact, "individuals make the future, and they do it by imagining that things can be different." This book represents my humble attempt to create a better future by imagining a more empowering past.

It's my best hope that readers of *The Vanishing* who have little knowledge of the Holocaust find themselves, after meeting Sophie Siegel, motivated to investigate, for themselves, some of humanity's darkest days.

Thank you to my supportive early readers: Sasha Perrins, Susan Ellenberg, Nurit Wildenberg Stites, and Kathleen Marshall, as well as my generous proofreaders, Linda Levy, Jen Tuttle, Elizabeth Coronella, and Melissa Pruyn. Jennifer Rasmussen, thank you for going above and beyond by helping with research. And many thanks for your comments and corrections, Scott Denham. Katie Vincent and Sara Hamilton, your careful editing was most appreciated. Usher Morgan, I am grateful for your belief in and support of this book.

Heidi Slater, I love you always and forever.

—DMS

For my old friend, Jonathan Zigman

Dedicated to all those committed to *Never Again.*

Made in the USA
Monee, IL
01 November 2022

304040c3-bb48-44d6-852b-1834bbc53e74R01